Unheard, Unseen...

Unheard, Unseen...

A Novel

Daniel Lloyd Little

iUniverse, Inc.
New York   Bloomington

Unheard, Unseen...

Copyright © 2006 by Daniel Lloyd Little

All rights reserved. No part of this book may be used or reproduced by any means, graphic, electronic, or mechanical, including photocopying, recording, taping or by any information storage retrieval system without the written permission of the publisher except in the case of brief quotations embodied in critical articles and reviews.

iUniverse books may be ordered through booksellers or by contacting:

iUniverse
1663 Liberty Drive
Bloomington, IN 47403
www.iuniverse.com
1-800-Authors (1-800-288-4677)

This is a work of fiction. All of the characters, names, incidents, organizations, and dialogue in this novel are either the products of the author's imagination or are used fictitiously.

Because of the dynamic nature of the Internet, any Web addresses or links contained in this book may have changed since publication and may no longer be valid. The views expressed in this work are solely those of the author and do not necessarily reflect the views of the publisher, and the publisher hereby disclaims any responsibility for them.

U.S. Navy imagery used in illustration without endorsement expressed or implied.

ISBN: 978-0-595-41542-7

Printed in the United States of America

Chapter 1

▼

From the cold reaches of its low orbit in space, a shiny metallic object continued on its slow, endless journey circling the earth. Far below, six white lines moved slowly across the surface of the Atlantic, but the lens of the spy satellite's camera did not follow them, nor did it zoom in on what was obviously a naval formation. If it had, the now outdated technology would have discerned the flat expanse of an aircraft carrier with its attending battle group.

The once proud hammer and sickle painted on the side of the old satellite was now barely visible above the letters CC_P, the third 'C' having been replaced with a jagged hole. A small piece of space debris had done the damage that today a quick laser shot would accomplish.

The satellite's controllers and the small brick building they had occupied just outside of Leningrad (now St. Petersburg) were now gone, relics of a war long ended that history had ironically called 'cold'. Now in the year 2009, wars were fought on small battlefields and the threat of nuclear annihilation was history…almost.

∗   ∗   ∗   ∗

At the front of the 'line' in the center of the formation steamed the US Navy's newest aircraft carrier. The *USS George H Bush, CV-77* was the latest and last member of the *Nimitz* class of nuclear powered giants. She was a technological leap ahead of the old *CV-68* launched so many years ago. On her flight deck which stretched some eleven hundred feet in length, a carefully choreographed ballet of activity was playing out. A constant stream of aircraft launched by powerful steam catapults lifted into the air. Amongst them were F-18 Super Hornets, tasked with protecting the skies around the battle group, while a pair of S-3 Vikings circled slowly around the ships, searching for submarines that might be attempting to stalk them. Farther out, almost out of sight, a venerable Grumman E-2 Hawkeye, long past its 'best before date' as the crew liked to say, described a lazy figure eight in the sky; its powerful radar seeking anything that might dare enter the airspace near the fleet it protected.

Those long gone Soviet controllers would have seen immediately that the huge carrier was leaving less of a wake than her escorting mates. Many serious hours of super computer time had gone into accomplishing this feat in an attempt to avoid, or at least confuse, shadowing submarines. On most submarine sonar sets, the *Aegis* class missile cruiser steaming on her port side would appear to be the larger target, acoustically at least. A fact not lost on the captain of that ship.

Even now he was studying the huge grey mass of the *George Bush*. It would be his responsibility to protect this leviathan from air threats and he had complete confidence that his charge was more than capable of doing so. It was still not publicly known how many incoming targets the ship's Aegis weapons system could detect, track and eliminate, but it was unlikely that anything short of the rebirth of the Soviet Union would allow the sophisticated radar system to ever be tested to its full capabilities.

For Captain Frank Pettigrew, commanding officer of the *USS Vincennes*, that was just fine, especially as they were now finally heading home on the last leg of a three month deployment. Returning to their homeport of Norfolk, Virginia, only one mission remained. A last minute change from high up the command ladder had delayed their return home while unidentified 'assets' were put in place. No doubt another test of the *Bush's* new systems, he thought.

✳ ✳ ✳ ✳

On board one of those 'assets', the Canadian submarine *HMCS Corner Brook, SS-878*, Commander Michael Simpson was enjoying what would probably be his last operational posting. Now in the 31st year of serving his country, he was looking forward to the successful completion of this exercise, after which he planned to make the very best of what would hopefully be an uneventful few years sailing a desk at Maritime Forces Atlantic (Marlant). This chasing around under the water's surface was a younger man's game now, and he felt it in his muscles every time he climbed the ladders between the two decks; that and how the hatches on these boats were surely being designed smaller these days.

Mike had made it a priority to keep up with all the new technologies and had been an integral part of the submarine acquisition team that had first gone over to England in order to inspect the four *Upholder* class boats. They had been floating there lifeless, except for *Upholder* which was fully powered and open for inspection. The others were hermetically sealed against moisture and dust as though they had been wrapped in cocoons.

Launched in 1986, the four submarines had been ordered for the Royal Navy as a needed addition to their nuclear boats, but changing times and a worsening British economy soon gave question to their continuance. Remarkably under protest from the navy it had been decided to take them out of service when the last one built had been commissioned for less than a year. They were offered to Canada in the late nineties and after seemingly endless foot dragging, a deal had been struck to acquire all four boats which were then renamed the *Victoria* class.

The *Victoria's* were shorter in length than the old *Oberon* class boats Canada once possessed, but had been designed with two levels or decks making them much roomier below. Mike had found the tall slab sides, a British submarine characteristic, odd, but he knew that made them better sea keeping boats.

Retired for more than a decade now, the *Oberon* class boats had served Canada well in everything from fisheries patrol (overkill surely, Mike had thought, but the *LOOK* on that trawler captain's face when they had surfaced close alongside the ship which had been illegally fishing in Canadian waters!), to things that were never, ever alluded to. Canadian submariners took the submarine fraternity's 'Silent Service' tag seriously.

Now *HMCS Corner Brook* was his, or at least that's how Mike felt about her. Fully modernized, she was a deadly weapon but he knew in his heart that sadly, her career would outlast his.

Leaning over his sonar operator, who hated it when he did this, Mike watched the screens that took the minutest noises picked up by microphones located on the submarine's hull and along the towed array trailing behind them, and translated the sounds to lines on the screens laid out in front of him. Another screen on the console in front of him informed of any 'friendly' units within miles of his submarine using a new technology that redefined how submarines and surface warships would operate in the future.

HMCS Corner Brook had been the first unit equipped with the Canadian Navy's new Laser Communications System, or Lazcom as it had been nicknamed by the sailors tasked with its operation. The small screen installed to the left of the submarine's sonar suite allowed her communication or sonar officers access and control of the new system.

A row of icons ran down the left side of the screen. One of them, designated *Fred'ton* identified the Canadian navy frigate *HMCS Fredericton*, along with her bearing. Now and then the icon would flash either green or blue, indicating information being sent or received by the new system. If it turned red, that would tell the crewman manning the system that the Lazcom had lost its lock on that ship, and they were no longer able to communicate with it.

"Contact is an *Aegis* missile cruiser sir," Lt. Smith announced, bringing Mike back to the present.

"Which one is the carrier?" Mike asked, without removing his gaze from the screen.

"That one," replied Brad, pointing to one of the lines visible on the display in front of him. "See how little noise she's making?"

Lt. Brad Smith was as unique as the high tech systems he operated aboard the submarine. As with most sonar operators, he was a little high strung and some of his crewmates would say a bit eccentric as well. Too many hours staring at fuzzy little lines they thought, along with the other love of his life, his Playstation3, connected to the television in the junior ranks mess below. The shy twenty-four year old was well liked by the crew if for no other reason, his insistence on buying the newest PS3 games as soon as they were released combined with his generosity in lending them out to his fellow shipmates.

"So the new system on *Bush* really does work," mused Simpson, stating the fact rather than questioning it.

"Yes, but the info from *Freddie Beach* made it easy to distinguish them," replied Brad, using the nickname given to the ship that was the namesake of New Brunswick's capital city.

Mike looked down at 'Ears', as he was affectionately known throughout the boat because of his acute hearing, though not to his face, less the source of games for the boat's Playstation dry up.

"Sure Brad, but you would have figured it out anyway."

* * * *

HMCS Fredericton, FFG-337 was riding shotgun on *USS George H Bush's* starboard quarter. The Americans, as usual, had requested at least one of the *Halifax* class ships to be part of the escort for their carrier battle group. The Canadian multi-purpose FFG was a little out of place next to its US Navy cousins as the Americans seemed to prefer building warships in a 'mission specific' way. They had excellent anti-submarine warfare ships, and powerful anti-air warfare units, but they seemed unwilling to try to develop a good all-round ship that would be capable of more than one task.

Years earlier, US Navy admirals had stood with their tongues hanging out as the name ship of the *Fredericton's* class, *HMCS Halifax*, had shown her stuff in the Chesapeake Bay, adjacent to the sprawling Norfolk naval base. Her crew spoke in terms usually associated with the National Hot Rod Association when they discussed *Halifax's* speed and manoeuvrability. More than once a bar brawl had nearly broken out when some Canadian sailor looked his American buddy in the eye after a few too many brews and said "Is that ALL your ship can do?"

Currently *Fredericton* was 'silent'. A vulnerable state with all her radars and active sonars locked down. All the ships of the battle group were sailing in this mode so that whoever was conducting this 'exercise' would not easily detect them coming over the horizon.

Of course her sonar operators were still hard at work as their mission was usually one of listening and not pinging with active sonar. Once you went 'active' and started sending sound waves out into the ocean, everyone within miles would know where you were and probably who you were as well. *Freddie's* Lazcom was also operating, but only until a prearranged point in time, when it too would be shut down to let the exercise play out as accurately as possible. The crewman operating the new communications system was still being careful to transmit only in *Corner Brook's* direction lest some other ship's sonar operator detect the peculiar interference the Lazcom System's transmissions caused.

"Bridge, operations, we have *Corner Brook* at three one five degrees about five thousand yards."

The CO of *Fredericton* knew not to ask if they could do any better than 'about'. It was only because of the shared technology on the two Canadian warships that they were able to detect her at all at this distance. Some day, range measuring would be added to this new technology and then instead of being a communications system, it would also become an integral part of the fire control system for the ship's weapons. But for now, Commander Bill Hudson was more than impressed with its capabilities.

Bill was another commanding officer who was older than most of his compatriots. He was proud of his maturity however, and of the respect it earned him when he met with the younger officers commanding ships in the Canadian Navy. At his age, it was not uncommon for others to think that it was time that the 'old horse' was put out to pasture. That was fine with him. His 'pasture' was just outside Sydney, Nova Scotia where a small, warm cottage awaited him, along with Sheila, his wife of thirty-two years. Some said that his heart was really attached to the thirty-seven foot sailboat tied up at the small dock on the lake his property overlooked, but anyone seeing the name 'Sheila' in gold script lovingly painted across her stern soon realized otherwise.

This exercise would be Canada's first operational test of the navy's newest technology, the Lazcom Communication System. The system was comprised of a control panel, four transmitter/receiver antennas (two on surface ships) and a two foot square grey box housing the unit's electronics and computer. For decades communication with submerged submarines had been a combination of painfully slow Morse code and pure dumb luck using very low frequency radio waves transmitted from huge antenna systems that in some cases filled a valley. That was about to change forever.

The idea of shooting a laser through the ocean any distance was not a new one. What was though, had finally been perfected in a building sitting on the shore of Nova Scotia's Bedford Basin, across the harbour from the city of Halifax. The scientists working diligently in the top secret laboratories there had perfected the ability to accurately aim and track a narrow beam of light between warships at sea. The technology to transmit information and messages along this beam was developed shortly afterwards. The system was now installed aboard only a few Canadian warships and the navy anxiously looked forward to the remaining ships and submarines acquiring it as well.

HMCS Fredericton, now linked with *Corner Brook* through the Lazcom, was sending continuous positioning data to the hidden submarine, allowing her to approach the battle group unheard, unseen and much like the shark she closely resembled...a deadly predator.

* * * *

Soon after the first of the new submarines had arrived in Halifax, Canadian Navy engineers had looked at different ways to lower the noise signature of the boats. They had found not surprisingly, that there was little more they could do to improve on the excellent job already achieved by the designers and builders, VSEL in Britain. The *Victorias* were quiet boats; sometimes a little too quiet. Four years earlier at Maritime Forces Atlantic, in Halifax, Nova Scotia, concealing that proof had been a number one priority when *Victoria*, during one of her shakedown cruises, had chanced across another submarine. In spite of measures in place to prevent the resulting events from happening, things had gotten decidedly out of hand...

* * * *

"Sir! High speed screws! Bearing one four zero! Damn! Torpedo in the water!"

The young sonar operator could be forgiven the panic in his voice. *HMCS Victoria* had been playing a deadly game of cat and mouse with the other submarine for hours now. Its acoustic signature and their position south of Sable Island had indicated that in all likelihood it was an American SSN but now a torpedo was speeding through the water at them, fired by the other boat.

"Computer IDs it as a '48 sir!" This time the sonar operator's voice was lower and steadier; his instincts taking over, demonstrating that he deserved to wear the dolphin insignia on his work shirt.

"Helm! Hard right to zero degrees! Make your depth six hundred feet!"

The submarine's commanding officer would have given anything at that moment to have a working decoy dispenser. That would have given him a fighting chance, albeit a slim one against the high tech weapon hurtling through the water directly at him.

Given the luxury of time, he would have asked what the hell the Americans thought they were doing—firing at his boat without provocation. Right now though, their very survival was being measured in seconds and his reaction would either save or spell peril for him and his crew.

"Sonar! Three pings! Full power! As soon as it dies, give a holler on the UCD! Hopefully some jackass over there will ID our sonar!"

The sonar officer simultaneously punched the 'transmit' button on his sonar consol three times and reached for the microphone attached to the boat's underwater telephone all NATO submarines are equipped with. This scenario had not exactly been part of the planned use for the short range communications device.

"This is Canadian submarine *Victoria*! Check your fire! I repeat, check your fire! We are Canadian submarine *HMCS Victoria*!"

A short distance away, the sonar operator standing watch aboard the *USS Jimmy Carter* sat up abruptly.

"Damn! Captain! Positive ID! It's Canadian!"

"Weps! Disarm that Mark-48! NOW!" In that same split second of realization, the captain had disarmed the torpedo and given his last operational order as the commanding officer of a US Navy warship.

"Sir!" called the young Canadian sonar operator. "The other boat has acknowledged! They have disarmed the fish!"

It was too late however to stop the momentum of the now impotent torpedo from its headlong rush at the Canadian submarine. A few seconds later, it slammed into the side of *Victoria's* hull, the impact tossing crewman to and fro.

"Sonar, hail the Yanks that we're surfacing to check for damage," ordered the CO. "Lieutenant! Surface the boat! I want a damage report the minute the divers are out of the water!"

Shit, thought *Victoria's* commander as he mentally prepared his report to Halifax. O'Hanlon's going to have my balls for this. His new boat getting a 'ding' on one of its first cruises after finally arriving in Canada would not impress the vice admiral.

Months later, a court of inquiry absolved *Victoria's* commanding officer of any wrong doing. He was subsequently given command of one of the other four boats to arrive in Halifax.

In Norfolk, Virginia, the US skipper fared much worse. A JAG investigation found the *Carter's* captain had reacted far too strongly to the unidentified submarine. However, as the Canadian boat had appeared to be on a direct course to New York City and given the post 9/11 climate, the American captain was spared a full court martial.

The subsequent inquiry and results were classified 'top secret' and filed away, never again to see the light of day. But at the Pentagon, quiet notice had been taken of the abilities shown by the Canadian submarine in shadowing the US Navy's most stealthy boat.

After *Victoria's* return to Halifax, the subsequent damage caused by the torpedo had been examined by navy engineers who were now trying to unearth a way to mend it without compromising the boat's hull strength. So far the navy had been successful in keeping the event under wraps but as the boat had been readied for repair, a solution finally in hand, someone had forgotten to cover the damaged hull before it was lifted from the water, and with hundreds of sailors and civilian employees coming and going throughout the dockyard, it was only a matter of time before someone noticed and word leaked out.

The next day at Marlant, this disclosure had not been taken lightly...

"What???!!!"

"I'm sorry sir. It was in the Daily News this morning. 'A pizza pan sized dent has been found on the side of *HMCS Victoria's* hull.'"

The petty officer was thinking only one thing; please do not shoot the messenger! Vice Admiral Brent O'Hanlon was livid. He had made it perfectly clear that *Victoria* was not to be lifted out of the water by the huge Syncrolift in the Halifax dockyard, until the 'dent' had been repaired or covered. Surely someone would have noticed the dent, come to his senses, and quickly ordered it covered or the boat lowered into the water again!

"Dent", Brent murmured, half out load. His mind raced. At least none of the press had thought to compare the size of the 'pizza pan' dent to the business end of the Mk-48 torpedo currently in use by all Canadian and United States submarines; and the *USS Jimmy Carter* in particular.

A 'pizza pan sized dent'! Brent fumed. With nice footage of it being broadcast on the ATV Evening News, this might not be easy to make go away.

"Okay, ignore it! No comments, not even an acknowledgement. Something more newsworthy will come along and I'm sure the press will let it go." And if not, Brent surmised, and the opposition party demands an inquiry into why we accepted an obviously damaged submarine, we will be in very deep trouble. He imagined how it would play out on both sides of the border. 'The Canadian Navy today admitted that while playing with one of their new toys, they caused an unidentified submarine, to fire upon it.' Of course once word got out that the 'unidentified' boat belonged to the US Navy, that would be nothing compared to the thrashing the American media would give the crew of the *USS Jimmy Carter* for being either too trigger happy or sound asleep at their sonar scopes. Ah, yes, he thought. The sequel to the War of 1812!

If it had not been for Subtalk, the short range, rather limited communications system shared by all NATO submarines, the story might have had a terrible and tragic ending and Brent would probably not be sitting here pondering the consequences.

Fortunately, the American press had never acquired the story or it would have been all over the major networks, with Hollywood producers vying for the screen rights. The *Jimmy Carter* had extended her cruise; her crew sworn (again) to secrecy and other than one Mk-48 that would forever be missing from the US Navy's inventory (along with a couple of sonar operators who were probably learning a new trade associated with Antarctic postings), nothing would ever be said of the incident again. Or so it was hoped.

Brent had recalled how the new submarines had been a continuing sore spot within the Canadian Navy because of their delayed arrivals. Reactivating them had also consumed considerably more time and money than originally budgeted.

It had been a long and rocky road to say the least getting the Canadian submarines fully operational. Apparently a great many people had thought they would simply sail across the Atlantic to Halifax and be put right into service. Anyone with experience in the lengthy process of mothballing or reactivating a warship knew better of course, but when delays with the 'Canadianization' of the boats continued well past the expected time of their predicted 'in service' dates, both the government and the press started circling like hungry sharks.

Then the horrible disaster on board *Chicoutimi* had occurred while she was heading home to Halifax, with the tragic loss of a life and injuries sustained by the crew when their boat caught fire. That almost spelled the end of Canada's submarine program. The bravery exhibited by her crew dealing with all submariners' worst nightmare had earned them untold respect in the tight knit submarine fraternity. Indeed, after that event, there had been more than one day when Brent had wondered if they were doing the right thing and if these 'used' boats, as the press liked to call them, would ever see a real operational patrol.

Of course the navy couldn't simply forgo security and appear on television explaining how incredible the new systems being installed on the boats actually were or how valuable they would be for use in 'special' operations. The navy just quietly pressed on.

Brent smiled as he remembered some of the operations he himself had been a part of, for he also proudly wore the gold dolphins separating him and his kind from the 'regular' navy.

The tenacity of the men and women working on the submarines had paid off and finally the time had come when three of the boats had been fully transformed into stealthy black weapons of the deep.

Looking up again, Brent O'Hanlon had glared at the petty officer still standing in front of his desk. 'Pizza pan' indeed!

"Dismissed!"

The young man had turned smartly on his heel and strode from the office, wondering when it would be safe to speak with the admiral again.

Brent smiled. He'd pick up a 'double-double' at Tim's for his aide later. He was a good kid...for a 'skimmer'.

* * * *

Leaning back comfortably in his 'throne' on the Flag Bridge of the aircraft carrier *USS George Bush*, Vice Admiral Clive Henderson gazed serenely out to sea. It was a calm day, perfect for sailing, something he would have lots of time for in about five more years when he finally returned home for good to his wife Becky. He was looking forward to it with much the same anticipation that a top scorer in sports looks forward to the end of a successful season, excited about winning a championship, but sad that it would all be over for another year. In Clive's case, it was going to be over for good unless some horrible act of war caused his retirement to be rescinded.

The pinnacle of his career lay spread out in all directions for almost thirty miles. As a battle group commander he had more fire power under his command than most theatre generals had controlled during World War II. If you included the 'special' weapons (nuclear was not a word used in polite circles), more than ALL the theatre commanders in World War II.

The heart of the battle group, the *USS George H Bush* was a proud and powerful ship or 'asset' as the Pentagon liked to call her. Named after President George Herbert Bush, who had rallied the world against Iraq in the 1991 Gulf War, she would probably be the last of the huge 'big deck' aircraft carriers constructed. Now the US Navy was looking at the idea of smaller, more cost efficient carriers, and more of them, increasing the US Navy's geographical flexibility.

Around her, in the cold mid-Atlantic, steamed the battle group escorts, spread out in a wide formation lest some unknown enemy tried to attack the huge leviathan, which for all her potential power, was vulnerable to many things. Almost out of sight on the horizon, half a dozen destroyers and frigates watched and listened for anything that might pose a threat to the group and especially to the carrier in the center of the force. Circling above like some noisy vulture, one of the carrier's E-2 Hawkeyes flew in endless patterns. Its long range radar, housed in a flat dish attached to the top of the aircraft's fuselage, searched for anything that dared to fly into the airspace extending over one hundred miles from the ship. A second E-2 flew distant cover outside the battle group, poised to detect an airborne threat long before it was in range to attack the warships.

One last 'asset' played guard to this menagerie of grey. The nuclear attack submarine *USS Salt Lake City, SSN-716*, moved quietly through the water ahead of the group, one hundred and fifty feet below the surface, her sonar operators keeping a vigilant watch for the sound of any other ships or submarines in the area.

Clive thought about the *SLC* and the coming exercise, wondering if her crew had any idea that they were about to have an unexpectedly exciting day. Right now they would be going about their duties, no doubt thinking about soon returning home to Norfolk and their families, and not anticipating anything untoward happening this close to the end of the cruise.

Looking at the Rolex on his wrist, Clive checked the time. It was not a 'showpiece' so much as a rugged and practical watch that had survived many knocks passing through close passageways on whatever ship he was calling home at the moment. It had been a gift from Becky, his wife of...well; he'd remember to check his PDA for that info later. His record of unmissed anniversaries was the envy of all his buddies and he was not about to let it be ruined now.

1300 hours…any time now he thought, remembering the call from his old friend Brent O'Hanlon, who was now sailing a desk in Halifax. They had discussed the exercise at length and how it might play out. Of course a small wager was involved out of pride for their respective navies; Clive being very confident that the *USS Jimmy Carter* would arrive in time to send the Canadians and their untried boat ducking for cover.

Although serving in different navies, he and Brent had a lot of common sea between them. Being of similar age and having many common interests, they soon became good friends and had seen each other through some pretty tough times.

Brent had been there to celebrate with him when Jake, Clive's only son, had received his wings from the US Coast Guard and the two middle aged sailors had spent long hours simultaneously toasting and taunting the young man for not joining the 'real' navy. A few years later, when a Coast Guard search and rescue mission had gone horribly wrong, Jake had failed to return. Clive never forgot the morning of the funeral when Brent, having dropped everything, unexpectedly showed up at his door after hearing that his son had gone missing.

Pushing that memory from his mind, Clive looked off to his right and spied the *Fredericton* keeping her position perfectly as part of the close in escort screen. She was a fine ship and those Canucks sure were a tough bunch of sailors. Not tough like we were back in the fifties and sixties, he thought, when tough meant you stumbled out of the bar just before the shore patrol arrived to clean up the ones who couldn't. No, today they were tough in a different way—'brain tough', as Brent liked to say.

Brent O'Hanlon had impressed him the same way the first time they had met and still did, even though at some point in his career he had been swayed by the dark side and had successfully trained to become a 'bubblehead'; preferring to be crammed into a tiny metal tube underwater instead of enjoying the fresh sea air. The situation now was eerily similar to when they had first met.

Clive had been captain of the *Essex* class aircraft carrier *USS Intrepid* and one of his escorts had been Brent's command, *HMCS Fraser*, sailing in almost the same position as *Fredericton* was now. Then as now, captains of the valuable, yet vulnerable aircraft carriers had often requested one of the Canadian navy's destroyers to act as escort. The Canadian crews seemed to have an uncanny ability, almost a sixth sense really, to find and track down even the most elusive submarines.

Surprisingly, both of their old commands had escaped the scrapper's torch but in very different ways. The *USS Intrepid* was kept pristine and served as a fine Air & Space Museum on the New York City waterfront, visited by thousands of people every year. Sadly he remembered seeing the *Fraser* while on vacation in Canada a few years ago. She was an eyesore; her paint peeling and faded, sitting on the Lahave River in Bridgewater, Nova Scotia. There had been no one around for him to ask what she was doing there and he had driven away thinking that no warship deserved such a terrible fate.

Maybe when old admirals died, they were reunited with their ships in some sort of aquatic heaven, or so he hoped. The bridge crew noted the smile on his lips and wondered what the 'old man' was thinking about.

* * * *

Now THIS is the life! Leaning back on the balcony of his hotel room on the tenth floor of the Econo Lodge, Atlantic Avenue, Chief Petty Officer 2nd Class Darren Cole relaxed with his feet up on the railing and took another sip of Coke. Spread out before him, the warm sands and surf of Virginia Beach stretched out in both directions as far as the eye could see. And to think, he was getting paid for this to boot! The air was warm, the ocean was calm and schools of dolphins joyfully swam up and down just off the beach. Darren wondered at them as they appeared to stop and play at random. He had an affinity for the friendly little mammals. A pair of them, one on either side of a red maple leaf, adorned the left breast of his uniforms. Today however, he was wearing a colourful shirt purchased earlier from one of the many gift and souvenir shops that lined Atlantic Avenue, across the street from his hotel.

Even the colourful shorts completing his outfit had caused the girl at the Econo Lodge's front desk to take a second look at the tall, fit young man as he had signed the register earlier. Looking at his closely cropped hair, she had no doubt pegged him as a military 'dude' from one of the many bases in the area. She had acted totally cold to him until he'd handed over his Royal Bank Visa card, and asked how she was, with what seemed to her, a slight foreign accent, and a wide smile. She had returned his smile cautiously.

Darren had seen right away that she was very pretty in a natural way. Her long brown hair was neatly tied up and she wore just the right amount of makeup. Not like the tanned-to-death bikini clad girls walking up and down the street who seemed intent on frustrating the young guys driving by who simultaneously had to keep an extra eye out for the cops because of Virginia Beach's anti-cruising laws.

Heather liked foreigners. They seemed more civilized and cultured than the guys hanging out around the beach, and she absolutely loved their accents. Perhaps someday one of them would whisk her off to some exotic location. This young man, who obviously spent time keeping himself in shape, didn't have much of an accent, but he did have one of those mischievous twinkles in his eye. The kind that makes you think he's planning something naughty.

His clothing definitely stated he was no James Bond, but they did fit him well, unlike the baggy ones worn by the last date she'd had. Perhaps he was British. No, she had answered in her mind. The accent was wrong, but it did have a musical ring to it. Her eyes met his and she felt herself blushing. Oh great, she'd thought! Now he knows where my mind is!

Darren, unaware of what she was thinking at the time, had averted his gaze, embarrassed that she'd caught him staring at her.

"Where are you from?" she had asked him.

"I'm Canadian," he smiled, returning his eyes to hers, "here on business from Nova Scotia."

"Really?" She was more interested now. "I have a friend who lives in…Halifax? I think that's what it's called. She's always telling me how nice it is there".

"That's where I'm from!" Darren had tried not to appear too eager and failed miserably. Calm down now, he'd told himself. She's probably married or engaged to one of those muscle guys walking up and down the beach.

"Oh cool! She goes to university there! I keep meaning to pay her a visit some day." Her smile deepened.

"Great! Maybe we can meet for coffee while I'm in town? I can tell you all about Nova Scotia." It had been much more a question than a statement and she had looked away as he waited for a response. No doubt committed, he had thought again. She's far too pretty to be a single woman in this town, especially with a zillion navy guys around.

Surprising him however, she had looked up at him and responded, "Sure. How long are you here for?"

Darren's mind had raced. There would be no time for anything until he had completed the task he'd been sent here to accomplish, but surely that wouldn't take more than a day or two.

"Well how about I call you? I have meetings to attend for the next couple of days or so and then I'm free." He had found it very difficult lying to her. "Oh, my name is Darren, Darren Cole."

"I saw it on your card," she had smiled coyly, while writing her name and phone number down on the little envelope she placed his key card in. "My name is Heather."

"Pleased to meet you, Heather!" Darren had again felt like an oaf.

"Elevators are right up there," she had smiled at him again, pointing down the hall to his left. "Your room is on the top floor and the pool is open from eight in the morning until eight at night. Enjoy your stay with us."

"Thanks! I'll call you later!" he'd answered, grabbing his bags before he embarrassed himself any further and heading for the elevator where he punched the button for the tenth floor, hoping he'd have a chance to call her and spend some time together.

The two room suite was certainly more than he needed but it had been the only room available on such short notice. He admired the view out the balcony doors as he walked in and noted the full service kitchen along with the large television in the living room and bedroom as well. Unpacking his shaving gear and a few clothes, he had attached his cell phone to its charge adapter and found an outlet in the kitchen to plug it into. The room sure beat his tiny bunk on *HMCS Corner Brook*. This was going to be nice. Nicer still if things worked out with the cute girl working at the front desk. He looked down at the key card holder. "Heather", he had said aloud to the room, "nice name."

Now as he leaned back in the white plastic chair and took another sip of Coke he gazed out at the horizon. The sky was crystal clear, a deep blue reflected in the ocean. It would be easy to spot the *Carter* from up here when she left the Norfolk Naval Base.

The *USS Jimmy Carter* was arguably the quietest SSN in the world, which was why he had been sent down here and was now sitting on this balcony with a view of the harbour entrance. One of the sister ships to his boat was submerged just off shore awaiting the *Carter's* appearance. He knew that *HMCS Victoria* would be hovering quietly just below the water's surface with only a small antennae poking above the water. Her commanding officer was no doubt waiting patiently for a satellite signal from Halifax advising him that the *Carter* had left port. He needed to know exactly when the American boat was leaving in order to set up an intercept course. Once in deep water, it was unlikely 'Rene's Raiders', the tag given to *Victoria's* crew, would find the *Carter*, unless lightning did strike twice in the same place and there was a repeat of that little 'episode' of a few years ago.

Remembering the first time the two boats had met, Darren chuckled to himself. That had been his first cruise aboard a submarine and while some of the guys had made it their last after that and had requested transfers to the skimmer world, he had found the whole thing quite exhilarating. Soon afterwards he had been transferred over to the *Corner Brook* when she entered service. Darren would have given anything to be a fly on the bulkhead in *Carter* when the *Vic* nailed her.

Information from Halifax indicated she was to join the aircraft carrier *George Bush* and her battle group in three days. That meant she would probably depart tomorrow, sometime around first light. Just in case however he had set the clock radio on the desk next to the bed for 3:00 am. The thought of calling down to the desk and asking Heather if she was going to be on duty had popped into his mind but he just as quickly dismissed the idea. Stay with the mission, he thought—stay focused.

Hopefully the weather would remain clear, or he'd have to go park on the Chesapeake Bay Bridge Tunnel lookout with the young people who favoured it as a 'parking' spot, and that might appear suspicious. He didn't really want to deal with the local police as to why he was parked there all alone in the early hours of the morning.

The roar of jet engines suddenly engulfed him as a pair of F-18 Super Hornets swept down the beach at low altitude turning on final for Oceana Naval Air Station.

"Awesome!" he yelled against the loud roar of the two jets.

Grabbing his binoculars, he tried to get a closer look at them but they had flown out of sight in seconds. That's when he noticed the sound of yet another aircraft and leaned carefully over the balcony railing, looking to his left to see what it was. The unmistakable shape of an E-2 Hawkeye flew into view. No mistaking that one for anything else. Darren knew a Hawkeye always flew out ahead of a submarine departing the Norfolk naval base to make sure…"Shit!" Equally unmistakable coming into view on the water's surface was the dark, low silhouette of a submarine slowly heading out to sea. A quick look with the binoculars showed him the large fairing built into the front of the sail making her one of the newer classes. Even more obvious was the submarine's length. The almost one hundred feet added to the hull was a dead giveaway for the *Carter*. She was certainly a very different submarine from when she had been first launched a few years earlier. Capabilities never before tried had been added to her original design, including the ability to change 'packages', actually plug in sections of the hull, to fit the particular mission she was assigned to.

Flying out of his plastic chair, he rushed to the kitchen, grabbed for his cell phone and turned back to the balcony. Forgetting in the moment that it was plugged into the charger, the tiny phone ripped from his hand as he exceeded the reach of the charging cord. "Damn!" Dropping to the floor he grasped for it and quickly hit the power button waiting for what seemed an eternity before the display finally came on. Rapidly punching the #1 menu button he noted the display flash 'Marlant' and start dialling.

*   *   *   *

"Vice Admiral O'Hanlon's office," answered Chief Petty Officer Jody Fletcher, sitting at his desk just outside the door of Brent's office.

"Fletch! Get a message to the admiral ASAP!"

"Darren? What's up my man?"

"*Carter* is departing right now!"

"Now? Hang on!"

Jody dropped his headset and threw open Brent's oak door without bothering to knock. "Sir, sorry to barge in but Chief Darren Cole is on the phone from Virginia; *Carter* left early." Waiting for one of Vice Admiral O'Hanlon's famous outbursts, he half cowered in the doorway.

"Ah, figures! Tell Cole 'good job' and instruct comms to send the action message."

"Right away sir!" Jody returned to his desk, hit a free line and buzzed Marlant's communication facility in the building up the street. Someone as always answered immediately.

"This is Vice Admiral O'Hanlon's office. Send signal bravo to *Victoria*," he instructed.

Nothing else needed to be said. The message had already been pre-loaded into the communication system's file list which only required someone to enter the proper code and then the 'transmit' command. That was done almost immediately after the petty officer manning the phones gave a thumbs up to the seaman at the console across the room. A few keystrokes on his computer sent the proper command to the transmitters where it was received and assigned to the Satcom filer. There the priority code was recognized immediately, bumping it ahead of all other signals waiting their turn to be transmitted.

Punching another button on his phone, Jody returned to Darren who he had hurriedly put on hold. "So Cole. How's life on Va beach? Tough duty, eh?" They chatted for a few minutes until the intercom called Jody away.

CPO 2nd Cole, having completed his 'secret' mission and now with nothing else to do, headed across the street to the 'Oh Fudge' store he had spotted on his way into the hotel. After acquiring some of their tasty morsels he returned to his room and called the front desk to inform Heather that 'surprise of surprises', his meetings had all been postponed and he was now totally free. Having agreed they would chat later when her shift ended, he grabbed another Coke and with his fudge returned to the balcony to enjoy the view.

Chapter 2

▼

Also enjoying the view of Virginia Beach, but from a very different angle, was the Commanding Officer of *HMCS Victoria, SSK-876*, hovering at periscope depth just outside the main entrance to the Norfolk Naval Base.

"Commander, message from Marlant coming in"

Commander Rene Bourgeois ducked, as he usually did, to get his six foot plus body around the many low hanging devices that littered the overhead and watched as his communications officer touched a few buttons, making sure they were properly linked to the navy communications satellite. This was accomplished using the antennae at the top of the ESM mast which was just barely extended above the relatively calm surface of the water. The young able seaman watched as the message came up on his communications screen. His captain, he knew, was reading it over his shoulder but proper protocol dictated that he read it aloud anyway.

"*Carter* has sailed and is just clearing the beach."

"Okay, she's early but we're ready. Confirm and acknowledge the message, Sam." Rene gave the young man's shoulder a pat, letting him know that he'd done well and his captain was pleased. Sam typed 'confirm' and hit the 'ENTER' button transmitting it back up to the orbiting satellite. The same message flashed on the screen again with no changes so he typed 'acknowledge' and having done so, turned back to Rene, "Message confirmed, sir."

"Thanks Sam! Helm, make turns for ten knots and take us down to two hundred feet. Let's see if we can catch him before they get settled into their routines. Maintain this heading." He didn't have to 'quiet the boat' because they had all been living in total fear for days that someone would drop even the smallest object and alert the United States Navy to a foreign submarine sitting on the doorstep of its largest naval base.

Arriving at this spot had taken days of very slow, very quiet sailing, not to mention a lot of luck finding a deserted area every third night to raise the induction mast so the diesels could run and charge the boat's batteries back up to full capacity. All it would have taken was for some fisherman or recreational sailor coming across the masts poking from the water's surface to radio the US Coast Guard and *HMCS Victoria* and crew would have found themselves the object of unwanted attention. This close to the navy base, all unnecessary devices had been turned off to conserve the charge in the batteries as there was no possibility of raising the induction mast and starting the diesels. The last thing they needed was for some warship or aircraft transiting to or from the base to pick up the masts on radar in spite of their radar absorbent coatings which although lessoning the chance, did not eliminate it completely. *Victoria* was scheduled to receive the extended capacity battery upgrade previously completed on *Corner Brook*, but until that happened; the crew had to keep a close watch on their power consumption.

The submarine would have been discovered a long time ago had it not been running on its quiet electric motors. This incredible stealth was the trade off against the endless but noisier power of a nuclear propulsion system. While they were waiting for the signal from Marlant, the only sound heard throughout the boat were quiet whispers and the occasional dull thunk as someone hit against something solid followed by a muffled curse.

"Yokov, keep those phones on tight son."

"Yes sir," replied the sonar operator who was so engrossed in listening and watching the sonar scopes in front of him that he almost hadn't heard his CO.

Rene was forcing himself not to pace. He envied the 'skimmers' and their spacious bridges at times like this. This shouldn't be too difficult, he thought. Their part in this exercise was going to be over with very quickly and he certainly was happy that the *Carter* had sailed early. The crew was starting to show strain from being quiet for so long. Because of their conservation efforts, he had nearly full capacity in the batteries right now and his crew would not have to stay in quiet mode much longer. The average person could not realize how exhausting it was to consciously watch every movement to make sure it did not create any noise. For submariners, noise is death.

* * * *

Not far from where *Victoria* waited, with its rounded nose pushing a huge bow wave through which numerous dolphins jumped with glee, the *USS Jimmy Carter, SSN-23* had cleared the Chesapeake Bay Bridge Tunnel and was now picking up speed as she headed for the open sea.

The submarine's commanding officer, Captain Richard Seller or Rick as he was usually called, sat in the small space politely referred to as the Captain's Cabin, tapping information into his PDA. As in most submarines, the space was more like a closet than a cabin. Especially when the cot or so-called bed was dropped into position. You had to admire the designers though. They had managed to cram all the amenities he required into the tiny opening. Shame they hadn't included the captain's measurements in their plans! Reading over his mission brief, it was obvious to the forty-eight year old commander of the US Navy's stealthiest submarine, that this cruise would be a milk run. Sail from Norfolk, meet Battle Group Charley and escort them back to Norfolk. *USS Salt Lake City* was performing the honours at the moment.

Good for her, he thought. This was probably one of the last deployments for the *Los Angeles* class attack boat which, like others of her class, would be prematurely de-commissioned and turned into razor blades, as the old adage went.

The world had certainly changed a lot in the past ten years and because of that, the large numbers of submarines that once sailed the oceans had found themselves without a vocation. Today's missions went to boats that were far fewer in number, but much more capable. His command was one of them.

Looking up, as he did every few minutes, he noted the boat's heading on the repeater display built into the bulkhead of his cabin. Everything was running smoothly so far. Even with the dreaded 'Echo' pack the *Carter* was currently configured with. The problem with the 'Echo' pack, as he and the previous commanding officer had tried to explain to the powers that be, was the lack of weight in the damn thing. Made for cargo carrying, it was the most unlikely of the many 'packs' capable of being deployed as part of the *Carter's* unique hull, to ever be used for what it had been intended. No one would seriously consider using this boat to transport anything at the dollar per/pound ratio that would exist. Empty, it made balancing the boat a precarious task for the seaman assigned that job. So precarious in fact, crew assigned to that duty on *Carter* received a full two weeks of extra training for it. Still, she was a remarkable boat and brought a whole new meaning to the word flexibility as well as an incredible new ability to the submarine's most important mission aside from hunting down and killing other subs—spying.

Rick was mentally designing the 'Captain's Cabin' pack when the speaker, all of three inches from his ear, burst to life.

"Captain, con. We are thirty miles out."

"Thank you. I'm on the way."

Turning off his PDA and slipping it into his shirt pocket, he ducked through the narrow passageway and entered the control room.

"I have the con lieutenant."

"Ay sir, captain has the con!" This let everyone know who was now in charge or as Chief of the Boat (COB) Elijah Deal liked to kid; 'Who would take the blame.'

"How are we doing COB?"

"Good Captain. No leak on the E-Pack and the tail is out."

The leak problem with the packs on *Jimmy Carter* had been one of the worst engineering nightmares the people at Electric Boat in New London, Connecticut had ever come across. It was months before the yard had finally came up with a solution to the never ending little trails of water that kept managing to seep into the boat whenever they dived below three hundred feet. Finally, a small, inflatable bladder nestled into the pack's mating groove seemed to solve the problem. It was inflated automatically before the boat dived and then sea pressure did the rest. The deeper the boat dived, the stronger the seal became. It always seemed that the really simple solutions worked best. This short mission would be that particular solution's final test before the *Carter* got back to doing the things she had been designed for.

The 'tail' on the other hand was another matter. A long cable with microphones attached to it, the towed array's retraction system had not been functioning well. It worked great while the array was being deployed, but every now and then while being hauled back in, the motor or its gear system would squeak, just once…but very loudly.

The yard gang, and finally the designers, had torn it down and rebuilt it more than once finding nothing amiss. It always performed perfectly in port but inevitably at least once during the boat's next deployment, the thing would sing out and let everyone within a few hundred miles know that something was out there, and to skilled sonar operators, that 'something' was probably a submarine.

Rick longed for the simple design of the previous SSNs. They stored the cable in a housing that formed a bulge along the pressure hull, but that of course would be impossible with the *Jimmy*, as her hull was no longer uninterrupted due to the addition of the pack system.

"Anything out there, sonar?"

"Two targets…both commercial…ten thousand yards to the east of us sir," answered the sonar operator. "The E-2 reported everything clean outside of those for five miles."

"Sounds wonderful petty officer. Let me know if you trip over anything."

"Yes sir wi…"

Rick saw him lean forward. "What have you got?"

"Spike contact. Bearing two six zero degrees. Nothing there now."

"Keep an eye open." It was probably nothing, Rick thought. One of the countless snaps and pops picked up by the super sensitive microphones built into the hull of the submarine and attached to the 'tail' strung out behind the boat. Trying to decipher the assortment of sounds in the ocean depths made sonar operators slightly paranoid, obsessively trying to track down every single sound and identify it, no matter how irrelevant it seemed. Of course that was exactly what they'd been trained to do and with good reason. Above, the 'skimmers' say 'you never see the one that gets you'. Down here below the surface, it was 'you never hear the one that gets you'.

* * * *

Aboard *HMCS Victoria*, the spike picked up by the *Carter's* sonar, was laying on the deck of the junior rank's mess in a puddle of gravy and fries.

"Oh crap, Parker!" hissed Cookie.

"Damn!" breathed the young master seaman who was picturing the CO tearing his stripes off in a few seconds, "Sorry Cookie."

Cookie, whose real name was long forgotten, even at Marlant amongst the countless people he had served with, softened his glare and bent down to help Parker clean up.

"I don't think it was too loud son. Probably didn't go far, eh?" Cookie called everyone 'son'. It was even said he had called Brent O'Hanlon 'son' once when the vice admiral had awarded him a ribbon for something he'd done while serving aboard *HMCS Onondaga* years ago. O'Hanlon had turned red, and walked away from the portly petty officer but a week later a promotion had come down making Cookie a chief. The friendly Newfoundlander had taken it all in stride and explained to all who would listen that it was simply a matter of O'Hanlon recognizing a great talent when he saw it.

What Cookie was pretty sure about, but didn't say to Parker, was that the noise of the plate hitting the deck had in fact been too loud and he quietly left Parker to finish cleaning up the mess, while he headed up to the control room.

"What happened Cookie?" greeted him as he poked his head in.

"Sorry Cap. A plate slipped."

Cookie enjoyed the relaxed atmosphere aboard the boat. Calling the CO 'Cap' would get you keelhauled on a surface ship.

"'kay Cookie. Keep it together down there."

"Will do." He turned and headed back to the kitchen spaces. Rene noticed he hadn't mentioned who had dropped the plate. Nor would the CO ever find out. Cookie looked after his shipmates, sometimes treating them like his own children. That was one of the things that endeared him to the crew although none of them could have imagined Cookie as a father figure. More like a rambunctious older brother perhaps. He would make sure there was no more noise from below again any time soon.

"Nothing Sir," replied Yokov, to the question the CO had asked before Cookie's appearance had interrupted them. "If anyone heard it they're ignoring us so far."

"Alright, but spread the word again. Quiet ship!"

Rene knew he didn't really have to remind the crew, but someone always seemed to forget the moment and a friendly reminder might just make a difference. Again he was reminded how noise in this business could be fatal. A few minutes later, the moment they had been waiting for occurred.

"Got him sir!" Yokov called out.

As usual there was a quiet grunt and a French Canadian expletive as Commander Rene Bourgeois failed to navigate his tall frame around a protruding valve and added another bruise to the surface of his shaved skull. He had long given up trying to keep hair on his head, as little patches of it ended up stuck to the maze of things submarine designers insisted on hanging from the overheads. Besides, band-aids stuck much better to the smooth skin of his scalp.

"Where is he?"

"Right here. Sonar has him and I'm pretty sure I have him on Lazcom as well. I'll bet dinner he's two thousand yards out. Looks like he's running at about two five zero feet."

"Good work, Alex. Helm, make your depth two five zero feet. Let's see how close we can get before he clears his baffles. Yokov, deselect him on the Lazcom as soon as you can. No need to mess with his mind just yet."

Rene knew the *Jimmy Carter's* CO would be clearing his baffles shortly. That would involve her captain taking the boat on a lazy three hundred and sixty degree turn to give his sonar operators a chance to hear what was happening behind them, where turbulence from the submarine's propeller made it difficult to pick up sounds clearly.

Victoria had no need to replicate the manoeuvre as her mission in the scheme of things was solely that of spoiler. She would be detected by the *Jimmy Carter* soon enough, but Rene wanted it to be on his terms with a little element of surprise thrown in for good measure. Once found, the *Carter* would have little choice but to return to Norfolk. Without stealth, a submarine was pretty much a useless commodity and her captain would have no way of knowing who else had heard when she was located with active sonar. *Victoria's* portion of this exercise was to make sure *Corner Brook* had free reign to take on the US battle group without interference from the far too capable *USS Jimmy Carter*.

Rene watched the sonar screen and sure enough, there was a thin line solidifying a third of the way across the display. At that frequency, it almost certainly had to be another submarine. As if reading his mind, the petty officer reached over and touched the 'Unknown' icon that represented the *Jimmy Carter* on the Lazcom's touch screen, then hit the 'Deselect' button causing it to stop transmitting in that direction.

This was the good and the bad trait of Canada's new hi-tech system. It would continuously transmit in multiple directions seeking a like signal. This close, a good sonar operator on the other boat would pick it up as an odd, fuzzy sound in his headset. It wouldn't show up on his screens visually though, unless the Lazcom operator hit his 'LOCK' button. Then the brief, high powered laser pulse designed to lock onto the other vessel's Lazcom unit would totally obliterate the sonar screens, hopefully creating momentary panic to ensue in the other boat's control center. The Canadian sonar operators, familiar with the effect, simply waited a few seconds for the screens to clear again. By deselecting a target, the system remembered the bearing to the target it had previously acquired and avoided transmitting through a fifteen degree cone in that direction. Of course, if *Carter* were to make an expeditious turn or depth change, the Lazcom would again 'see' the target and follow it, waiting to see if any communication was forthcoming from the other vessel.

Rene, like the other commanders fortunate enough to have the system on their warships, had been briefed that an upgrade to the system was almost perfected which would remove the interference picked up on their target's sonar systems. For today's mission, however, the older system would do just fine.

"Target aspect changing. He's coming around to starboard." Alex watched carefully as the thin line representing the *Carter* moved to the right on his sonar screen.

"Helm, dead slow!" Rene smiled. Here was where the SSK or diesel/electric powered submarine was in its element. As *Victoria* slowed to a bare crawl, there was effectively no noise radiating from her. Until someone invented a passive sonar system that could detect the absence of noise, nothing could see or find her at this moment.

"Target is coming around…directly astern…passing to port now…he's picking up revolutions now. Okay…he's back on course…slightly to port," whispered Alex as he described what the others could not see. He loved how the crew was hanging on his every word.

Rene patted him on the back. "Good work!"

His control room team was one of the best; almost all of them qualified submariners. There was very little banter amongst the crew while they were stalking a target. Unlike the way it was portrayed in some of the movies, tactical submarine operations usually took place slowly and very quietly. A noisy boat was a dead boat with the weapons carried today, plain and simple.

"Helm, come left five degrees and make turns for fifteen knots."

"Coming left five degrees and turns for fifteen knots aye sir," responded the young master seaman who, like all those in his position, found it amazing that the navy trusted him with driving this powerful submarine at his age. Especially since his car sitting at the Halifax dockyard parking lot was scarred with more than one scratch and dent resulting from his inexperience behind the wheel.

But he wouldn't let them down, thought Master Seaman Dwight Williamson. He had earned his Dolphins on the *Vic's* last cruise and could still remember hearing the pride in his dad's voice when he had called home and told his parents about the accomplishment. His dad, who had sailed on the old steamers in the navy back in the seventies, had kidded him about trying to have his insurance premiums reduced since he was obviously such a fine driver now, at least by navy standards! The next day, Dwight had bought the 'My Other Ride Is a Submarine' bumper sticker from the base Canex and had proudly stuck it on his back bumper, hiding a few dings and scratches in the process.

"Helm, come right five degrees," Rene spoke into Williamson's ear, shaking him from his day dream.

"Right five degrees, yes sir." Dwight slowly brought his wheel over and watched carefully so he wouldn't slip past the ordered heading, bringing it back just before the red digits on the display in front of him stopped on eighty-three. "New course zero eight three degrees; depth two five zero feet."

"Sonar how's the range?"

"We're closing on him. He's about fifteen hundred yards now. Solid line on sonar."

Alex referred to his scope with the line representing the *Carter* now showing up clear and sharp in the high frequency range usually emitted by submarines.

"Sir, we just cleared the shelf. He'll probably go deep now," Dwight observed as he noted the coordinates on the panel in front if him. In the 'good old days', he had learned during training, the guy driving the boat only did the driving and someone else worried about where you were. Someone else still backed him up manually on the charts, but computerized navigation made the many rulers and dividers only items of curiosity to the younger crew members. That old slide rule thing bothered him though. It was scary the way the Captain and Lieutenant Jemsen could do stuff with the funny looking white ruler. Not even a display on it anywhere. Scary!

"Okay Alex, it's time to wake 'em up over there. Lock Lazcom onto the *Carter*."

"Yes sir!" replied the sonar operator making sure the icon for *Carter* was the one highlighted and hitting the 'LOCK' button. Inside *Victoria* there was no indication of anything happening other than the icon for the American submarine flashing blue for an instant and then back to red, telling the operator that this unit did not posses Lazcom capability.

* * * *

On board the *USS Jimmy Carter*, pandemonium broke out. "Sonar is down! Wait! It's back again. Stand by!" Although Taylor was punching keys as fast as he could, everything now seemed to be operating normally.

* * * *

"Hit him with the Lazcom again Alex." Rene imagined the scene over on *Carter* right now.

* * * *

"We're down again captain! Something is really messing up the electronics! Okay, we're up again."

"Taylor, run a complete diagnostic on the system and make sure the self check is working!" Rick was getting worried. If they lost the sonar suite it meant surfacing and returning to the base.

"Self check confirmed. It's working fine captain."

* * * *

"Okay Alex, go active and let's see who messes his pants over there," laughed Rene. "Full power!"

He knew the control room crew was loving every minute of this at the expense of their compatriots across the water. For the remaining crew members who had been on that ill fated voyage a few years ago, when these two boats had first met, this was sweet revenge. Alex flipped open the small plastic cover protecting the sonar transmit key and sent out three quick pulses at maximum power. From the sonar transducer on *Victoria* three high frequency sound waves flowed out and in seconds struck the *Carter's* towed array and her stern section, sending an echo back to the Canadian submarine that was audible throughout the boat.

* * * *

"Captain! Active sonar! Directly astern! He's REAL close!" Taylor's ears were still ringing so he was unaware how loud he had yelled. "System says it's British!"

"Helm, come left ninety degrees!" Rick ordered. "Make turns for twenty-five knots; take us down to six hundred feet! Taylor, you okay?"

"I'm fine sir. Still no contact, but he was close!" The church bells in his ears were subsiding now and he spoke in a normal tone as he strained to listen for the submarine that he knew had to be close behind them.

As the *Carter* turned, her towed array would slowly swing around, but right now it was being drug through the increasing turbulence as her huge propeller sped up to increase the boat's speed.

"Anything at all Taylor?" Rick was perturbed that anyone could sneak up on him. This was not going to play well at the Officer's Club in Norfolk. A Brit managing to pull this off!

"Nothing captain. Wait. I think I have him. SSK! Oh crap! It has to be Canadian!"

Rick knew he could easily outrun the diesel powered submarine tailing him but there was no point. The active pings would have been heard for miles and now anyone else out there knew that there were at least one and more likely two submarines in the area. With other unknown boats probably already heading for this spot like sharks sniffing blood in the water, there really wasn't any point in trying to continue his part of the exercise.

Damn! Those Canadians had made life hell for this boat! He didn't want to be the second command casualty after a run in with the Canucks. Even as he was thinking it, two other submarines, one American and the other a Russian *Akula* which had been cruising off the Norfolk naval base for any tidbits that might show up, changed direction and started in, hoping for some left over spoils.

"Helm, all stop." Might as well be neighbourly, thought Rick.

* * * *

"He's stopped engines sir!"

"Helm, all stop! Alex, are we in Subtalk range?"

"We will be by the time we stop drifting. Give it twenty seconds."

Time seemed to pass slowly as Rene stood next to Alex at his console with the Subtalk headset on.

"He's back to our depth. You should be good to go now."

"*Carter*, this is the Canadian submarine *Victoria*, do you copy?" It was hard to talk with such a huge grin covering his face.

"*Victoria* this is *Carter*, read you clear." Rick laughed out loud upon hearing who it was. "Weapons are safe." He was referring to the last time these two boats had met when that Mk-48 torpedo went 'missing'.

"Roger the safe captain. My crew wishes to inform you that they select steak dinner for their prize."

"Steak it is sir!" Rick made a note in his PDA for some future date when the Canadian boat would be in the same port as his. The old tradition of serving dinner to the crew who 'sank' you was one of the things that made living in a small steal tube a little more bearable.

"*Victoria*, is there anything else I should know? Perhaps in regards to our passive sonar?"

Rene smiled. He wasn't cleared to divulge anything regarding the Lazcom System and answered, "No, why do you ask?"

"We had a glitch over here just before you went active. Thought maybe you might have noticed something." Rick was sure that whatever it was, *Victoria* had been the cause, but if her captain was not cleared to say anything, there was no point in asking again.

"Commander, we'll be going." It was time to head home and face ComSubAtlantic. "Congratulate your crew! You guys got us fair and square!"

"Thank you captain. It wasn't easy." Rene had to quiet down the control room as the crew broke out in laughter, knowing the sonar operator on *Carter* probably heard it.

"*Victoria* clear."

"*Carter* clear."

* * * *

Aboard the *Carter*, Rick gave the orders that brought his boat about for the trip back to Norfolk. They quickly headed to periscope depth and sent off a Satcom message to Commander Submarines Atlantic, which he knew would not be well received. It had been expected that he would make quick work of the Canadians and come sailing in with the *Bush* battle group. That certainly wasn't going to happen, he thought to himself, as he informed the crew that he was leaving the control room. Retiring to his cabin, he dug into his Jane's Fighting Ships for some clue as to what those Canucks might have added to their boats that would interfere with his sonar.

Aboard *Victoria,* having confirmed the battery state and ordered his comms officer to send a message to Marlant when they reached periscope depth, Rene had his executive officer plot a course south to the Panama Canal and back to British Columbia before retiring to his cabin for a well deserved nap.

* * * *

To the east, aboard *HMCS Corner Brook*, Mike was checking their progress on Lt. Beals' navigation chart.

"Incoming from *Fredericton* sir," reported the communications watch. "Relayed from Marlant, *Victoria* reports 'revenge is a dish best served cold.'"

Commander Simpson laughed out loud at the *Victoria's* message. "Excellent chief! That is great news!" Mike knew it meant that the *USS Jimmy Carter* would not be taking part in the exercise after all. He'd have to remember to ask Admiral O'Hanlon where he'd gotten the Intel on the US sub's location. He hadn't been party to his crewman's mission to Virginia Beach which had come about after *Corner Brook* had sailed. Darren had been on shore course and in the middle of one class had been plucked away by an officer and brought directly to O'Hanlon's office to inform him of his upcoming 'vacation'.

Petty Officer 2nd Class Jake Trask punched a receipt over to *HMCS Fredericton* and returned to his equipment. He enjoyed his current duty on the boat for the simple fact that he was pretty much assured of being the first to know what was going on outside the confines of the hull and everyone knew that a sailor with information was automatically the most popular person aboard ship.

"Okay, Trask, send to *Fredericton* that we are ready to begin the exercise," ordered Mike. "Oh, and be sure to thank them for the help."

"Aye sir." Jake typed the message faster than some people could speak and punched it through the Lazcom system, watching the lights go through their blue-green-blue cycle.

Amazing stuff, he thought. This almost doesn't seem fair, he thought, but hey, all is fair in love and war and especially if it involves embarrassing the US Navy.

"Message sent and receipted captain. *Fredericton* sends that *USS Salt Lake City* is on station about thirty-two hundred yards ahead of the carrier, depth unknown, and that they are shutting down Lazcom in five minutes as per the ROE (Rules of Engagement) for this exercise."

"I already have the *Salt Lake City* sir." Brad announced "Depth about three hundred and fifty feet." He had picked her up a few minutes ago but had been busily trying to identify which of the *688* class boats she was before reporting her.

"Good work guys," Mike answered. This was going far smoother than he had anticipated it would. "Helm, take us down to three five zero feet and change heading to two two three degrees. Make our speed twelve knots."

That should set them up nicely on the American boat and perfectly for the *George Bush*. Taking on the *Salt Lake City* had not been part of their original plan but it was just too big and fat a target to pass up. Besides, embarrassing two US sub drivers in one day would be worth a lot of drinks back in Halifax from the skimmers who detested US 'bubbleheads' even more than Canadian ones.

* * * *

Two hours later, the two crewmen at the *Salt Lake City's* sonar suite were surprised to see their scopes go completely blank and flicker back on again.

"Err, captain. Something is…"

PING!!!

"SIR! Active sonar! Thirty degrees! About three thousand yards and…"

PING!!!

* * * *

"Okay Brad, secure active. What's he doing?"

"Wiping his butt….sir", replied *Corner Brook's* best set of 'ears'. "Sorry sir. He's diving fast! Ejecting decoys—lots of decoys. I'd say he's about out of them now." Brad had lost the other boat completely in the mess of bubbles and turbulence. But that was all right. The fleeing submarine wasn't their target.

"Helm, bring us to one nine five degrees. Slow to five knots. All hands; quiet boat!"

Mike, watched as the instruments indicated his boat slowing and as a result, making much less noise as her hull slipped through the water. The Americans knew he was here now and the more wide awake sonar operators probably had a pretty good idea where. The question was who would lose this game of 'acoustic chicken', and go active first?

"Sir, active sonar! It's *Fredericton*! She might have us."

"Okay Brad, let's give her a few moments and be sure." Mike was confident that the noise generated by the *Salt Lake City's* escape was probably confusing the surface ship's sonar and he hoped that by going quiet, the escorts might just chase after their own submarine.

The thick acoustic tiles covering the *Corner Brook's* hull would not reflect sound waves from anyone at a distance, and he was hoping they hadn't lost any of them on the voyage down here. Someone had to come up with a better adhesive for those things. Worse of all, the holes created by any missing tiles created noise at almost any speed as the water flowed over them.

"*Fredericton* has changed course. She's heading after the other boat sir!" Brad nearly fell out of his chair turning towards the captain. He was excitedly watching the line representing the Canadian frigate start to grow fainter on his scope. Too bad for her sonar team, but they should have known better. Skimmer ears, he thought. Sad bunch. Maybe someday he'd go over and offer to teach them a few things. More likely he'd find himself treading water in Halifax harbour if he did.

"Brad, how far to the carrier?"

"A bit over twenty-one hundred yards sir. Solution is locked in. He's ours."

"Weapons, open outer doors on one and two. You have the solution."

This was it, Mike thought. All their hard work and the best engineering minds in the navy had come down to this moment. He listened and watched as Brad made sure his headset was perfectly adjusted over his ears, avoiding the tendency to push them down lest he start hearing his own pulse amongst the sounds coming through the microphones arrayed along the hull and down the 'tail'.

"Nothing sir," Brad whispered, looking to his right to make sure the CO heard him.

They had worked. The outer doors on the bow of the submarine had opened without a sound on their newly designed hinges, while the updated complex plumbing had allowed the tubes to fill with water without a single swish of noise. In the past, the sound of water flooding a submarine's torpedo tubes or the opening of the tube doors were easily picked up by sonar operators anywhere in the area.

The weapons officer was watching the displays in front of him and noted the green lights flashing on the panel just above his head.

"Tubes one and two, ready sir. Connect test on both 'fish' positive," he informed the captain. It was crucial that the computer ran a quick test to make sure the tiny wires attached to the torpedoes were connected properly, or a very expensive piece of hardware would be totally useless the moment it left the tube. Down these wires would travel the control signals from the submarine, giving the torpedo its course to target as it tore through the water.

"Sonar, one hundred percent power! Hit her!" Mike looked back to make sure his command had been heard before Brad had a chance to echo it.

* * * *

The sound waves traveled rapidly through the water. Heard on *Fredericton*, her sonar crew knew immediately that they had goofed. Aboard *Vincennes*, the captain was relieved to know that although his ship was leaving the larger wake, some 'bubblehead' had figured it out and gone for the carrier. On board the *USS George Bush*, momentary panic ensued as they realized a submarine was sitting virtually in their lap from the strength of the sonar 'ping'.

Chapter 3

▼

"Helm, take us to periscope depth! I need a picture!"

Mike moved aside as one of the crew prepared the search periscope for the photo that would prove *Corner Brook's* success in 'sinking' the carrier. Using the digital imaging equipment integrated into the scope, the photo would soon be sent off to Marlant via satellite, where it would probably soon hang on the wall in Vice Admiral Brent O'Hanlon's office.

"Periscope depth sir", announced PO 1st Charley Poulin.

"Raise everything chief." Mike waited as the two scopes rose from their wells in the deck, the attack unit moving twice as fast as the larger search scope, designed that way in case they had to lower it fast in the unlikely event that they would perform a periscope attack. Above them, the sea seemed to be sprouting a metal forest as the scopes pierced the waves, followed by the induction, exhaust, radar, and ESM masts.

"Jake, we up yet?"

"Yes sir. You're on."

Mike plugged his headset into the jack on the side of the attack scope and grabbed the handles projecting from either side. Next to him, Able Seaman David Jones, a name that was surely a cruel twist of fate for a seaman, was busily snapping away at the camera system that was part of the search periscope. The boat's youngest crew member enjoyed photography more than anyone Mike had ever met and more than one of his photos adorned the home he shared with his wife Anne. Mike pushed the small button on the right handle as he zoomed in on the grey expanse of the *USS George Bush*.

"Warship *George Bush*, this is the Canadian submarine *Corner Brook*. Note you have been targeted and 'hit'." Although 'hit' in this case was only a euphemism as no torpedo actually entered the water. For the *Bush's* captain however, that was cold comfort.

*   *   *   *

Captain David Lee looked over at the young seaman to his right and nodded. "Acknowledge the message Clark and ask him if he needs any stores. I guess we can at least reward them with some goodies." With that said Lee walked over to the starboard side and grabbing his binoculars, scanned the water for a sign of the Canadian submarine.

"Helm, make turns for ten knots. Maintain course."

The inevitable echo of his orders was correct and Lee could feel the great ship start to slow, although it would be several minutes before she reached the slower speed. Aircraft carriers did nothing fast.

*   *   *   *

"All hands prepare to surface!" Mike made yet another scan around the compass with the scope and satisfied there was nothing presenting a possible collision threat, gave the order to surface the boat. Compressed air blew the last of the water from the ballast tanks and the crew felt the customary wobble as the boat broke through and became temporarily at least, a surface ship, albeit not a very stable one.

"Surface crew, to your posts! Helm, stand by for instructions from the bridge."

Commander Simpson climbed the ladder to the lower hatch and disengaging the locking device, turned the wheel, freeing it from its seated position. It moved remarkably easy considering its heavy weight, and he climbed through the opening up into the conning tower's 'lockout' chamber, continuing up to the cramped bridge. The fresh ocean air was almost intoxicating and he took a deep breath before fastening his ever present headset into the waterproof jack set into the side of the tiny space submariners called a 'bridge'. Calling down to the control room to test the communication's circuit, he received a reply, after which he grabbed his binoculars to examine the gigantic grey monster sailing alongside his comparatively puny boat.

"Helm, I have control. Come right to two eight zero degrees on my mark. Mark! Maintain present speed."

Simpson turned and watched the huge rudder poking from the water behind the submarine's hull slowly move, bringing his command on an even course with the carrier looming above his left shoulder. The sea was calm today or they would never have tried this manoeuvre without good reason.

Looking up at the huge expanse of windows lining the *Bush's* bridge he could see a figure that was undoubtedly her captain looking down at him through binoculars. He reached down and unclipped the small radio he was carrying on his belt.

"*Bush,* this is *Corner Brook,* do you copy?"

"*Corner Brook,* roger, we have you five by five. Vice Admiral Henderson sends his regards. Captain Lee was wondering if you'd like some fresh food."

That was the ultimate offer to a submarine crew of course, who on any extended cruise often ran out of perishables.

"We'll take some ham and sausage if you throw in some eggs," laughed Mike, knowing they wouldn't be able to transfer much on the light lines he'd be able to attach to the boat.

"On the way sir! Admiral Henderson also sends that he would like to be there when you run into *Fredericton's* skipper."

Yes, that would be interesting Mike thought. That was one part of the exercise that didn't quite go as planned. *Fredericton* was supposed to stay with the battle group and try to run down *Corner Brook* when she attacked, but in the confusion of the turbulent water, her sonar operator had assured the frigate's commanding officer that he had the Canadian submarine dead to rights and the CO had ordered the ship after it, thinking it would look good for him to save the carrier before *Corner Brook* had managed to attack it. Yes, Freddie's skipper would no doubt be the butt of some serious jokes when he returned to Halifax, thought Mike, smiling.

* * * *

Vice Admiral Henderson, having been in the loop on this test, was also surprised when 'combat' had informed him that *Fredericton* was claiming they had the target on sonar and that they were now making a hard right turn and steaming away at high speed in pursuit of it.

Right now, however, his mind was on a much more serious matter. The message in his hand from Norfolk claimed that the *USS Jimmy Carter* had been caught by the Canucks as well. He had not for a moment considered the Canadians capable of pulling that part of the exercise off successfully. Getting up slowly, he patted Captain Lee on the back and smiled. "You didn't have a chance this time Lee. Don't take it personally."

Heading through the hatch to CDC, the heart of the carrier's communications and weapons control, Henderson heard the 'Admiral's off the bridge' announcement called out behind him. Approaching the communications consol he looked down at the young seaman sitting there and asked for a secure communications link to Admiral George C. Carroll, Chief of Naval Operations at the Pentagon. In seconds the young ensign had the connection established and relinquished his chair to the Vice Admiral, wondering if he noticed how quickly contact had been established.

"Fast work son," smiled Henderson, making the young man's day.

"George?" Henderson waited a moment for the characteristically gruff voice of his old friend.

"Clive, you old seadog! Good to hear from you!"

"Good to hear you too George. We have a problem though."

"I heard." The voice was gruffer now. "No chance it was dumb luck?"

"No, the Canadians played it very smart. Their new communication system works as advertised and I don't doubt they could have taken out the whole battle group if they'd had more than one boat involved." Henderson paused a moment to let that sink in.

"The *Corner Brook* made it through the outer screen and none of the escorts reported even a slight contact. They even managed to out-fox their own frigate which wasn't part of the exercise. If the operation is going to go, *Carter* isn't the boat we want. Especially if she's still reporting that problem with the 'tail' winch." He hoped his old friend on the other end of the communication would know where he was heading with this. He did.

Sitting back in his large, padded chair, Admiral Carroll thought for a moment. Last minute changes were never good for a mission. Besides, there really wasn't enough time. Any change to an operational plan could jeopardize the operation which was in the final stages of being set up, but he knew what Clive was getting at. He was sure that the White House would never agree to it, but then again, this new President liked to include his allies on matters of world security so just maybe. George figured the President looked at it as a case of making your friends feel needed and possibly a little bit of having someone else share the blame if things went wrong. He huffed to himself. If things went wrong on this mission, Canada being involved would only make it that much more of a disaster.

"Clive, I know what you're thinking. Leave it with me and I'll go see what the 'Boss' thinks. You know, there is a small chance he'll buy into it. He likes this sort of multinational thing."

"Thanks George. I've worked with these Canadians for years. They're professional and damn good operators. I think they'll do a good job for us if Washington and Ottawa can come together on it."

George grimaced. They could have the most beautifully executed plan in history on their tables but if the politicians didn't like it, it was shredder time. But hey, they were the ones who wrote the pay cheques.

"Okay Clive. I'll let you know as soon as I hear. Take care old man!"

"Wha…" Clive started to comment but the line was already dead. Vice Admiral Henderson laughed out loud at the remark. Old man indeed! All of two weeks difference in their ages. Replacing the headset on the console, he stared at the displays in front of him without really seeing them, deep in thought.

The CO of the *Corner Brook* did seem to have his wits about him and it wouldn't be the first time a Canadian boat had nosed around somewhere it didn't belong.

Maybe. Just maybe…

* * * *

At the same moment Clive was pondering the Canadian's abilities, the precious cargo of tomorrow's breakfast was carefully being brought down the transfer line which stretched from the carrier to the deck of the submarine and then safely stored below in *Corner Brook's* fridges. After trading greetings and jokes, it was soon time to end the 'visit' between the David and Goliath of warships.

"Helm, come right to three four zero degrees." Mike ordered. "Prepare the boat to dive. Surface crew, below!"

There was no rush, as the days of diving to avoid enemy aircraft were long a part of history. No submarine would be found on the surface today if there was even the most remote possibility of danger. Submerged, her incredibly sensitive sonar would usually hear anything out there long before it became a threat, anything except perhaps another submarine.

* * * *

At Maritime Forces Atlantic, Vice Admiral O'Hanlon was studying the reports on his desk. *Victoria's* ambush had made surprisingly easy work of the US

Navy's stealthiest boat and she and her crew were now headed south to the Panama Canal, beginning their journey home to British Columbia.

Simpson was bringing *Corner Brook* back to Halifax where she would no doubt sail in with the classic broom tied to her attack scope, signifying a 'clean sweep' of her patrol area. Submariners, he knew, liked to hang onto their traditions. He grinned at the Skull and Crossbones pennant hanging on the back of his office door. It had been presented to him by the man occupying this very office the night Brent had come home with *HMCS Ojibwa* from one of those cruises that no one ever talked about. He knew Canadian submariners were among the best in the world and he was very proud of his crews and the boats they sailed in.

In the past twenty years, he had seen a lot of changes in the navy and especially in the submarine service, but through all the transformations, the really important things stayed the same, as they should. The phone chirping brought him back to the present and he punched the 'answer' button.

"O'Hanlon."

"Admiral? How are you? This is Caroline Wheeler."

Unconsciously, O'Hanlon sat up. He didn't receive very many phone calls from the Minister of National Defence. Actually, Brent thought, he couldn't recall any from the woman who was now single-handedly trying to reverse Canada's military from shrinking into obscurity. She had served in the Canadian Air Force in 1991 during the Gulf War and after an early retirement following an injury received when her C-130 had been hit by a lucky anti-aircraft burst, had entered politics. Rapidly propelling herself through the ranks of her party, she had been intent on taking the portfolio that was both the most revered, and despised position in the Canadian Government, and she had succeeded.

"I'm fine ma'am. How are you?"

"Great Brent, and it's Caroline, okay?"

"Yes ma'am...err...Caroline," Brent stumbled out.

From her small office (they all were on Parliament Hill, except of course for the Prime Minister's) Caroline Wheeler, Member of Parliament for Saskatoon, Saskatchewan, smiled at the thought of crusty Brent O'Hanlon actually being uncomfortable. She had studied his record, as she had all the upper echelon officers in HER armed forces. Brent had stood out as being fearless in the face of the enemy...and politicians. Sometimes considered one and the same by many in the forces. Usually that would be fatal for a military commander, but he tempered his opinions with facts and solutions which had won him respect, not only on the ships of the Canadian Navy, but also throughout the halls of Capital Hill. Such was a rarity here in the nation's capital, especially when the military was always coming hat-in-hand, looking for more money. She knew from her experience in the air force that far too often the soldiers, sailors and airman had to make do with equipment that was simply too old, too used up or when it was modern, in too short supply.

She hadn't been there for the submarine acquisition; sitting as an MLA in the province of Saskatchewan's legislature at the time, but it had peaked her interest and she had followed the process intently. Caroline had watched as the navy tried again and again to convince opposition MPs and the press that these boats were an incredible deal and they just needed more time to bring them into service.

She had also watched as Vice Admiral Brenton A. O'Hanlon had carefully sailed through the minefields of opposition and steadily assured and convinced the government that they would someday look on these boats with pride. She bet that Brent wasn't aware how close that day might be.

"Brent, look. I need one of your submarines."

*   *   *   *

The people she needed the boat for were slowly and carefully moving through the darkened decks of a ship. Night vision goggles over their eyes and infrared sights on the silenced weapons they carried, allowed them to move smoothly and quietly through the dark.

"Five minutes."

Lieutenant Boris Martin spoke quietly into his headset. The five members of his squad, a unit of SEAL Team Eight, had entered the ship twenty minutes earlier and had taken far too long, at least in his mind, to find the crates that his men had been assigned to destroy. God knows they were big enough, but their intelligence had been faulty and they had wasted precious minutes entering the wrong hold in search of their target.

"Two," quietly replied Senior Chief Jamal Washington.

"Three," whispered Chief Jim Lewis.

"Four!" Ensign Stewart Cunningham quipped, speaking too loud, as usual.

"Five," Chief Markus Sanchez completed the radio check-in.

"Evacuate now," Martin hissed into the mouthpiece of his two way communications equipment.

Grabbing their gear and weapons, the SEALs rushed up the ladders from the dark hold to the main deck, being careful not to trip over the bodies lying in the passageways. It was a full minute and a half before they reached the ships stern where a black zodiac was tied to one of the ship's rails with a long rope ladder. The first SEAL had barely touched the rail when the shrill yelp of the ship's horn froze the men in their tracks and strong floodlights blinded them.

"Not bad SEALs! Not bad," Commander Ted Quigley hollered down at them from the deck above. The 'dead bodies', actually sailors stationed in nearby Norfolk, rose from where they had lain still, some hanging over the rails. The squad had made quick work of taking them out with blanks fired from their silenced automatic weapons. Along the shore half a mile away, the lights of the US Navy's Little Creek Amphibious Base reflected on the water. "Okay, debrief at 0230 hours and don't be late!"

"Not bad?" Chief Jim Lewis asked no one in particular. "I thought that was damn good considering our faulty intelligence on which hold the target was in."

Martin looked his men over. They had come a long way in less than a week of training. No information had been given to them regarding the coming mission, other than the need to board a ship somewhere and destroy some merchandise. There had been a lot of heat put on them and they had been working night and day, perfecting the operation with tonight's exercise being the most successful yet. Whatever was going on, somebody sure had their knickers in a serious knot over it.

They had been selected because of the squad's innate familiarity with the *USS Jimmy Carter's* Charley pack. It was by far the most advanced element of the submarine's many capabilities. Able to carry six swimmer units, small mini-subs that could launch from a depth of one hundred and fifty feet; it also had room for two full SEAL squads along with all of their gear.

When the *Carter* had been re-commissioned three months ago, it had emerged with an unheard of flexibility. The submarine's crew did have to stand a fair amount of playful ribbing from others in their fraternity however, because it had been the third time the 'spy' sub had emerged from General Dynamic's Electric Boat Division supposedly 'completed'. The second time had been in 2005 when after half a dozen cruises she had been brought back to Electric Boat for the latest upgrade. At this rate she would be twenty years old with practically no mileage under her hull.

Best of all, because the 'packs' could be exchanged at will, Martin's squad had been able to practice with the Charley unit here at Little Creek, while the *Carter* had been out to sea.

"Crew! Fall out!" Commanded Martin.

"Sir!" Came the simultaneous reply.

The men had been together as a unit for ten months now. They ate, played and trained together as one so that now each of them could predict the others actions with a fair degree of accuracy. An important trait that could save their lives some day.

Together, they climbed down the rope ladder attached to the side of the USS *Newport*, an older amphibious assault ship that was playing 'target ship' for them this morning, and dropped into the waiting zodiac. The sailors left behind were astonished at what little noise emanated from the speedy little craft.

"Beach in three!" Called out Chief Jamal Washington, who at six foot three inches was the tallest member of the group.

"Permission to swim in L-T?" Stu Cunningham called over to Martin. Stu was the typical All American athlete who liked to push his personal envelope to the limits. It had almost cost him the cherished Trident insignia worn by the few men who made it through the toughest training in the United States military, if not the world. His instructors had seen immediately that this one would not be ringing the bell, unless it was in the middle of the night as a prank. The 'bell' was indeed just that, a large bell where recruits could bring to an end the punishing, inhumane torture that was US Navy SEAL training. They had been right. Stu had shone throughout training and displayed excellent leadership skills, but they also saw his obsessive need to push himself harder than anyone else. Some of the instructors thought this a dangerous trait, and it had caused them concern.

"Granted, but don't miss debrief or Quigley will have your hide!"

"I'll be there with bells..." the last word was washed out by the splash as he flopped backwards over the zodiac's side.

"Jerk," muttered Chief Petty Officer Marcus Sanchez. One of these days, he thought, that boy was going to be propeller mush. Sanchez knew that in a tough situation, Stu would be one of the few men he'd want covering his butt, but there were times when the guy was just too much of a 'showboat'.

As promised, three minutes later the Zodiac swept up the beach and they hauled it out of the water and headed in to change into work dress before going on to the command building. Commander Ted Quigley, who at forty-one seemed ancient to them, would be waiting to debrief them on tonight's training mission. The debriefings were brutally honest and every man was expected to be totally forthright and blunt. Something left unsaid or overlooked could cause the death of a squad member later on.

The moon was just starting to disappear below the horizon, as the squad, running double time to make sure they were early, reached the command building.

Stu caught up to them, still in his TAC suit, as Martin opened the door to conference room four and stepped inside.

The commander was seated at one end of a long table centered in the sparsely furnished room. On either side of him studying a map were two officers who Martin did not know, but he did recognize the two stars on the shoulder boards of the taller of the two men.

"Attention on deck!" yelled Martin, who sensed rather than saw his men come to rigid attention behind him while noticing how rapidly the map on the table was rolled up.

"Lieutenant Martin and squad reporting for debrief sir!"

"Stand easy gentlemen," the tall officer with the stars said, turning to face them and unrolling the map again. "There has been a change in plans."

Martin really didn't like the sound of that. There was an old-school theory that changes in plans meant someone had not collected enough intelligence for the mission, and they had probably just discovered that. Changes were dangerous for him and his men. The SEALs were a brave lot but they were not suicidal or reckless. Boris could smell a bad mission ten miles away, and this one was starting to smell pretty rank.

"Guys," started Commander Quigley, seeing the doubt in his team leader's eyes and wanting to get started before he said anything, "this is Rear Admiral David Randall, and Commander Greg Newell. They will brief you on the changes and how they will affect you. They're all yours." With that Ted sat down on one of the metal chairs set around the table and let the Seals step up to the map he and the other two officers had been looking at. The Mediterranean Sea filled the center with all the surrounding countries' coastal areas in sharp detail around the edges.

"Martin, how was this morning's exercise?" queried the commander.

"Excellent! We were given bad Intel, yet still pulled it off in the time bubble," he replied, referring to the time allotted for them to enter, carry out their mission and disembark from the ship. "The packages were scored at ninety-seven percent, but the three percent loss was caused be a faulty fastener on one of them."

'Package' was the current euphemism for explosives devices. Usually they were contained in small, easily carried plastic boxes, with detonators, timers and attachment systems integrated into them.

"Good, very good," remarked Commander Newell. "That part of the mission is unchanged. Unfortunately the *Carter* won't be available to you due to one of its systems being unserviceable. We do have a replacement for you however and we are quite certain it will work out just fine."

Martin looked him straight in the eye, heard 'spook' in his mind, and decided this man's eyes would tell him nothing. The *USS Jimmy Carter* was the best 'spy' boat in the world so any replacement was going to be second rate, at best.

"I am unable to give you any details at the moment but you can expect to egress a five-man lockout chamber." Greg looked them over. It was obvious they didn't like the news he'd given them. Nor did they believe that the replacement would be suitable, but there would be no outward sign of protest. Newell hadn't expected any. After all, these men were SEALs.

Greg didn't care for the disguise he wore today. He would have rather sat down with these men and laid it all out for them. They deserved that much, but his boss back in McLean, Virginia, wouldn't go for it. The Director had a standing order to keep information disbursement as limited as possible. It probably made sense, thought Greg, but then again, it wasn't his life on the line. Well, at least not this time.

"One of the '*688*'s?" asked Martin querying what submarine they would be traveling in.

"Sorry," he answered, meaning it. "That's all I can say for now. You and your crew will be briefed as soon as possible."

"Men, I assure you that your new 'transportation' will be suitable in every way and you will not be placed in any greater harm," Rear Admiral Randall stated, signalling the end to the meeting. David knew the worst thing a leader could do to his men was to keep them out of the loop before an operation, but in this case, it was best considering the implications of the story getting out. One country sticking its neck way out there was enough for right now.

"Squad, you are dismissed. No more exercises will be held for thirty-six hours so have fun! But! Make sure you are available!" Commander Quigley smiled at the small group and gave them a 'thumbs up', his way of patting them on the back for a good exercise.

Yes! Thought Stu. A day off! A couple hours sleep, quick shower and shave and hit the main gate. Va beach, here I come!

The rest of the men headed for the Team Eight barracks and some much needed sleep. It had been a long night and the 'debriefing', if you could call it that, had left them feeling uneasy and even more tired.

* * * *

Two hours later and a few miles down the road from Little Creek, CPO 2nd Darren Cole was slowly waking up and planning his day with Heather, who while chatting with him last night had suggested they go for a drive, giving her an opportunity to show him around. He had tried to think of somewhere for them to go and explore together but decided it was best that he act as though he had never been here before and let her suggest a destination.

Looking down at the stretch of newly raked beach from his bedroom balcony, he saw that it was going to be another beautiful day. He was looking forward to spending it with the beautiful young girl who had checked him into the hotel the day before. Permission to take a few vacation days had been granted when he had called Halifax to check in at Marlant. Not that he had anticipated any problems seeing how he was there anyway and his boat was now returning to Halifax after the successful conclusion of the recent exercise for a light refit. Jody had filled him in on the details while waiting for personnel to clear the leave request. Yes, he thought, watching the dolphins playing in the ocean; life was good.

It would have been great to have been aboard at his weapons station when *Corner Brook* had taken out the heart of that American carrier battle group, but this day was shaping up to be even better! He grabbed the ironing board and iron from where it was stored on a rack by the back door to his suite. Side door he thought since in reality, it was just down the hall a few yards from the 'front' one.

Unpacking what he hoped were nice clothes that would impress Heather, he started ironing out the creases formed when most men and sailors in particular, attempted that mysterious task known as 'packing'.

The phone on the bedside table rang and he reached to pick it up, wondering who would be calling him here. Anyone he knew would have dialled his cell phone.

"Hello?"

"You awake sleepy head?" Heather laughed as Darren described his current mission.

"You know if you pack them right in the first place you don't get wrinkles!"

"I know, but I was in a rush to…to get to the airport." He almost said 'get off the base'. It was a good thing she didn't ask how his non-existent suits would have looked for the business meetings. He didn't like to lie to her. Well, it wasn't really a lie; more like a fib really. Well not even that he rationalized, because it was in the interest of national security, so…her laugh derailed his train of thought.

"I do have something I need to pick up at my parent's house. Would that be okay? They live just outside Williamsburg up the highway a bit, unless of course you had somewhere special in mind that you wanted to go…" She paused. "Hello?"

"Err...sure! That would be great!" he managed to say with some enthusiasm. Parents! Yuck! "I don't really have anything in particular in mind. A nice drive anywhere would be great. Is there anything touristy around Williamsburg?" Meeting the parents! This can't be good! Darren's mind raced as he stretched the phone cord to its maximum length, reaching for his suitcase in search of something nicer to wear.

"Touristy? In Williamsburg? Oh I'm sure we can find something 'touristy' for you to see around there." She laughed again. She liked this young man. He tried so hard to be debonair but he was obviously just a regular down-to-earth guy. They had spoken on the phone for almost three hours the previous evening and when she had finished chatting with him she'd gone to the kitchen for a bite to eat. While munching on a ham and cheese sandwich, she had decided to call her mom to say hi. Her dad had answered and reminded her that she needed to get her university application papers in and they were still sitting on top of the bed in her old room there at home.

They had talked for some time and she told him about the man staying at 'her' hotel. Heather's father, in typical dad fashion, had asked what the man did for a living and she had responded that she didn't really know, but since he was here on business it couldn't be too bad. Her father had relented, knowing Heather was careful who she dated, and upon hearing they would be dropping by in the morning to pick up her university application, he promised with a laugh that he wouldn't do anything to embarrass her.

"That's great Heather," Darren answered. "Maybe you can show me around down here, and when you get up to Halifax someday, I can return the favour." That was his second 'almost' invitation to visit Nova Scotia. This seems to be going awfully fast, Darren thought to himself, but in spite of that, he didn't feel inclined to slow it down any.

"We'll see," she replied. "When do you think you'll be here to pick me up?"

He had the directions to her apartment building carefully drawn out from their conversation last night, and allowing for the extra ironing time for his 'meet the parents' clothes, he told her around nine-thirty.

"Great! I'll see you then!" She smiled as she replaced the cordless phone in its base. Meeting her parents had not been part of her plan for the day, but they were good people and she felt sure Darren would like them. Besides, it wasn't like he was in the navy. That would never work out with her dad. Being the daughter of the Chief of Naval Operations for the United States Navy sure did limit the men a girl could date. Not daring to bring home a sailor wasn't easy when you lived just outside the world's largest naval base.

Darren finished ironing and after a shower, got dressed and checked for messages on his cell phone. No messages. That was good news! Grabbing his camera in case there were some good photo opportunities, he headed out the door and down the elevator. His rental car was where he had left it in the hotel parking lot, outside on the second level.

Feeling the morning sun warm on his face as he unlocked the car, he could see by the cloudless sky that it was indeed going to be another beautiful day in Virginia Beach. Tossing his camera bag into the trunk he got behind the wheel and carefully manoeuvred his way out of the parking garage, turning right to head north up Atlantic Avenue. Even this early in the day, the tourists were already beginning to line the side walk, checking out the seemingly endless rows of gift shops and tourist traps. He was careful to avoid the trolley lanes painted on the streets, designed for the nostalgic buses that catered to the many visitors. You had to give the city of Virginia Beach credit he thought, they made sure you left with a desire to return again someday.

Steering left to enter the little dog leg that Atlantic Avenue made before continuing north, he caught a red blur out of the corner of his eye. An old Mustang convertible, ignoring the red traffic signal roared through the intersection cutting him off. "Idiot!!" screamed Darren as he swerved to the right, his tires squealing in protest before hitting the curb. The other driver looked right at him and gave him the universally recognized sign of contempt.

I can't believe the way the tourists drive around here! Stu thought, seeing the other car come to a stop against the curb. What a bunch of...the SEAL's eye caught the red traffic light in his rear view mirror, ending the thought. Oh shit! Well, the other car looked fine, but man, that guy sure looked severely pissed off!

Chapter 4

Recovering his wits, Darren slowly pulled the car back onto the street and driving slowly at first continued up Atlantic Avenue to where it curved left and headed west, becoming Shore Drive. He made it the rest of the way without further incident and after a brief search, found the address Heather had given him. Thinking that perhaps he should have brought a flower, he got out of the car and walked around towards the pebbled walkway leading to her apartment. No, it's way too soon for that, he told himself. Before he reached it, the front door of the building swung open and Heather stepped out smiling at him as she came down the walk towards the car. Rushing to get there before she reached the passenger door, Darren rapped his right leg against the front bumper and limped painfully as he reached over to open the door for her.

"My, what a gentleman! Are you okay?"

Darren blushed, nodding. It was an old habit he had developed watching his mom and dad and it just came naturally.

"Are all you Canadians this polite?" Heather asked taking a look at the scratch on his leg.

"We are," he laughed, trying not to grimace from the pain. "It might be something in the air up there."

"I hope you don't lose that breathing the polluted air down here," she joked.

"No fear! I try not to inhale too much." Lame, he thought. Very lame!

"Good! Looks like you'll live." Again she laughed. "So you found my place without any trouble?"

"No trouble at all. You give very good directions." He recounted the incident back on Atlantic Avenue and how the driver of the other car had nearly run into him. After the near collision, he had stopped to sit for a moment while his knees and heart returned to normal. It had been that close.

"That's a really bad corner. They should just get rid of the curve and turn it into a normal intersection. Sounds like you handled it like a pro," she grinned and reached over, giving him a light peck on the cheek. "That's for keeping your cool. Shows character."

Darren blushed crimson. I hate when I do that, he cringed feeling his face go red. At the same instant Heather was thinking just how much she loved that he did that.

As they drove on, the conversation from the night before continued. She teased him about meeting her parents and how he would be the first man she brought home in over a year. She laughed at the nervous look in his eyes. Reaching Highway 64, she directed him to continue west over the bridge leading to one of the tunnels that would take them under the bay to Hampton, just across the water from Norfolk.

"Wow, look at the aircraft carriers!" Darren enthused, trying to look and drive at the same time as the dockyard of the naval base came into view on his left. He could make out the superstructures of two *Nimitz* class carriers as well at the *USS Enterprise* with its distinctively shaped island structure. The masts of dozens of warships spread out until they disappeared in the morning haze.

"Amazing," he sighed.

Heather was thinking 'YES!' He knows what an aircraft carrier is at least! Her dad wouldn't find him completely boring like the last guy she had brought home who's only apparent interest had been beach volleyball. Maybe she'd see if Darren wanted to take a tour of the base on the way back. It seemed like he might enjoy an 'up close' look at the many navy ships in port.

"Have you ever seen a battleship?" Heather inquired. "The *USS Wisconsin*, a World War II ship, is berthed downtown and you can go aboard and tour her"

"Once, when I was...on vacation in New York City." He caught himself again, but this time she had noticed the hesitation in his voice. He had been there during Fleet Week a few years ago, on board one of the Canadian Navy warships taking part, and afterwards, his ship had continued down the east coast to Norfolk, Virginia, where he'd toured the *Wisconsin*.

"I had to go home early," he continued, thinking fast. "After supper the first night, I had a really bad reaction to something I ate. It was pretty scary," he added, which was true. Just that it had happened at a 'greasy spoon' in Norfolk, not New York City.

"You poor thing!" she exclaimed patting his hand. "Did you have to go to the hospital?"

"Just long enough to have my stomach pump…er sorry. That sounds kind of gross I guess."

"That's okay," she smiled, touching his hand and holding it this time.

He really did have his stomach pumped, although it had been done at the base hospital at the Norfolk Navy Base. He'd been much more careful about where he ate after that episode and avoided any restaurant with more flies than waiters.

"There was a navy thing going on in New York at the time," he said, changing the subject. "It was pretty impressive."

"Oh that would have been Fleet Week. The navy just uses that as an excuse to go to the big city and get drunk," she frowned.

She must have dated a sailor, Darren was thinking, trying hard to suppress a smile. Oh well, she almost was again! He was starting to wonder where this could possibly go. Once she found out what he really did, he envisioned her throwing him out to the sharks that swam a little further out beyond the dolphins.

"It sure does get warm around here." He tried to change the subject while pushing any thoughts of the future out of his mind.

"I know. I just love it!" she gushed. "There is no place like Virginia in the summer time."

They continued driving through the countryside and a half hour later, highway signs indicated they were getting close to Williamsburg.

"Okay, the exit we need is coming up after the next corner," she directed. "Their place is just off highway five right outside a little town called Five Forks."

Following her directions, which were impressively accurate, Darren brought the car up a smooth gravel road that curved gently through a large grove of tall trees. A strong fragrance of flowers enveloped the car as they drove through a veritable tunnel formed by the boughs stretching from trees on both sides of the road. Rounding a corner the solid wall of trees suddenly spread open to reveal a huge white house, complete with a pillared front porch and a beautifully manicured lawn.

It's a scene right out of 'Gone with the Wind', he thought. Whoa! These people were definitely not poor!

"Nice house!"

"Thanks. It's so much bigger than they need, but Mom loves it. She fancies herself a throwback to the Southern Belles of the past. But don't let it fool you. My folks are real down to earth people."

"O…kay," he smiled. Darren didn't believe her for a second. Down to earth people lived in bungalows, about the size of the garage he was approaching that was dwarfed by the huge home alongside it. Pulling up in front of the majestic southern mansion on the large circular driveway, he saw her parents coming out the front door. Or maybe they're just the servants; he smirked, keeping the observation to himself.

"Mom! Dad! How are you?" Heather rushed out of the car, not waiting for her door to be opened this time, and hugged the handsome older couple. "This is Darren Cole. He's Canadian, but other than that he seems fine," she joked as her parents turned to greet him.

"Pleased to meet you, son!" Her father came over to him with an outstretched hand. The two men's eyes met and George Carroll liked the first impression he received. Good firm hand shake and the kid didn't avert his eyes. Years of commanding men had made the Chief of Naval Operations a good judge of character. It's a good thing he had spoken to Heather about this young man last night, he thought. Otherwise he would have bet money that Darren was a military man from the way he looked and carried himself.

"This is my wife Deborah."

Darren shook the woman's extended hand. She was quite beautiful and obviously kept herself in good shape. He couldn't help the old adage coming to mind that if you want to see what your wife will look like in twenty-five years; take a look at her mother.

"I'm honoured to meet you ma'am."

"My pleasure young man and you may call me Debby."

"I just started warming up the barbeque," her father announced. "You kids going to join us for lunch?"

Heather looked over at Darren who grinned hungrily and nodded. "Sure Daddy! Darren, wait until you've had one of Daddy's steaks. You will not believe how good a cook he is!"

"Sounds great," Darren answered. "I'm famished!" Things seemed to be going really good with this visit so far and to think he'd actually been worried about it!

"Your home is magnificent Mr. Carroll. It looks like something right out of a civil war movie."

"It should, son. Only what took place in this area was no movie. A few skirmishes happened right in those woods you drove up through. We still find minni balls and other stuff when we dig around in the garden. It's lucky the house survived considering the amount of fighting that took place around here."

"Incredible," Darren whispered as they walked through the front door into the spacious foyer. He stopped short for just a second as his eyes adjusted to the light, then realized he was looking at a large painting of a warship hanging on the wall to his right.

"That was my last command," George proudly announced, seeing Darren examining the painting. "The *USS Bainbridge*. She was a guided missile cruiser when I had her, although they called her a destroyer when she was originally launched. You know, she was one of the world's first nuclear powered warships. She's gone now. Scrapped, no…recycled they call it nowadays, but the end is still the same.

Darren's mind was racing. Heather's dad is or at least had been in the US Navy. He was probably pretty high up in rank too. They wouldn't give command of a nuclear warship to just anyone. He'd have to tread carefully.

"It…it's a nice ship," was all Darren managed to get out of his suddenly very dry mouth.

"She sure was," George replied putting the emphases on 'she' for to him each ship had a soul and were always referred to in the feminine.

"So, you were in the navy?" Darren asked, trying to sound interested but not too interested.

"Still am. Not for much longer though. In two more years I'll call it quits and spend the rest of my life trying to keep this old 'barn' standing," he laughed as he ducked a playful punch from Debby.

"George Carroll, you know that is not at all true. You will spend the rest of your life terrorizing the fish living in the Chesapeake!"

"Okay hon. But I'm holding you to that!" This time he didn't duck in time and was rewarded with a swat.

"Make yourself at home Darren. Would you like a soda?"

"Soda? Oh! You mean pop! Sure. Anything you have will be fine." He sat down in a huge arm chair and glanced at the photos hanging in the huge room and sitting across the mantle of the fireplace. One of them was obviously Heather in her high school graduation gown. She looked absolutely radiant. No need for any touch up work there, he thought, unlike his own photo which needed a master's touch to remove the many zits he sported all over his face at the time. Standing, he walked over to examine the rest of the photos on the wall. Two of them were of warships. One of which he recognized as the *USS Coral Sea*. He was pretty sure that she was also decommissioned now. He had toured her as a teenager when the aircraft carrier had visited Halifax on a 'good will' visit. The nearly endless expanse of the flight deck had impressed him along with the shear size of the ship and the feeling of power she emitted. That may very well have been the point when he had decided to join the navy. Perhaps Mr. Carroll had been aboard that same day and they might have met.

George came in with their sodas and caught him looking at the picture.

"The *Coral Sea* was my first duty," he said, with pride in his voice.

'Nope', Darren answered his unasked question. He wouldn't even have been born then.

"She was finally decommissioned and scrapped a few years ago. A group of us almost went to see her before the torches fell but we thought better of it and decided to just hoist a few in her honour instead." He stared distantly at the photo and it was obvious that he was reliving some event from the past.

"I was aboard her when she visited Halifax a while back," Darren broke the silence of the moment, happy to be telling the truth for a change.

"Really?" George turned to him, noting that the young man had not only walked his old ship's deck, but was also referring to HER in the proper way.

"I was in high school then and I can remember thinking how amazing it must be to control something so huge."

"It is that my boy." George put his arm around Darren's shoulder and led him to the couch. "Have some soda," he said handing over the glass. "So what do you do for a living?"

Darren felt a moment of panic, but the vibration from the cell phone on his belt distracted him before his mind had time to react.

"I'm so sorry. Would you excuse me for a moment Mr. Carroll?"

"Of course. Let me go check the barbeque while you talk. Heather will be back in a moment. She's just helping her mom in the kitchen."

"Thank you sir."

"It's George!"

"George," smiled Darren, waiting until the man had left the room before hitting the 'talk' button. "Hello?" Talk about saved by the bell, he thought.

"Darren? I'm sorry man, but your vacation has been cut short."

"Jody? You're kidding. You don't understand! Please tell me you're kidding!"

"Sorry pal. You need to report to the Little Creek base at 0800 tomorrow. When you get to the gate, ask for Commander Ted Quigley. He'll be expecting you."

"Little Creek? That's an amphibious base...commander?" Darren's mind raced. "What's going on?"

"Can't say, man. Sorry. So tell me…what does she look like?" Jody knew that Darren must have met somebody, especially the way he sounded so forlorn about losing his vacation.

"Very cute, not that it matters much now."

"Sorry again pal. Keep this under your hat. It's Level 1."

"Okay Jodster. Take care." He pushed the 'end' button and returned the phone to his belt. Damn! His mind was torn between hating this interruption of his time with Heather, and a powerful curiosity over what the hell was going on. He didn't even have Level 1 clearance! Well, at least he hadn't until now.

"Everything okay, son?" George saw the concerned look on Darren's face as he returned and thought it must have been bad news.

"Yes and no. I have to attend a meeting first thing tomorrow that had previously been cancelled." He felt his stomach knot at the lie.

"Well why don't you just stay here tonight as our guest and drop back tomorrow after your meeting is over. Then you two can have supper here and head back to the city afterwards."

"That would be great sir…George. Thank you very much. I don't want to impose…" As long as the 'meeting' didn't take more than the afternoon, he thought, extremely disappointed with the way things had turned out.

"Not at all!" George interrupted his protest. "It would be our pleasure."

"Thank you again! I'll go explain it to Heather. I hope she'll understand."

"I'm sure she will," George assured him. "She grew up watching me leave her mom behind for more cruises than I care to remember. She's a good girl."

Darren caught the half hidden warning there and acknowledged it; "I know she is. I'm looking forward to getting to know her better. If you'll excuse me, I'll tell her and be right back." Darren followed the direction Heather and her mom had gone and found them in the not surprisingly, huge kitchen, unwrapping the biggest steaks he'd ever seen.

"You must have made quite an impression on George," Mrs. Carroll remarked. "He brought out the 'good' steaks. He doesn't offer these to just anyone who drops by."

"They look delicious Mrs. Carroll! Heather, I just had a call and I have to attend a meeting tomorrow morning after all, but your dad suggested I stay the night and then just leave from here in the morning and come back afterwards for supper. Would that be okay with you?" He suddenly realized that it might not be okay with her at all.

Heather didn't try to hide the disappointment in her eyes and he felt thrilled and guilty at the same time. She really did seem to like him and in spite of the short time they'd shared, he was starting to like her as well.

"That's okay. It'll give Mom and me a chance to catch up on everything."

"I'm sorry. I should have lost the cell phone along the way."

"You're forgiven. But don't make a habit of it!" she laughed. Well at least her father must really like the guy. The prime steaks were one thing but asking him to stay over like that was a first. "Now here, give these to Dad and tell him I want mine well done, not charcoaled!" She handed him a serving tray with the thick steaks hanging off the sides.

"Yes ma'am."

"Polite young man," noted Debby, as Darren headed for the patio.

"Very. He's really nice. Dad seems to like him too."

"Yes…that is odd," her mom replied smiling. She thought back to the many times some poor fellow Heather had brought home had kept looking at his watch, fidgeting and anxious to leave and get away from her father's interrogation.

"Oh Mom!" Debby threw the towel she was wiping the counter with at her mother.

"Hey! I was just beginning to worry that you'd be a spinster or something!" she laughed throwing the towel back at her daughter.

In the living room, Darren handed the plate over to George and told him about Heather's instructions.

"Ha! She's too picky! Listen son, maybe you should run for it now, before it's too late!" He laughed as he headed for the patio doors leading to the back yard.

"Come on. I'll show you how a master grills a steak."

The two men went outside and again Darren was amazed by the scale of the property. The back yard, if you could call it that, stretched for what seemed like acres. The grass was meticulously mowed and the hedge that bordered the property was perfectly trimmed. Flowers of a dozen varieties grew in strategically placed spots, sprouting from both the ground and numerous planters of every size and shape. A cloud of grey smoke rose from the barbeque, the only regular sized thing around here, Darren noticed.

"So what was it you do for a living?" George asked once again.

"I'm in advertising." It didn't come out smoothly and he could see suspicion flicker briefly in the man's blue eyes for the first time today. Hell, thought Darren. I've blown it now!

* * * *

"Incoming Lazcom message sir," announced the sailor at *Corner Brook's* communications console. Commander Mike Simpson turned to his communications officer and studied his countenance. One thing about Petty Officer 2nd Class Jake Trask; he'd make a poor poker player. You could usually tell the gist of a message by the expression on the communications officer's face. The look this time was a combination of puzzlement and distaste. Odd, Mike thought. He hadn't seen that one before.

"It's from *Montreal*," Jake announced, answering the obvious question from his commanding officer. The message made no sense to him, but he had confirmed it and knew it would not be popular with the *Corner Brook's* crew who all expected that they'd be heading home tomorrow night. He handed the printout from the Lazcom to Mike who read it and swore under his breath.

"Confirm this petty officer."

"Already done sir. It's accurate."

Mike read the message again. 'From Marlant to *Corner Brook*. Rendezvous with *Montreal* for at sea replenishment at coordinates given. Afterwards, set course for Yarmouth, Nova Scotia, where you will conduct PR visit for three days while awaiting operational orders.'

This will not be well received, he thought, to say the least! Moving to the center of the control room he reached up and flicked a switch on the panel controlling the boat's address system.

"All hands, this is the CO. Prepare surface watch and replenishment details. We will be rendezvousing with *Montreal* for stores and we are then directed to Yarmouth for a three day PR visit." He heard a concerted groan from those in the control room and thought fast. "I guess they figured we'd be a bit too rowdy after our stellar mission, so they wanted to give us some time to cool down before letting you animals loose in Halifax."

It worked. The laughter, although forced, was slightly more pronounced than the groans had been and he watched as the control room crew returned to their jobs. Turning off the address system, he circled to his navigation officer, Lt. Fred Beals. He'd seen the questioning look in Fred's eyes when Mike omitted the part of the message that referred to 'operational orders'.

"I know what you're thinking Fred," he spoke quietly. "I'll wait and see what the orders are before ruining everyone's day. Plot us a line to Yarmouth beyond the rendezvous with *Montreal* and pass the course on to Charley." Then grabbing the mike again, he announced, "Crew stand by to surface! Sonar, check for traffic!"

"All clear sir. I have *Montreal* fifteen hundred yards north of us." CPO 2nd Derek Leaman announced as he double checked the screens and Lazcom again. With Brad, his immediate superior off duty, he wanted to make a good impression on the CO.

Yarmouth, Mike thought again…great! This would probably prove to be a boring visit, and after such a successful mission the men deserved to go straight home to their families. He knew better than to give voice to his disappointment as it was his job to set a positive atmosphere for the crew—no matter how he felt personally.

*   *   *   *

The sun had just started to peek over the horizon when the clock radio next to Darren's bed began blaring the six o'clock news. He looked up; exploring his surroundings through sleep filled eyes and fumbled for the 'off' switch on the radio. It had been late when Heather escorted him to the guest house tucked in under some flowering magnolia trees across the back yard. The so called 'guest house' would have easily accommodated a small family as their primary residence. He had chatted with Heather well into the night and during the conversation she had mentioned how well her father had taken to him. It's a good thing she hadn't witnessed her father's reaction to the lie about his job. The old guy was pretty wily and probably had suspicions about him now. He only hoped that he would be able to avoid any further scrutiny during the visit with her parents.

Once he finished showering, Darren dressed in the casual clothes he and Heather had bought last night at the local Wal-Mart. I should have thrown something extra in the trunk, he reflected. Looking in the mirror he was impressed. Heather obviously had good taste in men's clothing. They were not as snappy as his dress whites but they would do for this meeting and hopefully there wouldn't be any problem at the Little Creek gate when he showed up. Finishing up, he straightened the room and headed quietly out to his car. No point in waking everyone else this early, he thought while carefully closing the door. He did notice a light on in one of the upstairs bedrooms however. Probably Heather's father getting off to an early start at whatever it was he did with the navy. Darren had figured him to be sailing a desk at Norfolk, filling in space and probably checking off his calendar every morning, counting down to retirement day.

Driving slowly down the lane, the petty officer stopped off at a coffee shop and found himself once again explaining what a 'double-double' was to the girl behind the counter. Back on Highway 64, heading east this time, he found the morning traffic quite heavy, although moving at a decent clip. If he ended up late for whatever this meeting was, it served them right for giving him such short notice. He thought again of his cancelled trip to the beach with Heather today. He'd get whatever this meeting was out of the way and they'd hit the beach for some fun and sun tomorrow.

The traffic moved along very well for the time of day and in no time at all he found himself on Ocean View, and being early, decided to have a quick breakfast. Seeing a McDonald's coming up on his left, he pulled into the drive-thru and ordered a couple of Egg McMuffins. Ten minutes later, having finished them and downing the last of his luke-warm coffee, he had only to drive across the street to enter the amphibious base. Slowly pulling up to what he hoped was the right gate, he stopped the car when directed by a young sailor who he noticed was carrying a sidearm.

"Good morning sir. May I ask where you are headed?" Seaman Troy Bellingham was polite as always to civilians entering the base. You never knew who it might be. A friend of his had found that out the hard way when he had been too abrupt with the president of Raytheon Corporation.

"I have an appointment with Commander Ted Quigley," Darren told the guard while passing him his Canadian Forces ID card which the seaman studied for a few moments. Probably don't get a whole lot of Canadians dropping in, Cole mused. Even fewer dressed in civvies no doubt.

"Please park your car right there," Troy pointed to an empty parking space outside the gate marked 'Visitor', "and stand by."

The politeness had been replaced by a more hardened, professional bearing, Darren noticed. Now he was just another sailor to the man. Reversing the car into the space back outside the gate where he had been instructed to wait, he turned on the radio trying to find something other than a country music station. Finally settling for an 'all talk' channel, he relaxed and waited. What seemed like half an hour passed before a 'topless' Hummer pulled up behind him and an officer he thought must be Quigley, walked over to his window.

"Petty Officer Darren Cole?"

"Yes sir," replied Darren getting out. He noticed now that this man wore the twin bars of a navy lieutenant. Obviously not Commander Quigley.

"I'm Lt. Boris Martin. Do you have any belongings in the car?"

"No…I mean yes. Just my camera," Darren stammered, wondering why he might not be coming back to the car.

"Okay, grab it and come with me. The car will be returned to the rental location."

Darren grabbed the camera case and slinging it over his shoulder jogged over to the Hummer.

"I'm not going to be done here by sixteen hundred, am I sir?" He already felt that he knew the answer.

"Sixteen hundred…today?! I'm afraid not chief!"

Darren hung on tight as Martin manoeuvred the grey Hummer expertly around one of the concrete barriers protecting the base entrance. Not good, he thought. Heather was not going to be happy about this at all.

"Can you tell me what I'm doing here sir?" Darren asked, not really expecting an answer. Maybe the US Navy had gotten wind of his mission here and was really pissed off about it.

"Not yet chief. But don't worry," he laughed. "You'll be in good hands."

Darren didn't respond, not seeing what was so funny. Glancing to his left at the man behind the wheel, he noticed the metal pin on the 'A' uniform Martin was wearing; the Trident insignia worn by US Navy SEALs. If his future involved the SEALs in any way, Heather was now the least of his worries! Although he didn't know it yet, a much more immediate worry was now pulling up to the same gate that he had just driven through.

"Good morning sir!" barked seaman Bellingham as he came to rigid attention and saluted at the open window of the navy staff car.

"Good morning, seaman!" replied the Chief of Naval Operations, Admiral George C. Carroll, showing the young guard his ID card. "I have a meeting with Commander Quigley this morning."

"Thank-you sir. Please proceed." Troy opened the gate and watched as the staff car wound its way around the concrete barriers with smooth precision. Wow, he thought. The CNO! Something big was going down. He wondered if it had anything to do with that Canadian in civvies who also had a meeting with the SEAL commander this morning.

At the SEAL operations center, Commander Quigley was going over the last minute details which always seemed to crop up when one of his crews was about to depart. There was always some piece of gear missing or unavailable it seemed, just when there was no time left to procure it. A rap on his door came as he e-mailed what he hoped would be the final instructions to base supply.

"Enter," he hollered. The door swung open to reveal Admiral Carroll smiling at him. Ted jumped to his feet and stood at attention.

"At ease, Ted. Any coffee around here?"

"Yes sir," Ted replied, grabbing a couple of mugs from the shelf above his coffee maker which was, as always, at least half full. "Black?"

"That will be fine. So, how are Martin's boys doing?"

"Great, sir. The last exercise we ran was flawless, even though I threw a few monkey wrenches into it. They're ready."

"Good. The mission is cleared all the way up. The Canadians have diverted their submarine to Yarmouth, Nova Scotia, supposedly on a good-will visit."

"Why Yarmouth, Admiral?" Ted knew where Yarmouth was but couldn't see what that could possibly have to do with the mission.

"There is a high speed ferry; a catamaran called *The Cat* running between Yarmouth and Bar Harbor, Maine," explained Admiral Carroll. "That's how we're going to get your men over to the Canadian boat. They'll go across on *The Cat* masquerading as tourists, and then go aboard the *Corner Brook* which will be open to the public, with the rest of the civilians. They just won't be departing the submarine when the rest of the tour does."

Ted was impressed with the simplicity of the plan. He knew the importance of keeping operational plans as simple as possible. Simple plans didn't seem to unravel half as easily as some of the complex ones he and his men had been sent out on.

"Think you can make your boys look like tourists?" asked George, a hopeful look on his face.

"It'll be a stretch," Ted laughed, "but I'm sure we can pull it off. Fortunately really short hair is 'in' right now, and they'll like the idea of wearing something besides BDUs for a change."

"Good. No point in keeping them in the dark any longer. Are they ready for the briefing?"

"Yes sir," answered Ted. "And Lieutenant Martin just checked in with the Canadian sailor who was playing 'spy' on us down here." He looked down at his notes. "A Chief Petty Officer 2nd Class Darren Cole. Maritime Forces Atlantic in Halifax suggested he could return to Canada with the team. He'll be handy to have with them as he can point them out to his crew mates on *Corner Brook* when they board her in Yarmouth so…" His voice trailed off as Admiral Carroll broke into laughter.

"So that is what young Mr. Cole does for a living! Advertising my ass! Well Ted, you have to watch his face when we walk into the briefing room. I assure you it will be interesting!" He laughed again and admitted to himself that Cole had indeed played his part very well. Maybe he SHOULD be in advertising!

"You know of him, sir?"

"Yes, I had supper with him last night," the CNO replied, laughing again at the astonished expression on Ted's face. George sat down and ran over the previous day's events with Commander Quigley who broke into laughter as he realized what had happened.

"Oh my god! He's going to die a million deaths when you walk in!"

"Give me a minute, Ted. I have to call Heather and tell her. She'll be expecting our young spy back home for supper tonight and I'm sure your man hasn't let him near a phone with the security level on this mission."

"Take your time sir." Ted was wiping a tear from the corner of his eye. He hadn't laughed that hard in a long time. "I'll go join the men and wait for you in the meeting room."

"This won't take long commander. I'll be right there."

Ted stood and left the office as the Admiral called home. Debby answered and he explained that Darren wouldn't be returning tonight or anytime soon, and to please tell Heather that he was alright but that was all he could say right now. "Oh, and tell her I think he's more than okay," he added. Darren had won the admiral's respect; no small feat. After all, he couldn't be upset with the boy. Cole had only been doing his job and damn it, thought George, he had done it quite splendidly, even though it had been at his and the navy's expense.

In the meeting room, the men saw that a map of southern France now adorned one wall. They were locked into condition 'S', which meant no communication was allowed with anyone outside of the base. They had all looked over the 'civy' who Martin had brought in with him, and although they were curious, none of the men made an attempt to talk with him or sit close by. To SEAL standards, he was skinny and out of shape. Although Stu had looked at him twice thinking, damn, he looks familiar.

Darren sat quietly in a corner, keeping completely to himself. While waiting for someone to show up, he had been examining the map on the wall while Lt. Martin dealt with some papers on the large table at the front of the room. He had briefly considered going over for a closer look, but thought better of it and instead continued to sit, sure that he would soon find out what was going on and how it could possibly involve him. The four other SEALs had come in a few moments ago and sat down, chatting amongst themselves and as he saw, barely acknowledging his existence. He did notice one of them had given him a second glance, but dismissed it as nothing more than curiosity. Darren's mind wandered to Heather and what her reaction would be to him standing her up. When he didn't show up at the Carroll residence tonight for supper, especially without calling, it would be all over for that relationship. Too bad, he lamented. He had really enjoyed her company.

The door to his right swung open and Commander Quigley walked in. "Attention on deck!" somebody yelled and forgetting he was still in civvies Darren had snapped to attention with the other men in the room.

"As you were! Chief Petty Officer Darren Cole of the Canadian Navy, welcome aboard. I am Commander Quigley and this group of misfits is part of SEAL Team Eight." With that the SEALs turned as one and looked at him as if seeing him for the first time. One by one they came over and shook hands. Oh well, thought Chief Petty Officer Jim Lewis, he's almost one of us, although rather puny and in the wrong navy.

"Chief Jim Lewis." Spoken softly, but with authority.

"Senior Chief Jamal Washington." Darren thought his hand was going to come off as the African American's huge paw squeezed it.

"Chief Markus Sanchez, glad to meet you." He looked at Darren who was obviously very uncomfortable. "They mustn't feed you Canadians very well," he added smiling.

"It's those long winters up there," replied Darren knowing immediately that none of them would realize he was just kidding. "A Canadian thing," he added lamely. This was not going well. These guys had more muscles on one arm then he had in his whole body and it wasn't like he was in all that bad a shape, he thought.

"Ensign Stu Cunningham, chief," said the one who had looked twice at him upon entering the room. "Do you drive a blue chev by any chance?"

"I did but..."

Stu cut him off...verbally this time. "Sorry about yesterday morning, chief. But you did a damn fine job of avoiding me!"

Now Darren remembered his face even though it had been partially obscured by his middle finger. "No problem ensign. I'm always on the look out for reckless drivers. Too many fine looking women around to..."

"Attention on deck!"

This time Darren remembered to just stand still as he glanced towards the door to see who had come in.

"What was that about fine lookin' women, chief petty officer?" growled Admiral George Carroll, Chief of Naval Operations. Darren had to look twice after naturally focusing first on the stars and ribbons adorning the man's dress uniform.

"I'm sorry..." started Darren as he completed turning towards the door and then froze. This had to be a bad dream. A really horrible bad dream and he would wake up back in the guest house any minute now. He remembered that most of his worst dreams always seemed to happen just before the alarm went off. Okay, wake up, he thought. Now would be a good time. He wasn't waking up though so he thought he'd better say something...

"...sir...I...well..." To his astonishment the admiral broke into hearty laughter along with Commander Quigley. Darren looked at them both in astonishment.

"At ease, chief! Welcome to Little Creek Amphibious Base," roared the admiral. "Oh, and congrats on that mission you pulled off for your navy. I hear that it was a fine piece of espionage work! We'll see what we can do about getting you out of here before the *Carter* returns tomorrow night. Her crew just might want to have a 'chat' with you," he remarked, looking deadly serious. Then his face broke into a grin again as he added, "and another thing; I called Heather and explained that you would be 'busy' for awhile. Treat this young man well gentleman. He has my respect. Be seated."

Relief flooding over him, Darren sat down on the metal chair. The admiral certainly didn't seem at all upset with him, even knowing he was in the navy. Well, not his navy but...then his mind switched in mid thought again to wondering what Heather was thinking. He'd have some tall explaining to do when he saw her again—IF he ever saw her again. Deceiving a US Navy admiral was one thing, but would the admiral's daughter understand?

"Gentlemen, as you've already been told, the *Carter* is unavailable for this mission and has been replaced. She is still having problems with her 'tail' winch but we have found another boat that is just as stealthy." He didn't have to explain the terms relating to the submarine. Navy SEALs were all too familiar with them as submarines were usually their primary source of transportation. They often joked amongst themselves that they spent so much time on the boats; they should be qualifying for their dolphins. The SEALs looked at the CNO saying nothing of course, but their faces couldn't hide their doubt about this change in plans.

"Chief Cole here," the admiral explained, "was recently involved in a top secret, joint exercise demonstrating a new communications technology the Canadian navy has developed. He will be acting as your host for the first leg of the mission."

Darren thought he noticed a few of the SEALs look at him with a semblance of respect on their faces, although he couldn't be sure. What he was sure of is that they were probably wondering why the hell he would be acting as a host to them.

"You will be flying to Bangor, Maine where you will acquire ground transportation to Bar Harbor, a tourist town on the east coast. Once there, you will split into three pairs and then board a high-speed ferry, *The Cat* to Yarmouth, Nova Scotia. Chief Cole's boat, *HMCS Corner Brook* is on route to Yarmouth at this time and she will spend three days there on a good-will visit. You will be traveling as tourists and when you arrive in Yarmouth, still separated, you will take the public tour of the boat as curious visitors." Admiral Carroll paused, letting what he'd said sink in. "There, you will be discreetly pointed out by Chief Cole to the crew, who will then sidetrack you without the rest of the tourists noticing. It is imperative, I repeat IMPERATIVE, that you are not identified as US Navy personnel let alone SEALs during this phase of the mission and that you are not noticed staying behind after the submarine tour. You will understand why when Commander Quigley gives you the mission brief. Remember that you will be guests of the Canadian Navy and that they have volunteered to help us on this mission. Good luck gentlemen!"

"Attention on deck!" The room stood as one as the CNO headed for the door. Darren wondered what on earth Commander Simpson had volunteered *Corner Brook* for. If navy SEALs were involved it was obviously going to be dangerous.

"Oh," the CNO stopped short of the door. "I nearly forgot. Cole, turn in your hotel key card to Lt. Martin. The stuff from your hotel room will be packed and sent to Halifax later."

"Thank you sir," Darren replied. That hadn't even occurred to him.

Chapter 5

▼

"Okay guys," called out Commander Quigley. "Gather around. You too, Cole. You have the pleasure of being briefed before anyone on your boat, including Commander Simpson. I understand your CO is a fine officer."

"The best, sir," replied Darren, his voice confident as he expressed the pride he had in his commanding officer.

Ted walked over to the map, using the wooden pointer that he preferred over the more modern laser type, and tapped the southernmost tip of France. "This briefing and everything from this point on is top secret. NOTHING of this can ever get out or the international implications would be disastrous." Ted paused for a few seconds to let his words sink in. The SEALs just continued to look at the map. Most of their briefings started with that line.

"Toulon, gentleman, is your destination. It is a major seaport and vacation spot on the southern coast of France. It's also the Mediterranean naval base for the French nuke boats. Jim, will you hit the lights?"

Chief Petty Officer Lewis reached back without leaving his chair and dimmed the lights until the room was almost totally dark. A projection screen lowered from the ceiling with a whirring sound and when it was completely down, a bright rectangle of light appeared on it, almost immediately replaced with the image of an old cargo ship.

"This is the North Korean *MV Sariwon*," continued the commander. "She's 450 feet and displaces twelve thousand tons. Her cargo will consist of four M4/TN 71 rocket boosters. They are a submarine launched ballistic missile minus the warhead and targeting system. In spite of our protests to the French government, who by the way claim that there is no law preventing their sale, the North Korean government has been allowed to purchase the rockets from the French company contracted out to dismantle and dispose of them."

"Question!" Stu as usual was first to speak.

"Go ahead ensign."

"Was there a 'fire sale' or did North Korea win the lottery?"

"Good question. Our sources say the missiles may have been financed by a third party, although no one seems to know who. We haven't been able to find out how much they were sold for either. The French government is claiming its hands are tied as they do not constitute a weapons system, and therefore do not fall under any kind of international agreement."

"It sure doesn't take a rocket scientist to know that the Koreans don't plan on using them to launch weather instruments," Stu commented. All the SEAL teams had kept abreast of North Korea's failed missile program.

"That is a given," Ted returned. "Alright, the rocket boosters are disassembled and packed in eight wooden crates. Our operative on site claims they are the only thing waiting to be loaded aboard the *Sariwon* when she arrives there in three weeks."

"Will the Canadian boat be able to get us there by then," Markus asked.

"I'm assured that will not be a problem. Anything to add to that Chief Cole?"

"Just to agree that we'll have plenty of time," Darren assured them. "The *Corner Brook* had a new type of battery installed last year and she can now run at 15 knots submerged for one hundred and sixty hours without damage to the battery. More importantly, they can be brought from ten percent to full charge in just over four hours. Not quite as impressive as your SSNs with their nuclear reactors but I promise you guys won't be disappointed."

"Okay; you fly out of Norfolk NAS at 0700 tomorrow and land at Bangor International at 0945. Your aircraft will taxi to the Air National Guard section of the airport and you will disembark there. A vehicle will be waiting for you and you are to leave it at the ferry terminal parking lot and purchase your tickets as walk on passengers. Park it as far from the terminal entrance as possible so none of the other passengers notice you arriving together. Bring a civilian change of clothing with you. We need you to look like tourists when you board *The Cat* and remember not to congregate. Stay in pairs. Lewis, long sleeve shirts. I don't want anyone trying to figure out what those tats on your arm are all about."

"Yes sir," Jim said in his soft voice. "What about our gear and stuff sir?"

"All looked after. A Canadian Hercules will leave CFB Greenwood, Nova Scotia on a supposed 'search and rescue' hop, allegedly looking for a disabled lobster boat, but will instead fly to Bangor and pick up all your gear. It will land at

Yarmouth airport on the way back on the premise of dropping off a couple of spotters, where your gear will be unloaded and delivered to the submarine. The Yarmouth airport is very seldom used, so there shouldn't be many people around to ask questions."

"Why couldn't we just go across with our gear on the Herc' then?" Stu queried.

"For security reasons, Ensign. Word cannot leak out concerning what assets will be used in this mission and you guys flying in together as a group aboard a military transport would be far too obvious. Your gear is being packaged into small cases marked as food stores destined for the *Corner Brook* so no one will notice anything strange about that on the Yarmouth pier. *Corner Brook* is being restocked with real food stores from a Canadian FFG at sea before its arrival at Yarmouth."

"Do we just go aboard the submarine when we arrive?" Markus asked.

"Not all at once. They will be conducting tours aboard the boat. Again it is important that you keep separated in pairs. Keep an eye out and decide on the flight up who will go aboard first. Darren, of course, has to be in the first pair as he will be pointing you out to the boat's crew who will then direct you how and when to 'disappear' below."

"Sounds like the Canucks have it all together on this one, sir."

"Completely, Stu. And remember, you guys are aboard the *Corner Brook* as guests and representatives of the United States Navy, so govern yourselves accordingly."

"Always sir!" Stu smiled and ducked the dry eraser that sailed for his head. "Missed, sir. I'd suggest some time on the eraser range."

"Any more questions?" Ted looked at them, knowing that as usual, the joking always seemed to signal the end of a briefing. He couldn't help but wonder if they'd all return safely from this one.

The mission did seem like a 'milk run' but so had many others in the past that had ended tragically. The North Koreans were far from inept at protecting their assets and even though all the reconnaissance photos had shown a harmless, dilapidated old cargo ship, Ted knew that was only because it was what the owners wanted it to look like.

Martin's bunch was one if his best squads. Maybe even THE best, but they were still human and humans made mistakes. As usual, he would live out every minute of the mission in agony waiting for some word of its success, or heaven forbid, failure.

It would be doubly hard with the 'unknown' of the Canadian submarine. Although Canadian boats had performed remarkably in the past on special ops, this was a new boat and he too had heard the rumblings through navy channels of the problems the Canadians had been having with them. Admiral Randall and now the CNO had both assured him not to worry about the boat, but if he had simply accepted that, he wouldn't be who he was.

*   *   *   *

"Ahead slow! Docking party stand by! All stop!" Commander Mike Simpson brought the *Corner Brook* expertly to the dock and watched as the deck crew threw lines ashore to the men waiting on the pier. In minutes the lines were made secure and the submarine nestled against the makeshift rubber fenders that would protect her hull from brushing against the wooden pilings of the public wharf. The tide was in so the submarine's deck was almost level with the pier which made attaching the gangway an easier job for the boat's crew. Mike had previously ordered all the submarines ballast tanks blown dry as there was very little margin, according to the charts at least, for *Corner Brook's* draft. The last act of docking the boat was the tying on of the submarine's banner along the gangway rails with her name emblazoned over the Canadian Navy dolphins.

"All hands, the boat is secure. Engine room, shut down all but auxiliary machinery."

Mike took one last look from the bridge and headed down the ladder to the control room. Grabbing the address system microphone, he gave the order much anticipated by ship's crews over the centuries. "Off duty personnel, clear to leave the boat in ten minutes!" This would give him time to climb to the deck and greet the dignitaries who would be waiting to welcome *HMCS Corner Brook* and her crew to Yarmouth, Nova Scotia.

"Lt. Polanski, you have the con. I'll be back in about an hour and I have my cell phone…" Mike was interrupted by Petty Officer Trask calling out. "Sir, you have a message coming in from Marlant!"

"Thanks petty officer. What have you got?"

After waiting for the printout to finish, Jake handed him the message. Mike glanced at it quickly before stuffing it into his uniform pocket and heading to the forward hatch where he climbed to the submarine's deck. The boson's whistle announced his leaving the boat and seeing a small group of people waiting on the dock, he saluted towards the flag now mounted on the sub's stern and headed down the gangway to where a small group awaited him.

"Welcome to Yarmouth captain! I am Mayor John d'Entremont and these are my council members. We are all honoured to have you visit us and hope you and your men have a wonderful stay!" He shook Mike's hand firmly. It was obvious that they really were pleased to have the submarine visit the town which had once been a major port for shipping along the east coast of Canada and the United States.

One of *Corner Brook's* crew had researched the town's history and printed up a small folder for all the crew to read. Yarmouth was not normally a stopping spot for naval vessels, so little was known about the local area and its population amongst navy crews. The folder pointed out that besides a rich lobster fishery, tourism was also a serious business for the town and the off duty crew could expect to find many little shops where they could pick up trinkets to bring back home to loved ones. Submariners were unable to purchase anything of any size while on liberty due to the tiny storage spaces they had for personal belongings.

The folder went on to describe the area populace as a mixture of English and Acadian with their rich French heritage; the balance of the population being a mixture of many cultures, including Aboriginal and African-Canadian as well as East Asian. With a growing population, Yarmouth still had strong ties to the sea and the flotilla of fishing boats tied to the many piers along the waterfront bore proof of that. The final sentence in the folder simply stated: 'BE NICE!' The capitals had been added as a warning to the more 'rambunctious' members of the crew.

Mike returned the hearty handshake. "On behalf of the crew of *HMCS Corner Brook*, and myself, we are honoured to be your guests and appreciate your hospitality." He didn't add that he hoped the local Royal Canadian Mounted Police felt the same way, and might 'overlook' any small infractions carried out by his crew. They were good men but sometimes things happened and he never looked forward to the inevitable meeting in his tiny office with a crewmember who had misbehaved while on leave.

"You will find Yarmouth very friendly, captain," said the mayor, understandably mistaking Mike's rank. That happened a lot. "Will you need any special services for your ship or the crew while you are here?"

"No, thank you your worship. We are connecting the telephone and water lines now. Other than that, we are pretty self sufficient. We were thinking of opening the boat up for tours tomorrow afternoon, if you think anyone in the town might be interested."

"I have no doubt you'll find people here very interested in your ship. Anything that floats will be of interest to the folks around here. Just watch they don't try to find a way for you to carry lobster traps aboard!" Everyone laughed at that and Mike was imagining the cartoon opportunity for the local paper's editorial page.

"Well here is my card and if you need anything at all, please call me. Again captain, welcome to Yarmouth. We are so happy to see you and your crew!"

The mayor was so friendly Mike was beginning to think these people didn't get visitors very often until he remembered that with the ferry service between Yarmouth and Maine, strangers were far from a rarity here.

"Mayor d'Entremont, I would like to invite you and your council for supper this evening if you are free. I can give you a tour of the boat as well, if you don't mind steep ladders and small spaces."

"We would be honoured, sir!" The smiles and nods from the rest of the delegation showed all of them were excited about the invitation. "The last navy ship to visit here was *HMCS Moncton* and that was five years ago." Again they all shook hands and made small talk. Then came a few pictures for the local paper as well as a quick interview with a CBC News camera crew.

With the required public relations duties completed for now, Mike returned to the boat and headed for his cabin. Pulling the message from his pocket he read it again, while reaching for the phone which acted as a paper weight when the boat was out to sea and no shore lines were connected. "Call Vice Admiral Brent O'Hanlon upon arrival Yarmouth," he half whispered. "Well admiral," he muttered while punching the memory position for Maritime Forces Atlantic, "I don't suppose this is going to be a social call."

It wasn't.

"Vice Admiral O'Hanlon's office."

"Jody, don't you ever take a day off?" Mike teased the young petty officer who was well-known throughout the fleet for his ability to handle Brent O'Hanlon's wrath with good grace.

"Never, commander. I tried to once and the Admiral found out and had the MPs drag me back."

"Sure he did," laughed Mike. "Is he in?"

"In and awaiting your call I believe, sir. Please hold a moment." Petty Officer Jody Fletcher punched the intercom and announced that Commander Mike Simpson was calling in on line three.

"Thanks petty officer!" Brent had indeed been waiting for this call and punched the flashing yellow light on his phone. "Michael! How are you son?"

"Great admiral, how are things in Halifax?" he asked, noting that Brent used his Christian name, meaning it was definitely not a social call.

"Look Michael, I need you to rent a car and get up here first thing in the morning."

"I think it's about a three hour drive sir. What time would you like to see me?"

"Ten hundred would be fine commander. Don't mention where you're going to anyone though. Just tell whoever asks that you're taking a ride to visit an old friend and you'll be gone most of the day."

"Okay admiral. I don't suppose…"

"You're right! See you tomorrow!" Brent hung up. He liked Mike a lot. The man was very capable and other than a tendency to over evaluate at times, he was as fine an officer as the Canadian Navy had. Some day he might end up taking over this office, but that would depend on what happened in the next two weeks.

Brent envied the commander. In times of peace, there were very few real adventures for a navy commander, but Michael Simpson was about to have one. Brent didn't notice how he used the full names of his commanders when something serious was afoot. If he had, he would have forced himself to discontinue the habit immediately.

On *HMCS Corner Brook*, Mike replaced the dead receiver on the phone. Something serious was up, he thought. His first instinct, as always, was to rewind the past few weeks and try to find somewhere he might have made a mistake or a bad judgement call. Nothing out of the ordinary had happened though which meant that whatever it was, he would just have to be patient. Not one of Commander Mike Simpson's stronger traits.

*   *   *   *

"Bangor tower, this is Navy six three seven. We are five miles out. Request landing instructions—we have Sierra," the pilot announced, referring to the automated broadcast for Bangor International Airport, where the current weather and runway conditions were given.

"Navy six three seven you are cleared straight in approach, runway two seven. Winds are calm and the altimeter is two niner eight three."

"Navy six three seven, roger." The pilot of the US Navy C-17 had checked her VFR Flight Supplement for any special information she might need about Bangor International Airport but hadn't found anything that would require her attention.

"Navy six three seven you are cleared to land-check the gear—wind is calm."

"Navy six three seven." The dark grey cargo jet's tires barely squealed as the pilot brought it in for a perfect landing. Military pilots concentrated carefully on operations at civilian airports, trying to give the civvies the impression that all their landings and takeoffs were perfect.

"Navy six three seven, welcome to Bangor. Turn left at taxi way Bravo. You are cleared to the National Guard base. Contact ground control now on two seven five decimal eight."

"Roger, ground control on two seven five point eight. Thank you."

The aircraft taxied slowly to the Maine Air National Guard portion of the airport. In decades past, four engine KC-135 aerial refuelling tankers based here would have chased after the huge B-52 bombers from Loring Air Force Base halfway up the state whenever an alert came through. Now the few tankers remaining were on call for other missions as the bombers were long gone from Loring and that base, like many others from the cold war era, was now an aviation industrial park.

"Navy six three seven, Bangor ground, turn right now and you'll see a hanger directly ahead. Please taxi right to the doors and shut down. We have a tow ready."

"Roger that. Navy six three seven." Sounds pretty 'cloak and dagger' thought the pilot but knew better than to waste time wondering. She expertly taxied the large jet to the doors and shut the engines down. As promised a tractor appeared from the left and moved towards the nose of the C-17 cargo jet, disappearing from her view underneath. A minute later, a ground crewmember appeared and gave her the 'release brakes' sign before disappearing again under the aircraft's nose. A short tug a few moments later followed by a slow forward movement announced that the aircraft was being towed right into the hanger. In a few minutes the aircraft was safely inside and the huge hanger doors slowly ground shut behind it.

"Well that's that," the pilot announced to the other two members of her crew. There was only a small amount of cargo on board and a group of sailors, so for once the aircrew would not have to bother checking long manifests and supervising the ground crew to make sure some fork-lift driver didn't puncture the side of their aircraft.

Fifty feet behind her, Lt. Boris Martin unfastened the belt that had held him to the rather comfortable seat he'd been sitting in and stood up. "Alright! Listen up! Last time for ranks. Let's get going!" From here on in, they were a bunch of guys on vacation. Military titles and courtesies would be on hold.

"No problem Boris!" Stu laughed. He was going to enjoy this. It would definitely be like a vacation.

"Don't get carried away," Chief Petty Officer Jamal Washington said as he shoved Stu out of the door, causing him to trip down the short ladder to the hanger floor. "I'm sorry sirrr...err...STU! Damn!" He saw Stu limp slowly back to his feet. "Shit! I am sorry!" Jamal rushed down to help the ensign back to his feet.

"No problem!" Stu laughed, punching Jamal's shoulder, not believing he fell for his 'act'.

"Hey now, gang way!" Chief Petty Officer Markus Sanchez yelled shoving past the other two. "I seriously need to find a head!"

"Right over this way, gentlemen! Bathrooms are that way! Your ride is over there," announced an air force sergeant pointing. "Mr. Martin. If you'll just sign for the vehicle, you guys can be on your way."

"Thanks sergeant," answered Boris as he signed. Not bad, he thought, a Dodge Caravan. Nice and discreet.

"Darren! You want to drive?"

"Sure." He was going to find it difficult dropping the military ethics although to keep it simple they would use their real names. All these guys were above him in rank although petty officers were petty officers in any man's navy. "I'll see if there's a map in the truck."

"Sounds good! Start her up and we'll get going."

The five SEALs and Darren got in and after a little game of 'Who's Gonna Ride Shotgun', where Jamal almost threw Jim Lewis into the back; they drove out of the hanger into the sunshine.

"Whoa!" Darren yelled grabbing for his sun glasses; the only personal belonging he'd managed to salvage since leaving Little Creek.

Following the signs as they drove off the base, they soon reached I-95 and headed south. Five minutes later they were on Alternate 1 heading for Ellsworth when Jim announced, "I'm hungry! Let's stop for food at the mall over there." He pointed to the right at a large sign announcing the Twin City Plaza.

"Good idea man! Let's stop!" chorused Markus and Stu, sounding more like children on a vacation than highly trained servicemen.

"Sounds good to me too," said Darren turning into the parking lot. Once stopped, they all piled out.

"Now remember guys, we're tourists," cautioned Darren and then added with a smile, "Maybe I should have given you some 'Canadian' lessons so you don't offend anyone."

"Maybe we should give you some 'American' lessons," shouted Markus as he tackled Darren against the van.

"OUCH! You turd! Come back here!"

"Don't bother chasing him, man," spoke Jamal. "He's the fastest runner on the team."

"He's also the biggest…" Stu started.

"So," interrupted Boris. "How long do you think it'll take to get to Bar Harbor?"

"Not long. An hour and a half maybe. We should be there by two thirty," Darren replied, remembering to stop using 'military' time.

"Well gentlemen, let's acquire some sustenance and get going then." For practice, the group broke up into the pre-arranged pairs they would form aboard the ferry and headed for the small restaurant they had seen advertised on the sign board outside the mall. An hour later their hunger pangs had been satisfied and they were back on the road and following the signs to Ellsworth, only stopping once to check the map and pull into a gas station to pick up a schedule for the ferry along with another snack.

"Looks like highway three will take us right into Bar Harbor," Jamal announced, reading the map spread out in front if him. We'll have to find a place to spend the night though. *The Cat* leaves in the morning at 0…err…ten thirty."

"There must be tons of hotels in the area for the tourists. I'm sure we'll find something worthy of our greatness," joked Stu. "Besides, the navy's paying!"

"I'm sure it'll be better than the dives YOU usually stay in," laughed Jim, punching Stu in the shoulder.

"Hey!" Stu threw the bag of garbage from his snack back over his head hitting Boris in the face.

"Missed me!" Jim taunted. "Looks like someone needs time on the 'garbage range'!"

"Simmer down guys! I'd like to make it home in one piece thank you!" Boris reached ahead and slapped the back of both their heads. Oh god, please let me not kill one of these guys before we reach the sub, he thought.

The noisy and raucous group continued on and finally reached a small motel just outside of Bar Harbor where they settled in for the night after a supper of take-out pizza that found its way all over the motel room.

* * * *

The Mayor of Yarmouth was impressed. He, like many Canadians had followed the reports covering the purchase and reactivation of the submarines, and had half expected to find water swishing around his feet as he climbed down the ladder into a brightly lit area before being shepherded forward to what was obviously the torpedo room of *HMCS Corner Brook*. Everything sparkled and other then the overall light grey color scheme and the slight odour of diesel fumes, you would not know you were aboard a submarine that had once been labelled 'used' and 'rusted'. The others in his entourage gingerly lowered themselves down the ladder followed by Commander Simpson who then stood waiting for a couple of them to catch their breath before following them into the torpedo space and starting the tour.

"I'm glad you could all make it," he said, adding "this evening," hoping no one thought he meant down the long vertical ladder. "This is the torpedo room and as you can see, we have a full load of weapons aboard. These are Mk-48 torpedoes. They have a maximum range of 50 kilometres and are wire guided which means they actually have small fibre optic wires attached to them that are strung out while the torpedo moves through the water. We can then send information to the torpedo instructing it to make course corrections to the target or even to disarm it if for some reason we decide that should occur. Once the wire runs out, the torpedo has a built in sonar system enabling it to track the target on its own. Any questions?"

Someone asked the question he expected right off…"They seem to have names written…"

"Yes," Mike blushed in spite of himself. "An over exuberant seaman." He didn't go any further. "Any other questions?"

"I have one sir," spoke one of the councillors holding up her hand.

"Please, it's Mike. Go right ahead."

"How do you get these things in here? I had enough trouble getting down that ladder myself and those things are huge!"

"Good question!" laughed Mike. "See that door above the torpedo tube hatches? That is where we bring them aboard and we use these pulleys to lower them right onto the racks here. The racks slide out so we really don't have to handle the torpedoes manually all that much. You can see how they load into the tubes. This little plate on tube number one's hatch means that this tube is loaded now. We try to keep at least one tube loaded at all times, just in case."

"Do you have much opportunity to practice firing them," asked Mayor d'Entremont.

"Not as much as we'd like, sir," Mike responded. "They are very expensive but we do have practice versions that we train with. We constantly drill through the loading and firing procedures though, and my forward crew can load and prime them in their sleep. If there are no more questions, we'll move through this hatch back to the Control Room which is the 'heart' of the submarine." Mike stood by the hatch, ready to help anyone or to shield a head if it looked like someone was not going to duck low enough. Once the group had huddled along one side of the control room, Mike continued with the tour.

"This is my station when we are at sea and it is from here that the boat is controlled. We call submarines 'boats', which goes back to the very beginning of submarine history when they were very small and lacked most of the amenities we have aboard today. Back then if a vessel could be lifted up and placed aboard another vessel it was called a boat. Of course, with modern heavy lift ships, that no longer holds true as most large ships today can be lifted by vessels specially made for that purpose."

"What are all these television screens used for?" one of the group asked.

"They have different purposes. These two are for the submarine's radar which is only manned when we are on the surface or at periscope depth when we can raise the radar mast. This is probably a good time to explain what all those things sticking out at the top of the sail are for. Two of them are the periscopes which you see here. The larger one is a search unit and gives an excellent view as well as having video and still camera capability. Now the smaller one is what we call the attack scope. It is made as small as possible so there is little chance that someone on the surface will see it sticking up above the water. You can see that there are numeric displays built into both scopes. They read out the range and bearing information which is also tied into the submarine's targeting computer."

"So you have to look at your target through here before you can shoot a torpedo at it then, eh?"

Mike turned to the councillor who asked the question and replied, "Not at all. The periscopes are seldom used in combat anymore. That brings us to these screens which are connected to the boat's sonar system. Now you can see we have a demo running on this one. These lines you see all represent sounds picked up by microphones built into the hull of the submarine and also strung along our 'tail', which is basically a long piece of wire we drag behind us with microphones attached to it.

The reason for the tail or towed array as it is called is to get the microphones away from the noise our own boat makes and also to stretch the distance out between microphones allowing us to better calculate the bearing to the target. These lines you see represent different sound frequencies and trained sonar operators can distinguish what might be out there by the frequency of the sound waves being emitted."

"You're telling me that those fuzzy lines represent ships and such?" asked the Mayor.

"Exactly. See this one over here," he pointed at a portion of the screen where the demo was running. "That's a high frequency sound. Now watch what happens when I ask the computer what it is." Mike moved the curser over the line and hit a button on the console. Within seconds 'US 688 Cl SSN' appeared on the screen below the sonar display. "The computer has identified that particular noise as an American submarine. We have an extensive library of sound samples acquired through various methods and we guard them religiously. Now a really good sonar operator can even distinguish what particular submarine is out there. All ships have acoustic traits, something like fingerprints that set them apart from each other. That is why a tremendous amount of time and effort is put into making a submarine as quiet as possible."

"That must be why they call you guys the 'silent service'," commented the lady who asked earlier about the torpedoes. She had gone to the local library upon hearing of the dinner invitation and with the help of the head librarian had studied as much as she could about the submarines.

"That among other reasons," answered Mike with an appreciative smile.

"What's up there?" the Mayor asked looking up at the conning tower hatch.

"That's the hatch to the bridge on top of the sail. We call the narrow structure above, the sail or fin simply because it looks more like a sail than anything else. Directly above this hatch is the lock-out chamber from which up to five people can leave or enter the submarine while it is submerged. There are two other hatches, one forward and another one just like it aft, err…to the back of the boat. This is also where a rescue submarine would attach itself to this submarine and remove the crew if something was to happen to us and we couldn't surface." Mike's mind was thinking, 'fat chance', but he supposed under the right circumstances it might work.

"Does that scare you at all?" asked the torpedo lady.

"In all honesty, the thought seldom enters our minds. We are kept pretty busy when we're at sea, so there's not much time to worry about things like that. Team work is more crucial here than anywhere else in the navy and we all trust the man next to us to do his job properly."

"I suppose I shouldn't ask why women don't serve aboard submarines," laughed the Mayor.

"Okay…so if we go through here we'll go back past the hatch you came down, and on to the engine room," Mike laughed, avoiding the comment altogether.

They were shocked at the cleanliness of the engine room and impressed with the huge diesels that powered the boat and charged the battery. One of them questioned why they couldn't make batteries like the ones on the submarine for his car, so it would start better on cold mornings. He tittered sheepishly when Mike pointed out that the battery would cost more than his car did.

Soon they had been through the boat and were enjoying a 'home-cooked' meal of roast beef and mashed potatoes in the senior ranks mess. When they had finished, and everyone was standing on deck, the mayor turned to Mike and congratulated him on his fine ship, correcting himself and saying 'boat' with a hearty laugh. After shaking hands and waving good bye, Mike made his way down to his cabin where he finished the day's reports and pondered his drive to Halifax in the morning. At least he might get to see Ann and the kids for a quick visit.

Chapter 6

▼

Outside the most out of the way motel Darren and the SEALs had been able to find close to Bar Harbor, the morning dawned bright and sunny with a mild breeze coming in off the water.

After showering and getting into the one change of clothing they had been allowed to bring, Stu collected everyone's soiled garments in a large garbage bag, which he then shoved into the small space built into the floor of the van. The van would be left at the ferry terminal where someone would pick it up later. It was not unusual for vehicles to be left at the terminal's parking lot so the empty van would not appear suspicious to people passing by.

"Okay guys, last time. Try to look and act like tourists. Nice tourists," Boris looked directly at Stu. "No more than a few tries at the slot machines on the ferry and remember to try and stay separated in your pairs."

"Slots?" Stu perked up at the word. He hadn't been aware there would be gambling aboard the ferry.

"No more than a FEW games!" Boris didn't want one of them winning a jackpot, as that would draw too much attention to the men.

"Yes boss," replied a dejected looking Stu.

They had checked out of the motel and driven to the ferry terminal where the sleek ship waited for the next load of tourists heading for Nova Scotia.

Pulling into the parking lot and finding a corner where only a couple of cars were parked, Darren brought the van to a stop and turned off the motor. "All aboard gentleman!" he called out.

"Man, look at that thing!" Jamal exclaimed, admiring the sharp, sleek lines of *The Cat*. "We have GOT to get us one of those!"

"Yeah, but in navy grey with a few guns mounted on her," Stu offered.

"Well guys, remember to keep apart," Boris warned one last time. "We'll chat again when we get aboard the sub."

"Unless I get lucky on the slots," Stu smiled. "Maybe you'll have to pull this one off without my help."

He received a stern look from Boris in response.

"Or maybe I'll just sit back and enjoy the view," he sheepishly added.

They broke off into pairs, purposely letting other tourists get between them as they approached the terminal building. Darren and Jim chatted about high school and compared notes on some of the dates they'd been on. Jim laughed, remembering the CNO's speech back at Little Creek and Darren's run in with the admiral's daughter. During the drive from Bangor they had all enjoyed the story of Darren's adventure in Virginia Beach with Heather and her father, the Chief of Naval Operations.

"Wow, look at this," said Darren as they walked across a short ramp to the ship and entered a large lounge filled with comfortable seats and tables. Windows circled the front of the ship giving a beautiful panoramic view outside over the bow.

"Pretty impressive," agreed Jim. "Let's just sit right here."

Boris and Markus sat behind them in the lounge area but only for a few minutes before getting up to explore the ship and visit one of the souvenir shops on board. Stu and Jamal sat below near the slot machines which would be available once the ferry left United States territorial waters.

A short time later with a couple of blasts from its horn, the sleek blue ferry left the dock and started winding her way around the islands for the open sea. Once there, *The Cat* seemed to vibrate for a moment as she gained momentum and her water jets pushed a pair of 'rooster tails' high into the air as she picked up more speed. Everyone on board for the first time hung on, unaccustomed to the acceleration.

"It says here that *The Cat* travels around fifty-five miles an hour. Sweet!" Markus explained to Boris reading one of the hand outs from the ship. They had returned to their seats after picking up a few small gifts and a light lunch.

Boris looked out the window and could see they were moving along at a fast clip. He thought back to when the US Navy had experimented with a similar ship but then decided against it. The twin hulled catamarans were very fast in waters that were not too rough but out in the open sea during a storm, the speed advantage was lost, although they did remain very stable due to a complicated 'water wing' which steadied the ship.

The voyage across the Gulf of Maine went quickly, and in a few hours the Cape Forchu lighthouse just outside Yarmouth came into view. Everyone hung on a bit as the ship slowed noticeably before entering the harbour.

The Cat's captain brought the ship parallel to the ferry terminal pier and expertly guided the large vessel backwards to the huge ramps waiting to be lowered down to the opening in her stern. As the dock workers finished tying her up, the ramps slowly dropped into place on the ship's deck and the ferry passengers were instructed to return to their vehicles in preparation for disembarking.

As Darren and Jim gathered the refuse from their lunches and dropped it into the trash receptacle, they took one last glance out the huge windows before heading for the exit. They could see that the ship was secured to a large pier and that a long ramp led down from the passenger entrance into the terminal building. They couldn't help but notice the dark shape berthed at the public pier a few hundred yards from where *The Cat* was docked. Darren quickly looked away, his eyes showing warm recognition. Jim's eyes showed a different emotion—uncertainty.

"This is the captain speaking, on behalf of Bay Ferries my crew and I would like to thank you for traveling with us today aboard *The Cat*. We hope your trip was a pleasant one. The Tourist Nova Scotia representative would like us to announce that the Canadian navy submarine *HMCS Corner Brook* is visiting Yarmouth and will be open to the public for tours today until eight pm. Have a pleasant and safe journey."

"How nice. I'll just have to take that submarine tour," Jim voiced to no one in particular as he descended to the vehicle deck.

✳   ✳   ✳   ✳

As *The Cat* was tying up in Yarmouth, Commander Simpson was reaching the outskirts of Halifax in the rental car he had procured from Enterprise the previous evening. Mike enjoyed the beautiful scenery along Nova Scotia's picturesque south shore where he and Ann had often camped with the kids when they were younger. With very little traffic to slow him down on highway 103, he soon reached Nova Scotia's capital city and taking exit 0, drove along Joseph Howe Drive heading north. Navigating quickly through the early morning traffic on the Fairview overpass, and then heading down Barrington Street, he soon arrived at the main gate to the navy dockyard. Presenting his ID card to the seaman who examined it before waving him in, Mike drove around to the building housing the offices of Canada's East Coast Navy. Parking the car in the visitor lot, he quickly walked inside, wondering what this visit would bring and hoping the admiral's aide had a pot of coffee on.

"Good morning Commander," smiled Jody as he rose from his chair. "Two sugars and one cream?"

"You're a good man petty officer! I swear one of these days I'll get you on my crew!"

"That would be when hell freezes over with all due respect sir," laughed the young man as he poured Mike's coffee. "Take this in with you. The MOD and the Admiral are waiting for you. I buzzed him when I saw you come down the hall."

"The Minister of Defence is with him?" That surprised Mike. He checked his appearance to make sure everything was in place. His uniform looked good, except for the 'driving creases' in the pants. Damn! He thought. What is Brent up to?

"Yup. She got in early this morning, sir." And seeing the look on Mike's face as he tried to smooth the few creases in his uniform, he added, "You look fine sir."

"Thanks Jody."

Knocking gently first, Mike opened the door and walked in. Brent was sitting behind his huge oak desk, which was rumoured to have been stolen decades ago from the British Admiralty offices in London, and Caroline Wheeler, the Minister of Defence, was seated in an arm chair to his left. They had obviously been going over notes and a map which was strewn over the admiral's desk. Mike came to attention, looking at Brent with puzzled eyes.

"Rest easy, son. Commander Michael Simpson, this is Caroline Wheeler, the MOD."

"Honoured to meet you ma'am, I didn't…"

"The honour is mine commander and please, it's Caroline."

"Michael, we have a job for you. Have a seat." Brent waved him to the remaining chair in front of his desk. "This briefing is Security Level 1."

Mike looked at him and then over to Caroline who's expression revealed nothing. It didn't have to. Her presence spoke volumes. That meant there would be an 'international flavour' to whatever this mission was. He grabbed the chair from in front of Brent's desk and brought it forward, before sitting down.

"I take it we're not coming back to Halifax after we depart Yarmouth," Mike asked, although the answer was obvious.

"Not for a while…" Brent O'Hanlon knew Mike would have a hard sell to his crew when he returned to the boat. They had been out for some time and no doubt plans had been made by many of them, expecting to be home this week. "Have you ever been to the south of France commander?"

"No, but Ann and I planned to take a trip there someday," Mike smiled. "Where are we headed?"

"Toulon." Brent rotated the map so Mike could study it. The Admiral went on with the briefing, explaining how they would be transporting the SEALs and about the rocket boosters.

"North Korea? How can they afford SLBMs?" Mike asked. The small country had been on the verge of financial collapse for so long now that everyone was sure they had nothing of value left.

"Intelligence thinks they might be financed by a third party, or that the French company sold them dirt cheap to save the hassle of recycling them. These are older rocket boosters so they are not all that valuable except to an impoverished country that recently exploded their first nuclear weapon and now are in need of a way to deliver it.

The French government has tried everything legally that they could to stop the sale, but they are unwilling to go beyond that. We are." Brent added, with a stern look. He then went on to cover everything that was known about the transaction to this point. Both the CIA and CSIS had been working diligently to uncover as many details as they could in the past few days to help ensure the mission's success.

"The SEALs will be using a specially designed, shaped charge, on the crates holding the rockets. They explode inward and will cause very little damage except to the rockets themselves. This will also lesson the chances of anyone being injured or killed in the blasts. Our intelligence tells us that the fuel for the rockets is being delivered to North Korea separately by rail car," he explained. "So there won't be much of an explosion, other than from the charges themselves. In fact, all anyone outside the ship should hear is a muffled thump as the explosives detonate."

He then covered what had happened with the *USS Jimmy Carter* and how the results of the recent Lazcom exercise with the *Bush* battle group had convinced the Americans that one of Canada's SSKs would be perfectly suited for the SEAL insertion job.

Mike chuckled when the Admiral explained that after his successful 'spy' mission, Petty Officer Cole was bringing the SEALs to Yarmouth aboard *The Cat*. They also discussed ways to clear space for the SEALs on the already tightly packed submarine as they would need to work out on the long voyage. Both men knew that the preferred modus operandi would be to have the SEAL team rendezvous with their submarine transport somewhere reasonably close to the target area. Due to the time constraint and more importantly the security level on this mission, that would be impossible to set up.

"The Koreans certainly picked a good port," Mike noted. "Toulon is also the main French submarine base in the Med. No one would dare try and cause trouble while they are docked there." He didn't mean to sound disrespectful of course, but the French would not be impressed with any suspicious antics around their nuclear submarine base.

"We expect that the French might be on the alert for something like this," Brent responded. "Hopefully, if we're discovered, they'll deal with us lightly. Unfortunately, we can't warn them through intelligence channels and risk the mission being blown."

"I'm also sending along a crew member with you who might be of help if things get a little too exciting and your crew needs someone of their own rank who's been there. If he can make it to your boat in time, Chief Cookie Barnes will be TDY to *Corner Brook*," said Brent. "He's had a lot of experience with this sort of mission and nothing seems to faze him."

"That would be terrific, Admiral. I met Cookie in Scotland when we were updating the boats. He's a good man." Mike was indeed very grateful. If any of his newer crewmen became stressed under the pressure of the mission, Cookie would be a good calming influence on them, and heck, he'd heard that no one could make fish chowder like the portly Newfoundlander.

"Michael, this is the point where the leader would put a hand on his man's shoulder and say we picked you because we know it's damn near impossible, but if anyone can pull it off, you can," he smiled. "I won't play with you like that commander, but I won't kid you either. This is going to be a very tough mission, and if you're caught, there will be hell to pay. Not only in Washington and Ottawa, but worse, for you and your crew."

"I know admiral," agreed Mike. "Don't worry. We'll be fine."

"Thanks, son," Brent said smiling. "Caroline has been working very closely with her American counterpart on this and very few people are in the loop on it of course."

"I can see why admiral," Mike answered, thinking again of the implications if anything went wrong. Damn, he thought. If everything went right and word of this leaked, there would be pandemonium at the UN.

"My crew and boat are ready. You can count on us."

"I never doubted that for a second son. Caroline, unless you have anything more, the commander better head back to his boat."

Caroline had been listening quietly, letting Brent explain the mission and not interfering in any way.

"Commander, you know there can be no public acknowledgement for this mission," said Caroline, stating the obvious. "But I assure you that it is critically important those rockets do not reach North Korea."

"They won't ma'am. I guarantee it."

She let the 'ma'am' go this time. Looking into Mike's eyes, she saw that he meant what he said. Those rockets would not be leaving the French port in one piece.

"We'll leave you for a few minutes so you can call your boat and prepare them for their 'guests' commander. Come and join us when you're finished," said Brent. "We'll be just outside."

"Thank you, sir. I'll just have to give Lieutenant Beals a brief explanation. I think I already have an idea how we can pull off getting the SEALs apart from the tourists. I'll be right out." Mike reached for the phone and dialled the temporary land-line number to *Corner Brook* that he had scribbled down on the same piece of paper that held his message to call Admiral O'Hanlon. No wonder the admiral hadn't told him anything until this morning he thought, quickly punching the buttons on the phone.

"*HMCS Corner Brook*, how may I help you?"

Whoever answered the phone was certainly being polite. "This is Commander Simpson. Is Lieutenant Beals still aboard?"

"Yes sir! Just a moment and I'll get him for you," answered Leading Seaman Gary Steeves. He had transferred to the *Corner Brook* a few months ago and wanted to make a good impression on his new commanding officer. He grabbed the microphone for the address system and asked for Lieutenant Beals to report immediately to the control room for an urgent phone call. Dropping the microphone and grabbing the phone receiver again, he informed Commander Simpson that the lieutenant should be along in a moment.

"Who is this," Mike asked.

"Leading Seaman Gary Steeves, sir."

"Thank you seaman. Good phone manners."

"Thank YOU, sir! I'll put you on hold if that is okay with you sir."

"That will be fine Steeves. Thanks again."

Gary hit the hold button and after paging Lieutenant Beals, went back to the book he was reading. Standing communications watch had to be the most boring assignment a person could pull when the boat was dockside. Just sitting around waiting in case the phone rang or the even more unlikely event that one of the radio systems came to life was a poor substitute for his regular duty. His usual station was forward with his beloved torpedoes. He recalled his first few days on *Corner Brook* and his introduction to his immediate superior…

"But Chief! They are the only reason this boat and crew exists!" He had been trying to explain to Chief Petty Officer 2nd Class Darren Cole, when new and entirely unauthorized markings had appeared on all the Mark-48 torpedoes sitting in their racks.

"I understand what you're saying Steeves," Darren had responded. "But you can't be giving the 'fish' names like that. They'll cart you away when the commander sees what you did!"

Gary saw no problem with naming the torpedoes lying on their racks in the weapons space. It gave them personalities, and as he said, they were the only reason for the boat's existence. Darren had walked in on him just as he was signing 'Nadine' over the gyro inspection hatch of the last one and had yelled at him to stop. But he was far too late. All eighteen torpedoes had women's names neatly scrolled on their sides.

When he had tried to follow Cole's order to remove the names, the reason permanent markers are called permanent became abundantly clear. Reporting this to Chief Cole, Gary was told, "Fine! Leave them for now, but nothing; repeat NOTHING else aboard this submarine requires a name!"

"Yes chief," Gary had sheepishly answered. "It won't happen again."

Lieutenant Fred Beals' arrival in the control center shook him from his day dream and he pointed to the phone. "It's the CO, sir."

"On the phone?" Fred thought that was odd. "Good morning sir. What can I do for you?"

"Lieutenant Beals, you won't believe who's coming for supper." Mike went on to explain just enough so the SEALs arrival would be handled smoothly and discreetly. He explained how important it was that the five men staying behind were not obvious to the rest of the tour groups.

"Have they started touring yet?"

"Not yet sir. They are already lining up outside though. I guess the locals don't get to see a submarine everyday."

"Okay, keep the groups coming aboard small, say ten or twelve. Darren and the first SEAL should arrive around sixteen hundred hours and the other two pairs will be watching to make sure they join different groups. Once you get Cole and his buddy aboard he'll point out the other four guys so you'll know who to 'grab'." He then went on to explain that Fred would need to come up with a way to 'remove' the SEALs from the rest of the tour group without rousing suspicion.

"Sounds simple enough. When do you think you'll be returning to the boat, sir?"

"I'm leaving shortly and taking the 101 back so it'll be a quick trip," Mike responded, referring to the recently twinned highway that ran from just outside of Halifax right into Yarmouth. "I'll probably be there by sixteen hundred hours."

"Very good, sir. I'll inform the crewmembers who'll be conducting the tours."

"Thanks Fred. Oh, and Fred? This is all Security Level One."

"One, sir? Where…Never mind. I'll see you when you get here."

"Okay lieutenant. Good luck and I'll see you in a few hours."

"See you later, sir."

Mike replaced the receiver on the phone and sat for a moment contemplating the turn of events. It was going to be a tricky mission but he was sure his crew were up to it. Well, they would be once he dashed their plans for going home anytime soon. Standing up he took a look outside the huge window in Brent's office, staring down at the warships berthed along the dockyard. The only submarine currently in port was *Chicoutimi*, now being used for training purposes after recent repairs to the damage caused by the fire a few years ago. Rumours abounded that she might soon be joining the active fleet. It would be nice to have all four boats operational.

Mike brought his gaze back into the office and headed for the door to join Admiral O'Hanlon and Caroline in the outer reception area. He'd noted the 'skull and crossbones' flag adorning the admiral's office. A souvenir no doubt from one of his tours on the 'O' boats. Opening the door, he strolled out into the reception area.

"All set, sir," he announced to the Admiral. "It's been a pleasure to meet you Minister. Thank you for all that you've done for the navy."

"The pleasure was mine commander. I've been there and I know what it's like to rely on equipment that should have been retired long ago."

"Well you've gone a long way towards eradicating the problem, ma…err Caroline. I'd better hit the road and see about my 'passengers'."

"Good sailing Michael." Brent had taken the commander's hand and given it a hearty shake.

Caroline did the same, surprising Mike with her grip. Shouldn't be surprised, he thought. She had flown a C-130 Hercules transport during Op Friction back in '91 during the first Gulf War. He had also heard that some of her missions were not exactly 'milk runs' and more than once her 'Herc' returned to base with flak damage.

Returning to his rental, Mike had sat for a moment and pondered the mission. Then reaching for the key, he started the engine, while checking that he had enough gas for the return trip. The gas was fine but he'd have to drive a bit on the fast side to make it back to the boat before the SEALs showed up. Not a problem, he'd smiled. Enterprise might 'pick you up', but fortunately they didn't come along to see how fast you drove. It was too bad that he was so close and yet wouldn't be able to drop in on Ann, but it was probably just as well. She, like all the crew's families, would not be happy to hear that their men wouldn't be coming home as planned.

He checked his watch while driving through the gate and saw that it was just after thirteen hundred hours. Putting the car in drive, he left the dockyard, quickly drove through Halifax and finally headed north on highway 102 out of the city. Driving faster than his normal ten kilometres over the speed limit, Mike had soon reached the exit for Highway 101 which would take him through the Annapolis Valley and finally past Digby into Yarmouth.

Two and a half hours later Mike pulled up to the traffic lights where highway 101 came to an end at Starrs Road in Yarmouth. Turning right and driving much slower now, he continued on to the pier on Water Street where *Corner Brook* was tied up.

Pulling into the parking area, he saw that the local populace was indeed excited to take advantage of the tour being offered. A long line of people stretched off the pier and overflowed into the adjacent parking lot. Walking up the gangway he saluted the flag and stepped aboard. In the corner of his eye he saw *The Cat* tied up at the ferry terminal, the sleek ferry's bow pointing towards him.

"Welcome back, sir!"

Mike noted that Seaman Gary Steeves, who had a few weeks ago, bewildered him with the naming of the torpedoes, had managed to get an 'outside' duty. "Thank you seaman. Any special visitors yet?"

"Not yet, commander. Chief Cole is in the second group back though," Gary let his eyes shift indicating to Mike where Darren was standing, "and we've had to quicken the tours a bit to try and get as many people through the boat as we can."

"Good work. Carry on seaman." Mike strode over to the open deck hatch and making sure there wasn't a tourist on the way up, quickly dropped down the ladder to the usual announcement of 'commander's aboard!' Lieutenant Beals turned to him and Mike was sure he saw relief in his executive officer's face at the appearance of his commanding officer.

"How're we doing, Fred?" Fred's answer was cut short by one of the tour groups coming through the hatch from the control room. One of them, a young boy, looked up at Mike and seeing the gold insignias on his dress uniform, saluted. Mike returned the salute and smiled at him.

"Did you enjoy your visit son?"

"YES!" exclaimed the young boy. His face glowed with excitement at being spoken to by this adult, who must be an important person.

"Well here's a souvenir of your visit, son." Mike grabbed the baseball cap emblazoned with the submarine's name from his head and after adjusting the back strap as small as it would go, placed it on the boy's head.

"WOW! Thank you, sir!"

"You're very welcome!" Mike stepped aside; catching a wink from a woman who he supposed was the boy's mother, so the rest of the tour group could climb the ladder to the deck. He waited until the last one had cleared the hatch before speaking again.

"Chief Cole is in the group after the next one, Fred. Let's see what you've planned for the guys."

"Down below, sir. You'll like this."

Mike followed Lt. Beals as he lowered himself down the ladder to the lower of the submarine's two decks. He immediately saw what Lt. Beals had come up with.

"The head?"

"Yes, sir. It seemed natural enough and would explain the delay as the group was leaving the boat."

Back in Halifax, Mike had thought of a more complex plan involving one of the pair feigning sickness, but this was much better and simpler and he was a firm believer in the KISS principle.

"Good job, Fred. Nothing like a bathroom emergency to facilitate a SEAL 'kidnapping'," Mike laughed, and patted him on the back. "I have to stay here and see this for myself. Carry on lieutenant."

"Yes, sir."

Fred climbed back up the ladder to the upper deck just as the next group was coming down the ladder from the outside. He ducked into the engine room and listened as a leading seaman explained to the group how the *Corner Brook* had been originally commissioned as *HMS Ursula* by the Royal Navy but was now named after the city on Newfoundland's west coast.

"Now if you'll carefully step through that hatch," the seaman continued, pointing ahead, "you'll see the control room where all the major systems on the submarine are managed."

Fred timed them. It was almost twenty-five minutes before the first civilian's head poked through the hatch on the way back, changed his mind on his method of going through and backed out again. This time he put a leg through first while swinging his body through. That was the easiest way to duck through the hatches between spaces. The group was soon shepherded up the ladder and outside the submarine's hull and Fred ducked back down the ladder to await his first 'guest'.

Standing in line with the people waiting to tour the submarine, CPO 2nd Darren Cole was having a friendly chat with CPO Jim Lewis about who would take the National League pennant this year. Both men saw that their group was about to board the submarine and they were watching as nonchalantly as possible for some kind of sign from one of the crewman as to what they were supposed to do once aboard.

"Okay ladies and gentlemen, please follow me," Leading Seaman Gary Steeves announced while waving the group up the gangway. "Be careful and take your time when going up or down the ladders and through the hatches between spaces inside the submarine. If you feel claustrophobic or uncomfortable at any time, do not be alarmed. Simply let me know and I'll guide you off the submarine. Do not feel bad if this happens as a great many people feel closed-in when below decks due to the tight spaces."

He waited a couple of moments before continuing aft to the hatch. This was the opportunity for anyone with second thoughts about touring the submarine to take their leave. No one did however, and Gary led the group to the open hatch in the deck.

"Now take your time, especially on the ladders. They are all coated with anti-slip so you'll notice the rungs are not at all slippery," he explained as the first tourist carefully grabbed the ladder's extended rails and gingerly stepped down. He watched as one after another the tourists descended to the deck below where they had been asked to wait for him. Another crewmember below made sure that no one drifted off on their own. Finally they were all down or heading down except for Darren and Jim.

"Okay sir. Take your time and hold onto the rails tight," explained Gary as he leaned close to Darren. "You need the head as soon as the control room tour is over," whispered Gary into his ear.

"Got it," Darren said, barely audible to Jim who was right behind him. Great, thought Darren. That would be neat and simple. He'd make sure Jim understood what was to happen before the tour was over.

Twenty-three minutes later, Gary was about to shepherd the tour out of the control room when one of the guests spoke. "Excuse me, sir," his voice lowering to an embarrassed whisper but still loud enough for most of the tour to hear. "I REALLY need a washroom. Is there one on here?"

"No problem, sir. Just a moment and we'll let the rest of the group up the ladder first. The head...err washroom is just below us."

"Thank you," said Darren. "Jim, will you wait here for me?"

"Sure pal. I'll be right here," replied Jim, hoping the rest of the squad would be able to pull this off convincingly. They were good SEALs; but good actors?

Gary came back down after making sure his group was safely back on the pier and laughed at Darren who had just come up the ladder, "Have a good dump chief?"

"Yes sir. Your facilities are first rate! Seaman Gary Steeves, Chief Jim Lewis." The two men shook hands and exchanged greetings. "Jim, follow me." Darren led the SEAL down the ladder to the lower level where the tour groups were not permitted. As he reached the bottom, he found Mike standing there waiting for him.

"So Chief Cole. I hear congrats are in order?" Mike grinned at Darren. He liked the young sailor and wished more of the crew shared his level of dedication.

"Err, yes, sir! It went really well! You can assign me that kind of duty any time! Oh, Commander Mike Simpson, this is Chief Petty Officer Jim Lewis, US Navy."

Jim stood at attention, not sure what to say as he had never been on a foreign warship, or at least not officially.

"At ease son, welcome aboard. We apparently have quite the adventure ahead of us."

"Yes sir. I'm sure it will be that sir. And if I may say so sir, this boat is sure clean!"

"We try to keep her neat and tidy chief. Especially when company's coming," laughed Mike, thinking this boy would soon pick up on how casual things were on the boat—that was more 'sirs' than he usually heard in the run of a day. "Chief Cole will take you forward and find a place to bunk your team. We are open to the public until 18:00 hours so you'll have to stay below until then but I'll have some chow prepared for you and the rest of the men."

"Thank you, sir."

Excusing himself, Mike climbed up the ladder and squeezing by the next tour which was already well under way, made his way to the tiny space he called his cabin. Sitting down he thrashed the events of the past six hours over in his mind and found it frustrating to just sit, unable to meet with his officers and plot out the mission because of the tour groups traipsing through the boat.

They were due to depart at oh eight hundred tomorrow and he at least needed a course plotted so he could relay that back to Marlant where it would be stored in case the unthinkable happened. Naval leaders had decided long ago after the *USS Scorpion* went missing, that expected routes and plot times would be recorded to prevent the frantic, aimless search that had followed *Scorpion's* failure to return to Norfolk.

Scorpion's final resting spot had finally been located after investigators had found a strange noise picked up by the SOSUS system of microphones lining the seabed and had triangulated the source. Sure enough, a deep diving remote submarine had found the eerie wreckage of the boat and to this day no one knew for certain what had caused the submarine and its crew to perish, or at least if they did know, they weren't saying. He'd have to meet with Lieutenant Beals this evening and run a course plot then.

Mike was tired after the long drive to and from Halifax and he thought this was probably a good time for a quick nap. Dropping his bunk from where it was propped up against the bulkhead he lay down and was fast asleep in a few minutes.

Outside on the pier, a large civilian truck slowly backed up close to the submarine and as two of the sailors watched closely, crates marked 'food' and 'perishables' were unloaded from the back of the truck onto the dock. The crates had all been carefully sized to fit down *Corner Brook's* main hatch and Lieutenant Aaron Polanski, now acting as officer of the deck, organized a work party to begin loading the crates aboard.

Two hours later, the 'food' had all been stacked in the junior rank's mess and the SEALs were busily opening the crates and checking their gear over. The heaviest crate, holding the outboard motor for the team's inflatable raft had been the last one brought aboard. A few sailors gathered to watch as the contents of the packages were laid out carefully over the mess tables and along the deck.

"Wow," whispered one of the crew as the motor was unpacked. "That's one mean looking outboard!"

"Mean, but quiet," remarked Stu. "We could sail a hundred yards from you and your sonar would barely pick us up."

"Damn!" exclaimed the sailor.

As the unpacking continued, Lieutenant Polanski rapped on Commander Simpson's door. Hearing Mike call out 'Enter!' he slid the door open and reported. "Sir, the last of the SEALs are aboard and unpacking their gear down in the junior's mess."

"Thanks Polanski. I'll be down in a few minutes." Mike looked at his watch. He had not slept at all. Laying there he ran through the mission over and over again in his mind, wondering if the Koreans had chosen Toulon because of the French military presence or was it just coincidence. He wouldn't dare try to slip into the port submerged as the French were sure to have some kind of passive sonar system guarding the entrance. It was too shallow to risk that anyway, so the SEALs would have to make their way in by boat.

Climbing off his cot, he reached for his well worn copy of *Jane's Fighting Ships* 2008 to update his knowledge of what the French were sailing these days. He didn't have to worry too much about their surface ships but the problem remained that little was known about their submarine fleet's capabilities. The French didn't like to release information about any of their major weapons systems...well, not unless you wanted to buy them, Mike quipped to himself.

Half an hour later he strolled into the junior mess to find a few of his crew spellbound as the SEALs checked over their equipment and weapons.

"Attention on deck!" Boris jumped up when he spotted Mike.

"We don't do that here lieutenant. People keep hitting their heads on things when they stand up too fast." Mike grinned and extended his hand to Boris.

"Thank you sir. Just being respectful first time meeting you, sir," Boris returned the smile and introduced Mike to his men.

"Good to have you aboard gentlemen," Mike announced after greeting each of the men in turn. "I hope you find the accommodations acceptable. If the crew become a bit too nosey, just let me or one of the other officers know and we'll shoo them out."

"No, they're just fine, sir," said Boris. "We don't mind educating them about our equipment and getting to know each other, and besides, when we're out there pounding on the hull to be let back in, we want to think of the whole boat being interested in picking us up," he finished with a grin.

"Okay lieutenant. But don't go recruiting any of them. I understand you met one of my petty officers and brought him back to us."

"Chief Cole? Yes sir. Good man...or snoop as we call him," Boris laughed, then narrowed his eyes. "Of course the Chief of Naval Operations might not see it that way," he added.

"Excuse me?" Mike asked, not sure if the lieutenant was joking or not.

"Oh, you'll have to ask Mr. Cole about that one, sir. I'm not even sure that it's not 'need to know'." The whole team laughed this time and Mike made a note to have a chat with his chief petty officer and find out what he had done. The CNO? Maybe it's time for young Mr. Cole to join the surface fleet, thought Mike, afraid to even imagine what might have happened.

"I'll leave you and your men to finish unpacking Lieutenant Martin. We'll need this space cleared for the next watch, and I'll definitely have a chat with Chief Cole later on."

"Thanks for having us, sir. We'll be done here shortly and we're going to haul out the wood and packing from the crates afterwards."

"That'll be great lieutenant. I'll be calling a meeting of my department heads for thirteen hundred hours tomorrow to brief them on where we're going. I'd like you to be there."

"I will," Boris assured the commander and turned back to unpacking his personal weapon. It had been inside one of the crates marked 'perishables'.

Chapter 7

As the last rays of the sun were setting over Yarmouth, the SEALs were completing the task of unpacking all their gear and finding areas to stow it in the limited spaces of the torpedo room. All of them had stopped short upon passing through the hatch to the weapons space and seeing women's names neatly scrolled on the sides of the Mk-48 torpedoes. Darren had hastily explained about Seaman Steeves' apparent obsession with the 'fish'. It made for a light moment as the team members began to reminisce and recount adventures with various women whose names matched those on the torpedoes.

After dark, the SEALs would take the inflatable boat outside onto the deck where it would be stowed in one of the deck compartments just forward of the sail. The compartments were built into the submarine's false hull which gave it a flat deck above the rounded pressure hull of the submarine. Anything stowed inside them of course had to be unharmed by salt water or the huge pressures built up as the boat dived.

The inflatable black zodiac had been designed with built in air canisters, larger versions of the type used to inflate life vests, allowing the boat to be fully inflated in less than four seconds. Constructed of a very tough but amazingly flexible rubber compound, it was also coated with a substance that absorbed radar waves, making it virtually undetectable. More importantly, it also had a limited self-sealing capability in case the boat was hit by small arms fire.

In his cabin, Mike was going over the final details of the course plot with Lieutenant Beals, who had stared at him open mouthed, when Mike had asked the quickest route to the Mediterranean Sea and then on to Toulon, France.

"Are we going there for a good will visit…" the lieutenant asked, knowing better but still able to hope. "…and I don't suppose we'll be going home first?"

"No, and unfortunately, no," Mike replied. "Sorry, Fred."

"Yes sir." Beals tried to hide his disappointment. His wife Shawna was home with their six month old son who at this rate would not recognize his father, assuming he ever got to see him again. Fred had joined the navy right after graduating from Cole Harbour High School in Dartmouth, Nova Scotia. He had pushed himself hard, climbing quietly through the lower ranks and soon the navy, recognizing his natural aptitude towards leadership, had encouraged him to attend university, to further his career.

Fred never forgot his mother's tears upon learning that her only son was going to university and would become an officer. It seemed as though the whole neighbourhood of North Preston where he'd grown up had come to see him off. Looking back at the crowd and waving from the window of the taxi taking him to the airport, he had made a pledge to himself that he'd be a good example to the youth of the small community just outside Dartmouth. At the Royal Military Collage he had excelled in his studies just as his superiors had predicted, and he had kept that promise to himself and his community. Now he sat in Mike's office wondering if he'd ever see Preston again.

Mike went over the details of the mission with his executive officer and together they plotted the route that would take them through the Strait of Gibraltar and into the Mediterranean Sea. As they calculated the distance and worked out an economical speed, they also discussed potential problems that might occur during the voyage. Fully fuelled, endurance was not an issue as the new oxygen system let them stay comfortably submerged almost as long as a full battery charge could hold out. Finally after a couple of hours they sat back, satisfied with their sea track. Mike dismissed Lieutenant Beals and started writing into the submarine's log. Fred scooped up his charts and locked them in the safe built into the pod that served as his navigation table in the control room. His disappointment was fast being replaced with excitement over their upcoming mission.

∗   ∗   ∗   ∗

The first light of dawn found the crew of *HMCS Corner Brook* preparing to depart Yarmouth and head back out to sea. Mike was standing on the bridge supervising the procedures for getting underway and also thinking about the best way to spring the mission on his crew.

A few of them still thought they were heading back home to Halifax and for security reasons he could not yet tell them otherwise. A few officers knew, of course, and certainly the SEALs were fully aware of what was going on. No doubt some of the crew had figured out that they were not likely carrying a fully equipped squad of SEALs back to Halifax with them, and Mike could just imagine the 'scuttlebutt' that was spreading below decks. He'd have to fill the rest of the crew in right after the department head's briefing.

"Sir, in all aspects we are ready for sea!" came the shout from Leading Seaman David Jones, who was coordinating the lines detail.

"Standby! We'll be casting off in ten minutes!" Mike shouted back down to him from his perch high in the submarine's sail. "Prepare to remove the gangway!"

The white banner with the boat's name and insignia blazoned across it, had already been removed and carefully stowed, and the lines holding the gangway fast to the submarine and the pier had been loosened. All that remained was for the gangway itself to be hauled back onto the pier and the lines holding the submarine in place to be removed.

Surprisingly in spite of the early hour, quite a crowd had gathered to see them off and Mike noted the mayor had also come to say good-bye. Mike gave him a friendly wave and smiled as the mayor waved back. The town had indeed been friendly and more importantly his crew had behaved themselves. Many of them came back to the boat carrying souvenirs purchased from local shops which generated a lot of good will with the locals. That and the stories told to them by the young sailors.

"Remove the gangway!" he called down to the men waiting on the pier. They were starting to pull the small aluminium bridge away when a car careened into the parking lot adjacent to the pier and squealed sideways to a stop. On the submarine's deck two seamen, each carrying an assault rifle, dropped to one knee, prepared for anything.

"WAIT!" called out a slightly stocky man as he threw the car door open and rushed towards the pier. He was able to move at a good clip in spite of his size and as he drew closer Mike could see that his weight was more muscle than fat. As he reached the pier, Mike could see his face clearly.

"Stand down men!" he shouted to the seamen below. "Good lord Cookie! Are you lost?"

"No sir! Request permission to come aboard!"

"Granted!" Mike dropped quickly down the ladder to the control room and found Cookie catching his breath, seated at one of the sonar stations. "Jeeze,

Cookie! What are you doing here?" Mike tried to act surprised and from Cookie's unconcerned expression he obviously hadn't been briefed about where they were going.

"I've been temporarily transferred from the *Victoria*, but there was a problem getting a flight from Panama. The boat was heading back to British Columbia so I grabbed a United States Air Force flight up to Dover, Delaware and then tried to connect with anything coming to Nova Scotia. I phoned Marlant and found out you guys were here, but would be returning to Halifax today, so I told them I'd just get a commercial flight to Halifax and meet you there." He paused finally to take a breath. "After I landed in Halifax, I reported in at O'Hanlon's office and he told me to get my fat a…"

Mike laughed, cutting him off before anyone else in the control room overheard. "Well come up to the bridge and catch your breath Cookie. We can chat up there while I get us turned around and out to sea." Mike literally pushed him towards the ladder and waited while he hauled himself up.

When they reached the top of the sail, Mike gave the commands to finally remove the gangway and release the lines that held the submarine in place, while Cookie stood back and watched, grateful for the chance to relax. He'd only had a few minutes to get to a store and grab a few things before tearing up the highway to Yarmouth, although he did make sure a buddy in Halifax would arrange to pick up his car and drive it back home.

Speaking into his ever present headset, Mike gave orders to the helm that eased the boat forward and away from the pier to give him room to bring them around towards the open sea. Half an hour later, they were clearing Yarmouth harbour with the Cape Forchu lighthouse disappearing into the light fog behind them.

"So cap," Cookie looked at Mike and smiled. "I take it you didn't shove me up here just for the view?"

"No, most of the crew think we're headed home and I didn't want to burst their bubble just yet," Mike replied. "O'Hanlon thought it might be a good idea to have you along on this trip." Cookie's face showed serious concern now. "Most all the men know you and the ones that don't have heard about your reputation, so I'm counting on you to sooth any frayed nerves that might come along." Mike went on, giving Cookie a brief version of their mission.

"Shit cap!" Cookie laughed when Mike had finished. "Maybe you shoulda' just let the *Bush* get away! I'd better get below and stow my gear," remarked the man who had been born just down the road from the submarine's namesake. "Any requests for supper?"

"Yeah, how about some of that chowder you're so damned famous for," asked Mike, with a hopeful expression. "After the briefing, the crew might need something tasty to help them get over not going home."

"Consider it done, commander. I'll have it ready to serve up by fifteen hundred."

Cookie dropped out of sight down the hatch and Mike leaned back to enjoy the view as the submarine slowly moved through the water. The waves were becoming higher and soon the smooth wall of water created by the bow as it pushed through the ocean was replaced with jagged waves crashing into the bottom of the sail. The sea was relatively calm though and *Cornerbrook* surged ahead with the ocean swells causing the boat to sway slightly.

Soon the last of the seagulls which had escorted them since leaving Yarmouth had begun flying back to the disappearing shore with Mike watching them, marvelling at the grace with which they flew. The first light spray over the sail's small windshield took his attention away from the friendly sea birds and looking at his watch, he climbed down the ladder to the control room.

"Lt Beals," he announced to his executive officer. "You have the con. I'll be down in the senior's mess."

"Yes sir."

Fred watched as Mike headed down the hatch to the lower deck. He wondered how the crew would react as word spread throughout the boat about their mission. They would definitely be disappointed in the fact that they were not heading home, but Fred was sure there would also be some excitement as well over the mission. Most of them had never been on a special ops cruise and it would be interesting to see if any of them found the stress a little more than they had bargained for. He was sure there wouldn't be any problems with this crew though. They were a good team and Mike was an excellent commanding officer. Yes, he thought while climbing up to the bridge, they'd be fine.

Below, the last of the department heads had gathered in the senior's mess and anticipation filled the small space.

"Gather round guys," Mike ordered, while spreading out the charts he'd unlocked from their storage in the control room. His officers were trying to squeeze in close to see where they were going and more than a few grunts and expletives were heard as the commander started to explain the mission to his men. With the SEALs aboard, there had been rumours floating around of a special operations mission and more than one crew member returning from liberty ashore in Yarmouth, had been shocked to bump into one of Lieutenant Martin's men casually cleaning his weapon while watching a video on the television in the junior mess.

Mike was pleased that the groans upon learning that Halifax was not their next port of call were subduing quickly. Damn, he thought. They're a good crew. O'Hanlon had been right to request *Corner Brook* for this mission.

"This is where we're going," he announced, pointing at the chart. "Toulon is a major seaport and tourist destination. It's also home to the French boomer squadron," he added, referring to the ballistic missile carrying submarines called 'boomers' by most navies. It dawned on him that ironically, submarine launched ballistic missiles happened to be the SEALs target.

"Sir?"

"Yes Brad."

"Do we have any intel on the port's security?"

"All we know for sure is that a patrol boat monitors the harbour entrance, but not constantly," responded Mike. "They beef up security when a boomer is coming in or going out, but for the most part it's pretty light. We have no information that the French have laid any kind of a sosus system, so we shouldn't have to worry about microphones on the seabed picking us up but let's not count that out just in case. There is an asset ashore who has sent word that there will be no arrivals or departures of boomers while we are there so that should lesson the security level somewhat."

"I'll make sure again that all the latest French submarine cards are loaded into the system, just in case," said the sonar officer.

"Good idea, Brad. Hopefully we won't need them."

The sonar system aboard *HMCS Corner Brook* had recently been upgraded to allow new 'sound signatures' to be loaded from tiny XD memory cards. Brad would make sure all the available French ones were reloaded just to be sure none had been accidentally left out. Not much chance of that, he thought. But it would give Derek something to do during the long transit across the Atlantic.

"The ROE in this operation is as follows; we are authorized live loads and have authorization to use torpedoes if we confirm we have been targeted and fired upon." He paused for a moment before continuing. "But not until we have used all possible measures to evade." The officers looked at Mike and he detected the obvious unasked question in their faces. Under those 'Rules Of Engagement', by the time they were able to fire a torpedo, they would probably already be sunk.

"I know these are pretty ambiguous but it is crucial that we not be detected and if we are that we not be identified." The faces in the room seemed to soften a little, and Mike went on.

"Now as for the SEALs, our orders are very clear. If anything goes wrong, we leave the area immediately without them."

"We leave the harbour area and wait for a rendezvous time?" asked Lieutenant Keith Anderson, the *Corner Brook's* weapons officer. He had gotten to know the SEALs quite well as they usually hung around the torpedo space where all their gear was stowed.

"No, Keith. We leave the area completely. They will be on their own and if they're captured, that's not our problem."

"Hey guys!" Lieutenant Martin spoke up. "It's not as bad as it sounds. If anything really bad happens, we plan to make our way to Paris and vacation for awhile."

"Sure you will lieutenant," Keith chuckled. "Be sure to send us a post card!"

"You can count on it! Something with a pretty French girl on it!"

"Okay," Mike went on. "Here is where we plan to disembark the team. The depth at low tide is about three hundred and fifty feet so we'll have plenty of water below the keel. You can see here on the map that the bottom comes up sharply after this point, so we don't dare go in any closer in case the French have laid some kind of Sosus system. But we will be far enough inside the harbour mouth so the SEALs won't have a long boat ride to the target. The XO and I have already gone over the route and the only place we may have a potential problem is the strait. Lieutenant Beals came up with a plan for that though and I think it'll work great."

He referred to the Strait of Gibraltar, where only a narrow passage allowed ships and submarines to enter the Mediterranean Sea from the west. Mike waited a moment before going on to give anyone with a question the chance to speak up. They all remained quiet so he explained how they would get past this first challenge.

"The strait is obviously a problem in that it is constantly travelled by half a dozen different navies, and although we might be able to make it through submerged, we're going to try something less risky." Mike went on with the plan.

"*Corner Brook's* silhouette is so close to a British SSN that we're going to transit the strait at dusk flying a Royal Navy pendant and hope that no one comes up for a real close look. With all the traffic in the area, our diesels shouldn't stand out."

"Sir?"

"Yes Trask," Mike responded to his communications officer who had been silent throughout the whole briefing until now.

"Lieutenant Beals went over his plan with me, and I just wanted to let you know that I have found all the material I'll need and the Royal Navy pendant should be finished by tomorrow evening."

"Thanks petty officer. It doesn't have to be perfect since it'll be almost dark when we go through, but try to make it look good out to say…two hundred yards."

"No problem commander," he affirmed. "If they get close enough to see it's a fake, I'll just yell over in my best cockney accent and ask if they'd like to have some fish 'n chips," Jake added smiling.

"Speaking of food sir…"

Simpson turned to Sub Lieutenant Craig Devereux, his engineering officer. Craig was new to the boat, having transferred from *Victoria* a month ago. There didn't seem to be anything the man could not fix when it came to *Corner Brook's* many systems. He'd also been one of the first Canadians sent over to inspect the boats when they were still in British hands, and although they had flown over to England on the same flight, Mike had not had a chance to meet him until he arrived aboard his boat.

"Are you hungry lieutenant?"

"No sir," answered Craig. "But I ran into Cookie Barnes in the galley this morning. I was just curious as I hadn't heard any scuttle butt about him transferring aboard."

"Chief Barnes is TDY from the *Victoria* for this mission. Admiral O'Hanlon thought it might be a good idea to have someone around who's been on a few special ops cruises in case some of the crew get a little antsy. If I have my way," Mike continued, "we'll be keeping him."

"After eating his food, you'll lock him in the galley before you let him go, sir."

"You might be right Craig. I'll make you our official promotions officer in charge of convincing Cookie that he's much better off here than back on *Victoria*," Mike grinned.

"Consider it done, sir!" Craig smiled and leaned back on the table he was using as a chair in the cramped mess room.

"Okay guys," the Commander said. "That's all I have for you. Notify your respective underlings and unless Lieutenant Martin has anything to add, we'll break this meeting up."

"I'd say you covered it all, sir. I've nothing to add." Boris had been about to ask what would happen if they were identified transiting the straight, but thought better of it. He was sure the commander must have a back up plan in case of that eventuality.

"Dismissed gentleman. Jake, can you stay a moment?" Mike rolled up the charts and map he had been using and made room for the rest of the men to file out.

"Yes, sir," Jake responded, finding an empty seat after having stood throughout the briefing.

"Jake, I just wanted to go over the communications restrictions with you. Marlant has informed our families and the media that we have been sent to Faslane, Scotland as part of an exercise that is being called Northern Gamble."

"Good choice of name, sir," Jake smiled.

"Yeah, it sure is," Mike agreed. "That's our cover story so if any traffic happens to come in directed at us, that's where we're supposed to be headed."

"No problem, sir. I'll make sure the comms team is aware and we'll plan a few cover messages in case anyone asks any embarrassing questions." Pausing for a moment he asked, "Is there a name for the op we're actually on?"

"No. They didn't dare give it one," Mike replied. "That's all petty officer. Carry on."

"Yes, sir," replied Jake, getting up and heading for his station. He'd have to make sure no one responded to anyone contacting them over the communication nets without referring to him first. This was his first special op and he planned to make sure that his department performed well.

In the empty mess, Mike sat back for a moment and went over the notes he had made in his PDA. He had covered everything on his list and he was more than a little surprised no one had asked what they'd do if the British submarine ruse didn't work. Good thing, Mike thought smiling to himself; he had about a week to come up with something.

*   *   *   *

Sitting and standing among the Mark-48 torpedoes, the SEALs listened intently as Boris recounted what had been said at the meeting.

"Gee, skipper…," Stu looked around to make sure no one else was in earshot before continuing, "…do you think these Canucks will be able to pull this off?"

"I'm sure they will," Boris responded, lowering his voice. "Commander Simpson's been on special ops before and from what I've seen since we arrived, they're a pretty good team."

"They do seem to be that," Stu commented, leaning back to signify that he was satisfied and had no further questions.

"How's the gear?" Boris asked all of them. "Any defects or missing?"

"It's all fine," Jamal answered. "We've gone over everything and it's all accounted for and working."

He didn't have to add that the weapons and explosives would be gone over again and again before they reached Toulon. SEALs were known to wear out weapons by constantly stripping them down to make sure everything was clean and working properly.

"Great! Well the CO promised fish chowder that will make us want to desert and join them, so let's hit the mess."

Back in the galley, Cookie Barnes was just putting the last of what he liked to call his 'secret spices' into the large pot that had been simmering on the burner for almost three hours. In his mind, the trick to perfect seafood chowder was not to over cook the poor thing as he found everyone else seemed inclined to do, but rather to entice it to cook slowly, at a low heat until the steam lifting off the surface made you want to dive into the pot.

"Mmm...," he whispered, as he sampled the broth, "perfect."

*　　　*　　　*　　　*

In the senior's mess, a small group was admiring the unfinished Royal Navy Ensign 'constructed' by Trask.

"I'm not sure the Royal Navy will be impressed. Maybe they'll try to sue us for copyright infringement," laughed Lieutenant Beals as he showed Mike and Brad the Royal Navy ensign, created from patches of material scavenged throughout the boat by Petty Officer Trask.

"I think it's an excellent job!" Mike replied. "What do you think Brad?"

"From a hundred feet I doubt anyone could tell it wasn't authentic, sir." Brad enjoyed having someone ask his opinion on something other than what was making that 'noise' outside the boat. He sometimes wished he was more of a social animal, but that just wasn't in his nature. And besides, he thought, when I'm on duty everyone listens to what "I" have to say. That was true enough. Brad's ears were the boat's ears.

"Fred, tell Petty Officer Trask well done, and that we might just be coming to him for a pirate flag some day," Mike laughed letting out a pirate sounding 'Argggg'.

"I will, sir," Fred replied. "You can count on that." He smiled to himself. The reason he had assigned the job to Trask in the first place, had been the incredible 'skull and crossbones' flag he'd seen Trask showing off to one of his mates last month. It was now safely stowed with the other signal flags and Fred wondered if they'd ever get a chance to fly it.

"Ahh...finally. So Cookie," asked Mike as he saw the man enter the senior's mess carrying a tray of steaming bowls. "Is this stuff as good as I hear it is?"

"Better sir." Cookie answered.

"I already have the off duty bunch next door served, cap," he remarked, referring to the men in the junior mess. Commander Simpson, like all good leaders, insisted the regular ranks be served first.

"Thanks Cookie." Mike sampled a spoon full of the steaming liquid. "Damn! This is really good!"

"Best there is captain. You might find as good back on the 'rock', but I doubt it," Cookie said, referring to his home province of Newfoundland.

"You know, Cookie," Fred was trying to look dead serious. "I hear they plan to get rid of the ovens on *Victoria* and replace them all with microwaves during her refit next year."

"Nice try, sir," laughed Cookie. "When that happens I'll be sure to ask for a permanent transfer."

They all laughed as Cookie picked up the tray and returned to the galley where he was preparing a surprise of home made bread soaked in real butter for the men on watch.

Mike watched him leave and wondered to himself again why Cookie was insistent on running the galley on whatever boat he was assigned to instead of taking a more serious duty.

He knew that years ago, numerous suggestions and requests that Chief Barnes attend the Royal Military Collage in Kingston, Ontario had been made, but the man would not hear of it. Officially he claimed that his men would starve if he deserted them. Most of his commanders felt he was afraid he'd be taken off the boats if he was promoted any higher. Neither was the real answer, and that, Cookie kept deep inside. He didn't think anyone else would understand.

Well, it's his choice, Mike thought to himself. Besides, he was the next best thing to having a counsellor onboard the boat. Brushing the thoughts aside, Mike returned to his seafood chowder. Damn, he thought, this really is good!

*   *   *   *

The next morning a thick blanket of fog surrounded the boat, muffling the sounds of the waves washing over the submarine's deck and the low throbbing sounds of the diesels. They were now one hundred and fifty miles east of Sable

Island and finally in deep water where they could dive, making better time submerged than on the surface. The seas had become much rougher since they'd left Yarmouth, and the crew was looking forward to the smooth sailing beneath the waves instead of through them.

"Sir, depth below keel is over six thousand feet. Battery is at ninety-five percent."

Mike keyed the microphone button on his headset cord. "Thanks, Charley. I'm on the way." His routine before diving was always the same. Clearing everyone below, he took a few moments to enjoy the view one last time. Drinking deeply of the fresh sea air, he climbed down the ladder leading into the lockout chamber after making sure the upper hatch was secure. Dropping down the ladder to the control room, he stepped aside for the seaman who climbed up to secure the lower hatch behind him.

"Lieutenant Beals, dive the boat. Take her down to three hundred and fifty feet. Maintain speed and course."

"Diving to three hundred and fifty feet, aye sir. Maintain speed and course."

And so the repetitions began. Each command echoed by someone else to be sure they were understood correctly. Mike watched as Fred gave the orders and the crew carried them out. This would probably be Fred's last cruise on *Corner Brook* as a promotion for him was in the works and he'd soon be moving on to a command of his own. Mike would miss him. Lieutenant Beals had a good way with the men and they in return all liked and respected him.

"Sir, our depth is three hundred and fifty feet. Course zero nine five degrees," Petty Officer Poulin announced a few minutes later from his station at the helm.

"Thanks Charley. Make turns for fifteen knots. We'll maintain this course for a couple of hours." Mike mentally calculated where that would put them and decided this would be a good time to check on the guests in the torpedo space. "Lieutenant Beals, you have the con. I'll be forward if you need anything."

"I have the con, aye sir." Fred enjoyed the responsibilities frequently given to him by the commander and he always carried them out to the best of his abilities.

* * * *

Mike entered the torpedo space, carefully stepping over and around the gear spread out around the deck. He found the SEAL commander pouring over the deck plan of the Korean ship.

"Lieutenant Martin, everything okay?"

"Yes commander. We're just going over our final plans," Boris responded. Taped to the side of one of the Mark-48s was a large layout drawing of the *Sariwon*. Mike could see markings all over the drawing, some obviously showing routes onto and through the ship and others he could only guess at. He did notice with a grimace that they were using the torpedo named 'Susan' for the layout's backdrop. He dreaded the day he'd have to offload these torpedoes back in Bedford. Sanding off the names and touching up the paint was not an option or so Lieutenant Anderson, his weapons officer had explained.

"Do you guys have enough space down here?" The commander had always found the torpedo spaces cramped. Especially when they were carrying a full load as was the case now.

"Yeah, we're fine. This is wide open compared to some of the boats we've been on. The old *Skipjacks* were really bad and all the SEAL teams were really happy when the last of those boats was retired," Boris related.

Mike looked over the drawing of the *Sariwon*. "Not a very big ship, is she?"

"Nope, just big enough to be a problem. She's really quite old. I think if we just let her go, there'd be a fifty percent chance she'd keel over in a storm and sink," joked Boris.

"I wish," Mike said. "Keep me posted and if you need anything at all, let us know."

"Thank you, sir. We will." Mike left the SEALs to their briefing and headed for his cabin. He had an appointment with Chief Petty Officer 2nd Darren Cole, first to congratulate him officially on his successful 'spy' mission, and second to satisfy his curiosity about the Chief of Naval Operation's involvement. Somehow, knowing Darren, it would be an interesting story. Twenty minutes later, a tap on his cabin door announced the petty officer's arrival. Mike ushered him into the small space without speaking. Darren stood at loose attention, not looking forward to this 'chat' as Mike had put it when informing him of their meeting.

"Relax Cole. So tell me about the CNO."

"I don't really know where to begin, sir…"

"The beginning is always a good place chief," Mike answered with a smile. He saw Darren relax a bit.

"Well there was this girl at the Econo Lodge where I stayed in Virginia Beach and…" He went on, recounting the story to Commander Simpson, who couldn't help but burst out laughing when Darren reached the part about Admiral Carroll showing up at Little Creek to brief the SEALs. "…and that's how it happened.

Heather's a wonderful girl but I don't think her old man is impressed with me now."

"Damn it Cole. If anyone else was standing here telling me this yarn I'd call him a liar. O'Hanlon didn't mention anything about it when I was in Halifax, so chances are you're not in any real trouble. Well at least until you try and call…" Mike paused, "…what was her name again…Heather?"

"Yes sir. I don't suppose she'll want to hear from me now. I'm sorry if I've caused any problems commander."

"No problem, Cole. Now get out of here and let me get back to work…dismissed."

Darren turned and opened the thin door which allowed the barest of privacy to Commander Simpson. Stepping out into the control room he was surprised to see half the crew jammed into the tiny space.

"SURPRISE!" yelled the men. Darren was momentarily shocked and almost backed into the commander who was entering the control room right behind him.

"Attention on deck!" hollered someone in the background. The group as one snapped to attention smartly, surprising for submariners, who didn't often practice formal military courtesy.

"Chief Petty Officer 2nd Class Darren Cole, front and center!" Mike bellowed towards the bewildered young man. Darren spun around and came to attention in front of his commander, totally unaware of what was transpiring.

"Chief Petty Officer 2nd Class Darren Cole, in spite of numerous occasions when your actions have left your commanding officer and fellow crew mates perplexed and questioning your sanity, on this date let it be known that you have been promoted to the exalted rank of Chief Petty Office 1st Class with all the responsibilities and privileges accorded said rank. Chief Cole, congratulations on a job well done!" Mike couldn't help smiling as he reached out and shook Darren's hand amongst the cheers from the crew.

"Thank you, sir! Thanks guys!" Darren was sincerely touched by the surprise Mike had pulled on him. Obviously getting him into the office was a ruse to allow the crew to gather outside.

"Chief Cole, I believe you'll be needing these," Mike handed him a small box with an open lid revealing a pair of gold embroidered rank insignia to be sewn onto his dress uniform.

"Thank you commander. I appreciate this."

"Don't thank me Chief. You earned it. Now stop standing there gawking and get back to work!"

"Yes sir!" Darren came to attention and smartly turned on his heel to head forward to his post in the torpedo space. Cheers and cat calls followed him from the assembled crew, all of whom liked the gregarious young man.

"Hey Cole," Marcel d'Entremont called out as Darren ducked into the torpedo space. "I hear I have to actually treat you as an equal now," he laughed, referring to the rank they now shared.

"Only for now, my fine friend," laughed Cole. "I suspect the powers that be, recognizing my greatness, will soon bump me up to sub lieutenant before you know it."

"Oh yeah? In which navy? Ours or the American's, once you marry the CNO's daughter?"

"I doubt that will happen now," laughed Darren. "I just explained it all to the CO and he nearly shit himself laughing when I told him about running into Admiral Carroll at Little Creek."

Darren had already told Marcel the story and how he felt that he and Heather had connected, but any chance of a relationship was clearly out the window now.

"Hey, keep the faith my friend. You never know how it'll work out."

"Yeah," Darren responded hopefully. "You never know."

Chapter 8

At fourteen hundred hours the next day, Mike had just finished entering his personal log into his PDA when the speaker above his head buzzed followed by Lieutenant Beals' voice.

"Skipper, we have a contact. Submerged."

"On the way!" Mike jumped up and rushed to the control room, noting with satisfaction that Lt. Brad Smith had the sonar watch.

"What have you got Brad?"

"Submerged target bearing three four zero degrees. The computer thinks it's a Russian *Sierra*. I'd say he's about fifty-five hundred yards out."

"Where's he heading?" Mike asked, watching the screen in front of his sonar officer.

"His heading seems to be the same as ours, sir. A bit faster though...say twenty-two knots."

"Keep on him Brad. Helm, slow us to ten knots. Let's see if he pulls away from us and gets out of our hair." The helmsman echoed the command and entered the new speed into the little keyboard on his left. In response, *Corner Brook's* huge propeller slowed almost instantly.

"Sir, speed is ten knots. Maintaining depth, maintaining course," announced the seaman at the helm a few moments later.

Mike watched as the line representing the *Sierra* class SSN slowly moved to the right and almost immediately became lost in the 'waterfall' on the screen. At that same moment, Brad's body stiffened.

"Active sonar! Russian! Contact is definitely a *Sierra* and he's got us!"

"Helm! All stop!" Mike ordered. "Quiet boat!"

Fred joined Mike at the sonar console where they exchanged eye contact, both thinking the same thing…there was no way the Russian could have heard them when he sailed by, but in fact, it appeared that he had.

* * * *

Aboard K-621, one of Russia's *Sierra* class SSNs, the control room was deathly quiet.

"Captain, the other submarine is directly in front of us. No identification at this time," spoke the Russian sonar operator, barely whispering.

"Very good, Petrov." The Russian captain looked down at the sonar operator and then over to the new targeting device which had first picked up the unknown submarine. It had come as a shock to the control room crew when the device had emitted a quiet beep, indicating that it was receiving interference of some kind. The only time he had seen this previously was when another Russian warship carrying the new device was close by. That of course was impossible right now as there were no other Russian warships in the vicinity, and yet, the device had clearly picked up interference from another one.

"Are you sure it is not one of ours," he asked the sonar operator again.

"I am pretty sure captain. I cannot identify for certain who it is other than it is conventionally powered."

The captain pondered this for a few moments. Well there was certainly one way to find out and if it was another Russian boat, they would have to identify themselves.

"Petrov, go active. Control, turn to three three zero degrees, power ninety percent."

The sleek submarine came around and headed directly for the other boat, increasing speed as it turned. The captain of K-621 smiled at the speed with which his boat manoeuvred. Now they would see how brave their mysterious friend was.

* * * *

"Target acquired sir, depth about seven hundred feet," Brad spoke more calmly now. "Range decreasing. He's heading right for us. Less than five thousand yards now."

"Brad, did you pick up any noise from us before he came around?" Mike knew there was always a chance that something on the *Corner Brook* had made some noise and they hadn't heard it.

"No sir. Nothing."

"Okay, we'll stay here for a few minutes and see if he just gives us a sniff and goes away. We don't have time to play with him right now."

Fred checked the time. They had a thirty-six hour window for the SEAL insertion but neither he nor Commander Simpson wanted to chance making it to Toulon at the last minute. They had run into Russian boats before and usually a small game of hide and seek followed while the skippers tried to out fox each other using their boat's prowess and finally pinging at each other. That wasn't an option right now and not only because of the time constraint. They also didn't want anyone else hearing their active sonar and wondering where the Canadian boat was headed.

"Active sonar!" Brad winced as the sound waves were getting louder in his headphones now.

"Helm! Take us down to seven hundred feet! All ahead! Let's see if we can rattle this guy."

Mike braced himself as the deck tilted down. The submarine dove quickly, an attribute of the *Victoria* class. They were slower coming back up though and all the submariners would have preferred it the other way around. Shortly they were level again and it was time to play his hand.

"Brad, bearing to target!"

"Target is one five zero degrees, forty-five hundred yards."

"Helm, bring us left to one five zero! Give me all she's got Scotty!" Mike thought a little humour might calm things down in the control room.

"One five zero degrees aye sir." Seaman McFarlane responded, attempting a Scottish brogue.

"Should I ping him sir?" Brad asked, seeing the game of 'chicken' developing and knowing one of the first rules of the game was that both boats had to be using active sonar so they'd know the range and when to 'chicken out'.

"No," Mike replied. "We can't take the chance that someone will recognize us."

"Aye sir," Brad answered. He really didn't like this new version of the game.

"Active sonar! Target is thirty-nine hundred yards. Same depth. No aspect change!" Brad emphasized the last part, making sure everyone knew they were on a collision course. He felt Commander Simpson pat his shoulder, but that didn't bring much relief.

"Now Mr. Ruskie, how brave are we feeling today?" Mike asked, knowing how dangerous this manoeuvre was, but not daring to go active. If necessary he'd break off but that would only entice the ex-Soviet boat to try and hunt him down. No, he had to end this here and now.

The seconds ticked by. The combined speed of close to fifty knots would eat up the distance between the boats in a hurry. No one spoke and Fred knew it was probably the same over on the Russian *Sierra*. He wasn't too worried. The Russians were professionals and some of the best sailors in the world. The captain of the *Sierra* would surely write them off as careless and break off soon. Or so he hoped.

* * * *

The Russian captain had now had quite enough of this. Whoever the captain of the other submarine was seemed intent on taking unnecessary risks. It was time to put an end to this.

"Control, change course to one seven zero. Slow to half speed." He didn't like being the first one to turn away but the other captain was clearly being too reckless. He'd report this incident when he returned to Murmansk. It had to be another Russian boat equipped with their new targeting device. How unfortunate the scientists at Karaul had not been able to invent a way for them to communicate with this laser system. Perhaps Moscow has assigned another boat to test the new system against him. He would find out who the reckless captain was and pity the poor fool commanding that boat.

* * * *

"Sir! Aspect change on target! He's turned south!" Brad tried to sound cool but couldn't hide his relief. He'd need some serious time with his Playstation to relax after this.

"Yes!" Mike couldn't help but shout!

"He's slowing down sir! Continuing turn and now heading away!" Brad gave a 'thumbs up', looking comical sporting a huge grin with his headphones hanging off one ear.

"Helm, bring us back on course," Mike ordered. "Maintain depth. Speed twelve knots."

He looked down at the sonar screens and saw the line representing the *Sierra* slowly fade out again.

"Lost him, sir. He's probably heading for the Med too," Brad noted.

"If he is, that might work out in our favour," Mike noted. "He'll trip the sonar net when he crosses through the straight and everyone will want to play 'Find the Ruskie' while we try to slip in unnoticed." Mike patted his shoulder. "Let me know if anything else crops up."

"Aye, sir." Brad returned to his screens. It would have been fun to lock the Lazcom on the Russian boat, he thought. Oh well, not today.

Mike returned to his cabin to consider how the Russian had heard them. Certainly the Russian sonar systems were very good, much better than the west had admitted during the cold war. But they shouldn't have been able to pick up *Corner Brook* at their present speed. He'd report it when he returned to Halifax. No doubt the engineers would want to go over the boat with a fine tooth comb trying to find something that might be making some kind of noise.

The idea that perhaps someone else had developed a new laser based system never occurred to Commander Simpson. It would be the first thing however, to cross the minds of the engineers back in Nova Scotia.

* * * *

HMCS Corner Brook continued her slow journey across the Atlantic Ocean. Every few days, Commander Simpson would surface the submarine or come to periscope depth so that the diesels could be started, charging the batteries. The crew fell into their routines; thoughts of the coming adventure never straying too far from their minds. When it did, the sight of one of the SEALs cleaning a weapon or piece of gear in the mess was always an abrupt reminder.

Lieutenant Martin went over the plans repeatedly with his team. He was determined they would know the small freighter inside out by the time they actually stepped aboard her. Boris had assigned himself to checking and rechecking the explosive packages they would use, always marvelling at the small size of the devices. Because the rocket boosters were very fragile, it would take only a small charge to render them useless.

* * * *

At the same instant *Corner Brook* reached the half way point of her voyage across the Atlantic, the *MV Sariwon* was entering the Mediterranean Sea from the northern end of the Suez Canal near Port Said, Egypt. Her five man crew was looking forward to docking the ship in Toulon, where they hoped to experience all the delicacies of the French port city. The old ship picked up speed as it cleared the canal control area; mostly ignored by the usual group of tourists and on lookers lining the shore watching the ship traffic entering and leaving the canal. Those who did give the ship any attention noted the rust streaks and numerous dents along the old steamer's hull. Some took pictures, while most of them dismissed it completely, saving their attention and digital camera memory cards for something far more interesting that might come along.

One person however, did look twice at the venerable old ship. Wearing a loose fitting shirt and khaki shorts, Greg Newell hoped he appeared to be just another curiosity seeker watching the canal traffic. His flight from Toulon, where he had managed to find out enough information about the French navy deployments to satisfy his superiors, had just barely brought him to Egypt on time. He confirmed again the name, barely readable in faded paint on the ship's stern, and noted the time on his watch. Right on schedule. The North Korean ship had made it this far and with any luck the Canadian submarine was well on her way to the Med.

Greg noted there was little activity aboard the ship, and watched as the Suez Canal pilot boat pulled alongside to pick up the canal pilot who had been aboard during the transit through the canal zone. The Korean ship barely slowed as he watched a man lower himself down a ladder to the deck of the small craft waiting below. The transfer completed, the pilot boat pulled away towards a ship heading in the opposite direction for the canal entrance. What a life, Greg thought. The ship pilots got to experience every kind of ship afloat in the run of their careers.

Taking one more look at the disappearing stern of the *Sariwon*, Greg Newell of the Central Intelligence Agency, headed for his rented car. As he walked, he began to feel the effect of too many hours without sleep. He'd head back to his hotel now, where he would make a quick satellite call back to Virginia, informing those who needed to know that everything seemed to be going according to plan. He thought briefly of the SEALs he'd met at Little Creek and the dangers they now faced, and then pushed the thought away. In his line of work it was better not to become too familiar with anyone and making friends was completely out of the question. After making the call, 'Greg', the alias he was using on this mission, lay down for a nap. He had only one more assignment in regards to this mission, but that wasn't until a few days from now. In spite of his exhaustion, he slept lightly, like most of the people in his trade.

* * * *

"Level at nine hundred feet, sir. Course zero nine zero degrees at five knots. Battery is seventy percent," announced Petty Officer Charley Poulin, who would be 'driving the boat' into the strait.

Corner Brook had slowed on approaching the Straits of Gibraltar and now her crew was preparing for their transit through the narrow sea passage that separates the Atlantic Ocean from the Mediterranean Sea.

"All stop. Maintain depth," Mike ordered, thankful that they had made it this far undetected except for the brief skirmish with the Russian boat. Now it was time for the sonar team to conduct a thorough sweep with the passive sonars to plot the traffic in their area. This being one of the world's busiest choke points with ships cruising in and out of the Mediterranean, it was paramount that he have a very clear picture of the ships moving through the strait during their transit.

"Lt. Beals, position?"

"We're just under ninety miles due west of Tangiers, right here," he said, pointing at the end of the line representing the *Corner Brook's* journey so far.

"Okay Brad, take your time and give me a good picture of what's up there," Mike ordered.

Lieutenant Smith and Chief Leaman studied the screens in front of them, making notes of everything sailing above and around them. There was a lot of traffic moving around up there and finding the right ship for them to follow through the strait was not an easy task. Twenty minutes later, they'd found what they were looking for.

"Commander?" Brad called Mike over. "This one will be our best bet. He's making twelve knots and there's at least a ten thousand yard hole behind him where we'd fit quite nicely."

"Looks good Brad. Helm, make turns for fifteen knots. Course…zero eight five degrees. That ought to put us right behind him. Make your depth four hundred feet."

Charley echoed the commands correctly and brought the *Corner Brook* smoothly to her new speed, course and depth. Lieutenant Smith had found a ship entering the Mediterranean that they could follow safely, only surfacing when they were just north of Tangiers for their passage through the strait. Mike again considered running in submerged, but if they were detected by a warship which by chance happened to be transiting at the same time, there would be a risk that the sonar operator might be able to identify them from their sound signature. On the other hand, running on the diesels while surfaced would not be such a problem as the ambient ocean noises and other ships should mask the sound of the engines.

By masquerading as a British nuclear boat on the surface however, which would have had difficulty manoeuvring through the shallow currents submerged; they would attract less attention this close to the Royal Navy base at Gibraltar. Anyone looking really close would probably tell that there was something amiss, but hopefully no one would bother with them. Once they were through, Mike would dive the boat and they'd remain submerged until on their way back from the mission. Only then would they surface and make for Gibraltar, where they would refuel and provision the submarine.

His mind mulled over the list of things which could go wrong with this mission for the hundredth time. The worse scenario would be if the *Corner Brook* was detected by the French and forced to surface near the harbour. He wouldn't acknowledge there could in fact be a much worse scenario…that the French in protecting their nuclear base might simply sink him and ask questions later. Although his crew was the best at what they did, his mind never let him forget that this was going to be very dangerous.

"Sir," Brad called out to him twenty minutes later. "We're directly astern the ship and I suggest we come to zero nine five degrees and slow to twelve knots to maintain our position."

"Chief Poulin, turn to zero nine five degrees and slow us to twelve knots."

Poulin made the slight correction and reported that they were holding on the new course.

"Thanks Chief. Lieutenant?" Mike looked over to Fred who was busily adding to the markings on his chart. "Do you think he's heading for Tangiers?"

"Hard to say, sir. But he's probably just turning south to avoid the heavier current in the center of the strait. I'd give you odds he'll come left after he passes Tarifa," Fred offered, referring to the city on the southern tip of Spain.

"Let's hope," Mike replied, "although by then it won't really matter as long as he doesn't slow up so we catch him. I really want to avoid any close encounters."

Lieutenant Fred Beals understood perfectly what he meant. The whole 'British nuc' plan depended on their avoiding close scrutiny. Half an hour later, Fred smiled as Brad called out that the target was coming left and maintaining speed. Mike ordered a similar correction in their course and they continued to follow the unsuspecting ship.

A short time later, Mike announced, "Well gang, its show time! Brad, any contacts close aboard?"

"No, sir. Just the ship we're following and another one astern about three thousand yards."

"Very well. Surface the boat! Helm, maintain present course and speed! Sonar, bring in the tail! Lieutenant Beals, join me on the bridge," Mike smiled, "and dig out that British Ensign for the deck crew!"

"Yes, sir," Fred answered as he reached in the flag locker for the Royal Navy Ensign. In the red lights of the control room, used so their night vision wouldn't be affected when they were going outside on deck or to the bridge, the flag looked pretty good.

"Sir, we're up!" announced Charley from the helm.

"Raise everything!" Mike commanded, noting the quiet whirring sound as the two periscopes rose from their wells. Grabbing the intercom he informed the engine room that they could now switch to the diesels and start charging the battery.

"Helm, give me all the navigation lights on full. We want to look like we're a British SSN heading home to Gibraltar with no thoughts of hiding."

"Done, commander. All lights set to 'high'."

Climbing the short ladder to the lower hatch, Mike quickly unfastened it and climbed up into the lockout chamber, then further on up to the bridge at the top of *Corner Brook's* sail. Lieutenant Beals joined him a few moments later. Looking back they saw a seaman emerge from the aft hatch and set up their stern mast. Soon, the improvised Royal Navy ensign was fluttering from the pole. In the dimming daylight, from the bridge; neither Mike nor Fred could tell that it wasn't the real article.

"Looks good, Lieutenant!"

"That it does, sir."

Behind them the last red glow of sunlight was disappearing over the horizon. Although they would have normally struck the colors by now, they'd leave them up for the transit through the strait. Ahead of them, Mike could make out the navigation lights of the ship they were following and looking through his binoculars, he couldn't see anyone on the stern looking back at them. If there had been anyone watching, the navigation lights on the small sail would make the boat appear to be a ship farther away than they actually were. Most crew on a freighter such as the one ahead of them would not recognize the significance of the yellow beacon flashing from the top of the sail. The ship's officers however might have wondered what submarine was following them through the straits that evening but they would probably assume it was British being on the surface this close to Gibraltar.

"So far so good." Mike said, half to himself and not expecting an answer. He got one anyway.

"Sir! Radar. New target bearing zero four zero degrees. He's coming straight at us. Range, two thousand yards. He was running the reverse course of ours and just turned in."

"Sonar, can you make out what he is?" Mike could not see any lights in the direction they were indicating.

"It's small, sir and pretty quick from the screw noises. I hear some heavy banging on that bearing. Sounds like he's having problems. Best I can tell you right now!"

Mike noted the perturbed sound in Brad's voice. The young lieutenant did not like reporting limited information, but running on the surface as she was, the *Corner Brook's* sensors were being washed out by the boat's wake, making the sonar unreliable.

"Thanks Brad. Keep an eye on him. Radar, any change in his course?"

"None sir...wait...he's slowing down. Still no emissions coming from him."

"Bridge, sonar. Engine failure sounds now. I'd say his engine just blew. He's silent now. Last range, fifteen hundred yards."

Mike strained to see anything in the little remaining light, but saw only the twinkling reflections on the water from their own navigation lights.

"You see anything Fred?"

"Nothing, sir. They must be running without lights or they're really small."

"Wait, look." Fred held his hand out and Mike lined up his binoculars on the bearing it pointed to.

"Got it. Looks like a small fishing boat."

"I'd say so too," replied Fred.

"Bridge, comms. I don't know if this is good news or not, but we just picked him up radioing for help. He's saying that his engines are dead."

"Excellent! Thanks comms." Patting Fred's shoulder, Mike laughed. "Just what we needed! A small diversion to take any patrol boats away from us!"

"Couldn't be better if we'd planned it ourselves, commander."

"Bridge, comms. A patrol boat just responded and is on the way."

"Thanks comms. Have a color party go out on deck and as soon as the patrol boat is close by, strike the ensign. Tell them to make sure they look smart doing it."

"Will do commander."

"Nice touch, sir," Fred laughed. "You can bet the patrol boat will notice our lights and have a look. They'll hopefully report us as a Brit boat and we should be home free."

Mike spotted the patrol boat approaching and sure enough, about the time he thought they'd spot the flashing yellow beacon, the small craft turned slightly and headed towards them. Taking a quick look back, Mike smiled at the sight of four crew members standing rigidly at attention in the last vestiges of twilight, as a fifth man slowly untied their fake ensign, timing it carefully so he didn't remove it until the crew of the patrol boat were close enough to see it first in the remaining light.

Their curiosity apparently satisfied, the patrol boat sped off towards the disabled fishing boat and Mike and Fred watched as the navigation lights came to a stop in the distance, marking where the other boat had come to grief.

Clear of the patrol and the disabled fishing boat, *HMCS Corner Brook* sailed on in the gathering darkness. Her commanding officer and XO stayed on the bridge enjoying the warm night air. Mike had allowed the off duty crew the opportunity to come up on deck and relax a little while taking in the fantastic view of a night sky peppered with stars. It was a rare chance for the crew as the extended capacity battery allowed the boat to remain submerged for long periods unlike the previous 'O' boats which spent the majority of their time on the surface.

"Sure is a beautiful night commander. Reminds me of the times Shawna and I would drive out to Lawrencetown Beach at night and star gaze."

"Ann and I used to do that more when the kids were growing up," said Mike. "Now it seems that we appreciate night time more as a chance to relax."

"I guess now that we have Andrew, we'll be spending more time at home as well," commented Fred. "Starting a family sure does change your life."

"For the better I think," Mike answered.

"Yeah, that's the truth."

"One thing you'll notice as the kids grow up," Mike reminisced, "they don't seem to have grown as much when you return from a cruise. I remember the first time I came home and it seemed like the baby had gone from a tiny little helpless thing to a walking, talking bundle of energy."

"Scary, sir. I hope Shawna handles it alright."

"She'll be fine Fred. Our women are a lot tougher than we give them credit for. Comes from living with us warriors," Mike laughed.

* * * *

Four hours later, the Canadian submarine was south east of Gibraltar and alone on the calm waters of the Mediterranean. The cargo ship they'd been following had turned north soon after leaving the strait area and headed for the Spanish port of Malaga.

The crew was below now, and only Commander Simpson remained on the bridge, as usual, taking in the last of the ocean air before they submerged. The Mediterranean air was different from the cool, salty aroma he was used to in the north Atlantic. It had more of a dank, almost putrid flavour. Once submerged, the air was always the same no matter where the submarine sailed, the ventilation system usually managed to keep it around twenty degrees Celsius with a humidity of fifty percent, more of course for the boat's electronics than the comfort of her crew.

"Control, bridge; what's our status?"

"Heading zero eight zero degrees at twelve knots, sir. Battery is ninety-five percent."

"Very good." Mike took one more look around with his binoculars. Submarine commanders had learned the hard way to never completely trust the various electronic sensors built into their boats when diving, and even less so when surfacing.

Climbing down the ladders and securing the hatches, Mike dropped into the control room and walked over to the search scope. At its full extension the periscope offered a better view of the surroundings than the bridge which was considerably lower. Using the night vision system, nothing was visible close to the boat.

"All hands, diving stations!" The diving horn sounded throughout the boat, warning everyone to prepare for the submarine's dive.

"Helm, make your depth four hundred feet. Maintain course. Make turns for fifteen knots." Mike rattled off the commands and listened for them to be echoed correctly. Charley, who was just finishing his watch on the helm, coaxed the whale-like shape of *Corner Brook* beneath the waves with his usual smoothness. A few minutes later, he announced that they had reached the depth and speed ordered. A wordless pat on the shoulder from his commander signified he'd done well.

* * * *

The next day in Toulon, France, the sun shone brightly in a cloudless sky as the last crate carrying the body of an M4 rocket booster was slowly being lowered into the forward hold of the *MV Sariwon* by the ship's rusty old crane. In the cavernous hold below deck, the crew carefully secured the delicate cargo lest it shift and sustain damage on the journey home. From high above on the bridge, the ship's captain supervised the loading. It would be his responsibility to make sure the precious cargo arrived safely in North Korea, and he was not about to cause himself to suffer the wrath of Dear Leader, as some friends (whom he now denied knowing of course) had done. They were probably all dead now, but not before suffering a fate he did not even want to imagine.

A great deal politically rested on the safe delivery of the four boosters to the small communist country. Having perfected a functional and reliable nuclear device, only the ability to deliver it accurately over a long distance had eluded the North Korean scientists. Now all that would change. Although these rockets were not powerful enough to reach the capital city of the hated Americans, they would easily reach that country's Pacific coast. Soon Dear Leader would be respected by the West, or they would feel his wrath.

As the last crate was lowered to the cargo hold's deck, the captain smiled. His reward upon arriving home would no doubt be great. Perhaps he'd even share it with his crew for the fine job they had performed…or perhaps not.

He wondered what kind of reward lay ahead for the six mysterious men living below decks. They had not seen the light of day since boarding his ship the night of their departure from the eastern city of Hungnam. They carried automatic weapons but did not wear the regular uniform of his country's military forces. They had also refused to speak to any of his crew, except when food was delivered to them in their lair deep in the bowels of his ship. Having them aboard perturbed the captain more than the nature of his cargo. It wasn't their weapons that concerned him. It had been the look they'd given him and his crew upon boarding the *Sariwon*. As though he and his men were mere insects who these soldiers would crush under their boots without a second thought if need be.

It doesn't matter, the captain thought to himself. Soon they would be home. He'd receive his reward and those animals would be off his ship. Looking down, he yelled through an open bridge window at one of the crew who'd stopped working and was leaning against a deck stanchion. The man jumped up and returned to his job. No, thought the captain, he'd keep the reward for himself.

What he really needed was a night on the town, away from this crew of ignorants. Yes, he deserved that and besides, his ship was not sailing for two days.

*   *   *   *

As the North Korean captain was mentally spending his reward, *HMCS Corner Brook* was steadily cruising east beneath the surface of the Mediterranean. Commander Simpson was sleeping soundly after having posted the last of his personal log to his PDA. He knew sleep might be a rare commodity after today and left orders that he not be disturbed with Lieutenant Beals as he left the control room. Fred had laughed and assured Mike that he could sleep soundly and not worry about a thing.

"Lieutenant Beals, we are at marker sierra," Leading Seaman Jones announced.

"Thanks Jones." That would put them just Northwest of Bougie on the coast of Algeria. They had hugged the North African coast while heading east into the Mediterranean in order to avoid the major shipping lanes. Now they would have to head north across the sea, but because of their perpendicular course across the heavily traveled east-west routes, there would be little chance of them coming across anyone. Especially, some warship with a hot-to-trot sonar operator, thought Fred.

"Helm, bring us left to zero zero six degrees. Maintain depth and speed. Mr. Whalen, how's the battery?"

Master Seaman Craig Whalen, sitting at the control room's engineering console looked up from his laptop and read the display centered amongst the gauges, switches and displays laid out in front of him.

"Thirty-one percent sir."

"Okay, it will be dark in a few hours and we'll be charging it then. Let me know if it slips below twenty percent though." They kept a close watch on the life cycle of the new battery recently installed during the boat's last light refit. With the new submarines, the navy had decided to discontinue the tradition of long, costly refits where a boat would be laid up for months at a time while all the problems discovered in the past year or two were repaired. Now the boats were gone over after every deployment. It had been decided to upgrade *Corner Brook's* battery with a new type being tested for the Swedish navy. By all accounts so far, the new cells were amazing and the commander actually had time to consider other things besides the state of the battery every few hours. Of course the ultimate update would be the new air-independent system being installed in *Windsor* which would make the boats an even deadlier weapon.

Four hours later, Fred ordered *Corner Brook* brought to periscope depth and after confirming no other vessels were in the immediate vicinity, slowed the submarine down to ten knots. Just for good measure he altered their course to zero seven five degrees. Then if anyone did detect them while they were snorkelling and running the diesels, they would not appear to be heading directly for the French coast.

"Raise everything!"

"Coming up, sir." Master Seaman Craig Whalen, still manning the engineering console flicked the switches and levers that sent the periscopes, radar masts and snorkel masts poking through the wave tops.

"All up!"

"Sonar, keep a close watch. If you detect anything within ten miles, let me know," Fred commanded. "Radar, keep a sharp eye on the ESM and sing to me if you see anything."

They did not want to risk detection at this point, so they had the radar shut down but all the receivers were up and running allowing them to detect radar emissions from anyone else.

Punching the intercom button for the engineering spaces, Fred ordered the diesels started up and the battery charge to begin. Give it three hours, he thought. That'll bring us up to about ninety-five percent on the battery and his deviation from the planned course wouldn't take them very far off schedule. He was certain it was worth it, given the increased odds of detection with the comparably noisy diesels running. Even as he thought about it, he felt a small shudder as they were cut in and his ears popped as fresh outside air was pumped throughout the boat, replacing the clean, antiseptic environment they were used to.

Lying on the cot in his cabin, Mike awoke for a moment, detecting the change in the air, and feeling the slight hum of the diesels. Good, he thought. Fred must be charging the battery. He forced his eyes open and glanced at the small display screen above his desk. Ah…he changed course to throw anyone off. Yes, he thought as he drifted off again. That Beals was going to make a good CO some…and he was asleep again.

* * * *

"I wish we had our 'sled' for this one." Stu was voicing the concern that all of the SEALs felt. They were going to have a risky time entering the harbour in their zodiac without being seen by anyone.

"I know, but if we hug the coast and stay close in to the piers, we should be fine," said Boris. "Besides, it will be the middle of the night and we're not going anywhere near the navy base."

"Yup, but it'll be one hairy ride," replied Stu. "How good is the 'intel' on where the ship is supposed to be berthed?"

"Apparently very good," Boris answered. "Because of the cargo, the authorities want it tied up at a pier with limited access. That doesn't affect us very much but it does mean that if something goes amiss, there will be more time before anyone can get to the ship."

"Well that's in our favour at least." Stu smiled. He really did prefer to go in with the 'sled', which held eight SEALs and was for all intents a miniature submarine. Unfortunately, the *Jimmy Carter* was currently the only boat capable of launching the 'sled' while submerged. One of the other two SSN-21s was being converted along the same lines as the *Carter* had been, but that wasn't going to help them right now.

All SEAL teams were experienced using the stealthy inflatable boats like the one stored in the forward deck space, but none of them would chose it over the 'sled'. Well, thought Stu, at least with the boat we won't have to worry about what happened a few years ago in Iraq happening to them. SEALs manoeuvring one of the 'sleds' had been compromised and someone in a small surface craft had literally depth charged the small submarine killing half the team.

"Okay guys; let's go over it one more time. Then we'll run another weapons check and make a few more practice runs in the lock-out chamber." Boris listened as each man ran through his particular segment of the mission flawlessly.

An hour later they'd completed their weapons checks and were all grouped together around the charges that would be used to destroy the rocket boosters. It was imperative that all five men be fully versed in their use in case something happened to any of them before the charges could be set.

Chapter 9

▼

"You're kiddin' me!"

"No, seriously! I had no idea he was the CNO!" Darren sat back on the mess table laughing as Cookie looked at him in total disbelief.

"And he didn't try and throttle you right then and there?"

"You know Cookie; it was like he was all happy about it or something. I swear he didn't seem upset at all. By the time I came out of shock he was just going on with the briefing like I was one of the guys. He did tell them to treat me good though. Maybe he'll put in a good word to his daughter for me," Darren finished with a note of hope in his voice.

"Well my son, if she gives you the time of day after what you pulled off…" Cookie saw the look on Darren's face and changed his track. "…of course, you WERE under orders. I mean the woman's gotta respect that. Don't 'cha think?"

Darren smiled again. "I hope so." Then checking to make sure that no one else was in earshot he lowered his voice and asked, "So what do you think? These SEAL guys going to be able to pull this off?"

"Don't let their antics fool you son. The SEALs are the toughest bunch of professionals in the world. I've known a few of them and they live for this kind of mission."

Cookie did indeed know a few of them and one night he'd seen them in action. Of course no one else on the boat knew about that. O'Hanlon had been the only other Canadian there. Yeah, he thought, remembering that night on a cold desolate beach, when things had gone horribly wrong, tough is hardly the word.

"You plan on staying aboard when we get back?"

"Not sure Cole. Your CO seems to think so, but I'll see. Depends on how honoured you all act towards my cooking," he smiled.

"Well damn Cookie." Darren fell to his knees in mock respect. "I ain't tasted anything as good as your cooking since my mom…" He ducked just in time as a roll sailed for his head.

"Geeze Cookie. Think of all the starving kids out there and you tossing food around like that!"

Darren leapt to his feet running, but he was too slow as a second roll caught him squarely on the back of the head.

"You're lucky we're under noise control Cole, or it might have been a friggin' frying pan!" Cookie laughed heartily as he returned to his preparations for the evening meal.

Returning to the torpedo space after his break, Darren began checking over the torpedoes lying in the racks. Unfastening a small watertight door on one of them, just behind the warhead, he plugged a hand-held diagnostic device into its port and read the display as he checked each of the Mk-48's circuits. No problem with 'Carrie', he smiled noting the name beautifully scrolled on the side of the deadly weapon. That must have been a special woman. Gary had been especially artistic with the calligraphy while writing her name. Fastening the door back in place, he moved on to the next 'fish'.

"Torpedo room, control." The bulkhead speaker came to life.

Darren grabbed the handset from the bulkhead behind him. "Torpedo room. Chief Cole."

"Chief, the commander wants tubes two, three and four made ready and loaded."

"Aye, sir. I'll report when completed."

"Thanks Chief."

Darren looked across the space and saw Seaman Gary Steeves studying one of the boat's manuals. He was working hard to earn his dolphins this trip and in spite of his torpedo artwork, he'd probably succeed. "Steeves! Wake up! We're loading two, three and four!"

"Do you think the commander expects trouble?"

"Only when he has to off load these 'girls', seaman," Darren looked at him with mock contempt. "Now if we get to shoot them all, there won't be a problem."

The look on the seaman's face showed that he was still hurting from all the ribbing over the names. Someone had earlier posted an announcement on the mess bulletin board for a new 'Name the Fish' contest with the prize of a life time supply of permanent markers going to the lucky winner. Unable to help himself, Darren continued with the teasing.

"He's probably just being careful. If the SEALs don't pull this off, we'll have to go in and sink the freighter ourselves you know."

"Damn! Do you think there's a chance?" Gary looked a little too excited at the prospect.

"Geeze seaman!" Darren exclaimed, "I'm just kidding!" Maybe Steeves wouldn't be getting those Dolphins on this trip after all.

Opening the torpedo tube doors, Darren and Gary both inspected the tubes for any foreign material or visible damage. Finding none, they loaded them one at a time with one of the Mk-48's and made sure that all the control wires were properly connected and showing green on the test board. Confirming that the three tubes were in all respects ready, Darren signed off on the torpedo's serial numbers on the ready chart and slipped the metal 'tube loaded' placards into the slots on each of the three doors.

"Control, weapons room. Tubes one, two, three and four loaded and all circuits checked okay." Darren replaced the microphone, waiting for an acknowledgement from the control room.

"Tubes one, two, three and four loaded and ready. Thanks chief."

Replacing the microphone on its overhead clip in the control room, Lieutenant Fred Beals turned to his engineering officer. "Lieutenant Polanski, how are we doing with the charge?"

"Coming up on ninety-six percent now," he answered, as the display in front of him changed.

"Very good." Grabbing the microphone again and pushing the appropriate button, Fred informed the engine room that they would be submerging in five minutes.

"Engine room, submerging in five minutes, aye," came the response from the overhead speaker.

Fred held onto the microphone while looking down at his chart. Marking in a new line north to Toulon from their present position, he measured off the distance. About eighteen to twenty hours sailing from here, he thought. Crunch time.

"Helm, bring us left to zero zero five degrees. Engine room, dropping the masts now!" Again his ears popped as the exhaust and induction mast shut tight as they lowered down into the sail.

"Helm, take us down to four hundred feet! Make your speed fifteen knots!"

There was a perceptible tilt to the control room as the helmsman pushed the control column forward a bit steeper than usual. Fred watched the depth display and noticed how smoothly the young seaman pulled out with '401' just flickering before returning to '400'. He made a note to have Petty Officer Poulin commend the man.

"Depth four hundred feet, course zero zero five and battery at ninety-seven percent sir."

"Thank you seaman." Fred patted his shoulder and moved over to where Lieutenant Smith was gazing at his sonar screens.

"Any company, Brad?"

"Nothing close enough to worry about. I do have a submerged target to the east but he's a long way off. Sounds like he's testing his active sonar. I've got him marked," Brad assured him. "The system can't even take a guess at what he is yet."

Fred leaned over and sure enough, one fuzzy little line on the screen was a bit more solid than the others. He reached back and flipped the intercom switch to address the boat.

"All hands! Quiet the boat!" It was never a popular order. The crew would now have to think twice before beginning any task. Running on the electric motor, any noise emanating from the boat could only be caused by someone dropping or hitting something. Standing again behind Brad, Fred watched as the line representing the other submarine remained unchanged.

"Let me know if it appears to even think of heading towards us Brad."

"Will do. There's remarkably little traffic up there today."

"That's too bad. Maybe it'll pick up later on." Fred didn't like the sound of that. More commercial traffic on the surface would lessen the chance of their being detected.

There were usually a half dozen submarines cruising the Mediterranean at any point in time, from almost as many nations. Hopefully today, none of them would cross the *Corner Brook's* path.

*   *   *   *

Commander Michael Simpson awoke and immediately gazed at the status display. It showed they were at four hundred feet and back on course for Toulon. Looking at his watch, he realized that he'd been asleep for almost six hours but he also knew that it was probably the last sleep he'd have for a couple of days. Grabbing his PDA, he filled in his personal log and checked that he hadn't forgotten anything. That done he changed clothes and entered the control room.

"I have the con lieutenant. Better hit the rack and get some sleep."

"Okay commander. We're back to four hundred feet and heading zero zero five. We'll be twenty miles off the French coast in about fifteen hours. Battery charge went fine," Fred informed his CO. "Brad has a submerged contact to the east. It's too far out to identify at this time. He'll let us know if anything changes with it."

"Sounds good Fred, thanks." Mike didn't really think the contact sounded good, but kept that concern to himself. "I'll wake you if anything comes up."

"I think I'll see what Cookie has stewing before I sack out. Want me to bring anything back up?"

"Thanks, no. I'll slip down later and grab a sandwich or something."

Fred left the control room and went below to see what was available for lunch. He called all his meals lunch as he, like the commander, spent most of his awake time in the control room and soon lost track of which meal he was eating. Poking his head into the galley he saw that Cookie was at his usual spot.

"What's good today Cookie?"

"Hey Lieutenant! How about some pizza?"

"Pizza? Dare I ask?"

"No problem! I just use bread dough and we have everything else in some form or another."

"Bring it on chief! No wonder everyone wants you on their boat!" Fred smiled and strolled ahead to the senior rank's mess. Sitting back on one of the couches, he relaxed and sipped the Coke he'd grabbed on the way in.

A few minutes later, Cookie came in with a plate containing three slices of what indeed looked like pizza.

"Here you go Lieutenant! Take a bite and tell me what you think."

Breaking off a chunk, Fred was surprised at how good it tasted.

"This is really good! Cookie, you must have smuggled some spices on board."

"When I heard where I was coming to, I grabbed a bunch from the store before I left Halifax. I knew you guys wouldn't have much here. Glad you like it. I'll get some up to the control room in a bit."

"You'll never get off this boat alive Cookie. I'd start preparing change of address cards if I was you," laughed Fred.

"We'll see lieutenant!"

Cookie smiled and headed back to the galley. He would never admit it to anyone else but he was extremely proud of his reputation in the Canadian navy.

Fred finished the pizza and relaxed for awhile before downing the last of his Coke and heading off to his bunk. He knew he would find it hard to sleep with his mind racing through the various aspects of the mission, but he also knew he'd need rest for later on. Feeling a burp coming up he also realized that pizza probably wasn't the best thing to snack on before turning in, but it sure was tasty. Yes, he thought, he'd lead the posse himself to make sure Cookie stayed aboard when they returned home.

* * * *

Greg Newell was once again on the Port Said waterfront sitting back on one of the dingy green park benches placed there for the many tourists who liked to relax and watch the never ending parade of ships entering or leaving the Suez Canal. Seeing a light grey ship heading up the same channel taken by the Korean ship a few days earlier, he brought the small binoculars hanging around his neck up to his eyes.

They had worked well with his earlier 'tourist' disguise and fit in just splendidly with the US Navy khaki uniform he now wore. The gun mounted on the ship's forward deck was the first sign he looked for and as it drew closer, he could make out the number on the side of her hull, 331. He watched with satisfaction as the crew members lowered a grey zodiac over the warship's side and down into the water as the ship slowed. A few sailors were riding the inflatable boat and as soon as they unfastened it from the hoist the outboard motor was started and they pulled away from the frigate heading for the shore. Rushing from his vantage point, Greg barely made it down to the small public pier before the boat pulled in and tied up. Seeing the American naval officer looking down at them, one of the seamen in the small boat queried, "Commander Dennis Bishop?"

"Yes seaman," Greg/Dennis replied with a wave. "Thanks for picking me up!"

"No problem sir," responded the young man, as he helped steady the boat for the US Navy Commander while inspecting his proffered ID card. "We'll be back to *Vancouver* in a few minutes."

"Thank you. I'm looking forward to it."

The CIA agent liked this new name. It rolled easily off the tongue. He watched the warship grow larger as the zodiac approached from behind and to the left...port he mentally corrected himself. Once tied up, he climbed quickly to the main deck. There the ship's commanding officer waited with an outstretched hand.

"Commander Bishop! I'm Commander Chris Donnelly. Welcome aboard!"

"Thank you commander." They shook hands firmly. "I really appreciate the lift!" He added that for the benefit of the men standing close by.

"My pleasure! Come to my cabin and let me treat you to one of the pleasant differences between our navies."

Once behind the closed door of his cabin, Chris reached into the small fridge built into the bulkhead and handed the stranger a cold beer. Slowly sipping his Coke—no beer for him since he was on duty—Chris watched the man standing in front of him with a look that was all business.

"So commander. This must be where you tell me the story of why a Canadian frigate on its way to Japan, received orders to drop everything, race west at top speed and head up the Suez Canal to pick up a stranded US Navy Commander."

Chris was not really upset, but he didn't like being left out of the loop either. His crew was jubilant over the unexpected 'Med Cruise 09' as their quickly printed T-shirts read, but the ship's officers had lost fistfuls of hair arranging provisions and fuel for the unexpected detour to the Mediterranean. All of which was made even more difficult by their inability to disclose anything about where they were going—not that they knew anyway.

"I'm sorry commander," Greg/Dennis replied, and meant it. "All I am cleared to tell you at this point is that you are needed here." He pulled out what appeared to be a civilian chart and pointed to a small mark west of the Balearic Island of Mallorca, in the eastern Mediterranean Sea.

"And then?" Chris looked at him expectantly.

"We wait."

"We wait," Chris repeated. He knew better than to ask more of this man. He knew that in spite of the US Navy uniform, Bishop was a 'spook'. Chris really hated 'spooks'. They all seemed to exude an air of self-importance.

"Commander, I know this is a pain in the ass to you. Hopefully it'll all make sense soon. One more thing though, and this is critical. When we do reach that point, we have to be quiet, VERY quiet. No emissions of any kind"

"Quiet we shall be commander," Chris answered. "Come with me and we'll find a place for you to bunk. My XO is the only other officer aware of who you are…or should I say who you aren't?" He smiled. Greg/Dennis returned the smile. The CIA operative appreciated this officer's candour and that he was willing to play along. In past missions, not everyone had been so co-operative.

* * * *

HMCS Corner Brook slithered silently through the depths of the Mediterranean while the tension aboard the boat began to grow. It seemed to be taking on a life of its own as the officers and crew of the submarine faced the reality of the dangers that lay ahead. Commander Simpson had addressed the crew and brought everyone up to speed on the mission details and the dangers involved. He didn't hold anything back as he knew that their success largely depended on how well his men reacted to any situation that might materialize without warning. As planned, this excursion was dangerous. If anything went wrong it could indeed prove fatal.

"Brad, lock down the Lazcom."

"Lazcom secured sir," Brad answered, flicking the switch that would prevent another sub picking up the unusual signal the system generated on sonar sets. He would be pulling a long shift as the boat's 'A-team' was manning the various watches throughout the submarine now.

"Commander, we're thirty miles south of the Echo Buoy." Fred drew a line from their current position to the buoy that marked the entrance to Toulon Harbour.

"Thanks lieutenant."

Mike looked over at Fred and watched as he worked on his charts. Fred definitely preferred his callipers and compasses over the million dollar navigation system built into the boat. He laughingly joked that there wouldn't be as much as a pause in their navigation, even if they lost all power. He would just have to light a few candles so he could see his beloved charts and slide rule.

"Helm, slow to five knots. Maintain depth and heading. Lieutenant, you have the con. I'm going forward to check on the SEALs."

"Got it commander. Wish them luck from me too."

Mike made his way to the torpedo space. There he found Darren sitting on the deck chatting with the SEALs.

"Gentleman, we're thirty miles out," Mike announced. "I just wanted to take a moment and wish you all luck on behalf of the crew."

"Thanks commander," Boris reached over and shook Mike's hand. "It's been a pleasure to be aboard your boat."

"My pleasure lieutenant." Mike shook his hand firmly. "Now you guys take care and make sure you make it back in one piece."

"We will sir. Chief Cole here wanted to come along but we talked him out of it."

"You looking to go TDY with the SEALs chief?" Mike asked, feigning seriousness.

"No sir!" Darren responded. "I like my nice warm boat!"

"Well I'll let you guys be." Mike smiled. "We'll hit the debarkation point in about fifteen minutes. Is there anything else we can do for you?"

"Just be there when we come paddling up sir."

"You got it lieutenant."

Mike shook hands with the rest of the squad and returned to the control room. Darren stood aside, an uneasy feeling growing in his stomach. His 'personal sonar' was acting up again and he worried that all would not be well with this mission.

"Look guys, stay out of trouble up there." Darren reached out to shake Boris's hand.

"Hey now chief! Don't be going all emotional on us!" Boris grabbed Darren's hand and nearly squeezed it off in his powerful grip.

"Yeah Cole! What happened to that fearless spy who sank our boat?" Jamal laughed punching Darren hard in the shoulder.

"And don't forget you promised me driving lessons if the CNO doesn't kill you first," Stu grabbed him in a huge bear hug.

"You bet!" laughed Cole. "Someone has to make the roads safe from the likes of you!"

Markus punched Darren's shoulder and the five SEALs started gathering their gear. It was like watching an old war movie as the men applied camouflage paint to their faces and hands. Every piece of their equipment seemed to have a pocket to be stuffed into or a place to hang. Metal objects were all cloth covered to make them quiet. The last piece of equipment checked Darren noted, were the knives. Evil looking serrated black things that slipped into scabbards clipped to the harnesses each man wore.

"Damn, you guys don't need guns!" Darren smirked. "One look at you would scare anyone to death."

"If only," laughed Stu. "Hey, we'll be fine. If anything was going to go wrong, it would have happened by now."

What Stu didn't know was that it already had.

* * * *

"Oui," the French officer nodded over to the sailor sitting in front of him. Leaning closer to the console and holding the headphones to his ears, he concentrated again. Barely noticeable in the background, a tiny sound, just a bit out of place was audible. "I hear it as well."

Carmaux, a small town in southern France noted for its mining and rugged countryside was quiet at this late hour. The people who lived here were early risers and therefore went to bed early as well. Few people knew, or cared really what took place in the squat little building sitting just outside the town limits. Inside the cinder block structure was the French Navy's ultra secret listening post connected to the underwater microphones recently laid by the French navy in the Mediterranean Sea.

The officer clicked on the play button to hear the sound once more. It was recorded digitally of course, so there was no rewinding of tape, trying to find a particular spot.

Yes, he thought. It was definitely not the normal background noise ever present in the sea. He knew he would never have noticed it himself, but the young man standing behind him for whatever reason, had chosen that moment in time to be particularly vigilant and had picked it up. It was so faint, he had probably sensed more than heard the sound. A pity the new computer equipment that would complete the installation was as yet uninstalled or they might even have an idea who it was skulking around just outside their navy base.

"Very good work."

The officer turned and walked back over to his own console where he picked up the telephone. The information was now almost ten minutes old; an eternity in this business. He passed it on to the base closest to the source of the sound where another officer swore quietly under his breath as he listened to the report.

"No direction?"

"Nothing."

Again, a quiet oath. The French navy officer at the listening station regretted that he did not have more substantial information to give them, but that was often the nature of this game. Game? He smiled at the use of that particular term. It was anything but a game.

Hanging up his phone, the duty officer at the French submarine base in Toulon immediately punched a single button that would connect him with the base commander. No, he explained, after informing the admiral of the current situation, it was not the *Amethyste*. She was not due back until tomorrow and was presently west of Corsica on the sonar test range.

"Very well," replied the admiral. "Contact *Amethyste* and have her head back this way. Inform her captain why and have him approach carefully. If this is another little test by the Russians, I want to catch them at it."

"Yes sir."

The French Admiral reclined in his chair. Those Russians were becoming bolder every day he concluded. He would of course have immediately suspected a western nation's submarine, probably waiting to tail the Korean freighter when it left port with its cargo of ballistic missile rocket boosters…if he had been informed about it.

Minutes later, aboard the nuclear attack submarine *Amethyste*, her captain read the message just handed him, and also came to the same 'Russian' conclusion. He would love nothing more than to slip into a Russian's baffles and wake them up with a blast of his boat's powerful sonar. He ordered his sonar crew to be extra vigilant. Not really necessary as the French navy had a standing order for its sonar crews to take themselves off watch with no consequences if they felt the least bit incapable of giving the job their full attention.

The stubby little French boat left the testing range off the island that was once Napoleon's prison home and headed west back towards its base. Ironically, the submarine they were hunting was not Russian, but what turned out to be the 'second choice' for Canada's navy. Twenty years earlier, the Canadian Government had considered the selection of a nuclear attack submarine for its navy, and one of the final choices had been the French *Rubis* class of which *Amethyst* led an 'improved second group'.

The Canadian Government of the time had typically changed its mind and the Canadian Navy had sailed on with their aged *Oberons* until the four British *Upholders* had become available.

* * * *

"Helm, all stop. Make your depth fifty-five feet." Easier said than done Mike knew, in this area of the Mediterranean where the undersea currents failed to follow set patterns as they usually did elsewhere.

From this relatively shallow depth, the SEALs would be able to safely exit the submarine through the lock out chamber with no harmful effects as they made their way to the surface.

"All stop, aye sir." Petty Officer 1st Class Charley Poulin had the helm. He'd made sure his watch would coincide with their arrival at this point because after all, he thought, he was THE best helmsman aboard, and he knew how critical proper control of the submarine would be right now. A few minutes later he announced, "fifty-five feet sir."

"Give 'em hell lieutenant!" Mike called out as Boris climbed the lockout chamber.

"Will do sir!" Boris replied, continuing up into the chamber built into the lower part of the sail. It was made to safely hold five men, barely. Jamal being the last one in managed to just squeeze his 6'2" frame along with his equipment amongst the other four men.

"Last chance guys. Anyone forget anything?"

"Err, sorry sir. I think I have to use the head," Stu joked.

"If I could move in here, I'd pound you Cunningham!" laughed Boris. "Okay gang. Time to get wet!"

Reaching back, he hit the recessed button on the bulkhead behind him, and in moments water began to surge in and fill the chamber. The five men waited for the last possible second before donning their face masks and breathing from the tanks strapped to their backs. They were wearing their small 'transit' tanks for this mission. Made to hold just enough air to exit and re-enter a submarine with a few minutes of reserve, they added only a small amount of bulk and weight to the already heavily loaded SEALs.

A bright green light flashed from the bulkhead signalling that the lockout chamber was full and equalized to the outside water pressure. It was now safe for the men to open the upper hatch and exit. Half swimming and half climbing up through the sail, the team made their way out and back down the outside of the sail to the submarine's deck. Before he descended, Boris gave a 'thumbs up' to the periscope lens that was eyeing him from its barely raised position.

In the control room, Mike watched the greenish imagine of the SEAL on the low-light TV screen that was being fed from the periscope and sighed with relief as he saw the 'thumbs up'. The SEALs were on their own now, he thought. His job for the coming hours would be to make like a hole in the water and wait quietly, doing nothing.

"Good thing we have the night vision camera on the scopes now," Fred commented, while watching the occasional green glowing fish swim by. Turning away, he ordered the scope lowered back into its well.

"That's true. The scope was so low I don't think I could have reached the eye piece," Mike answered. "The old rap on the hull sure wouldn't work anymore," he smiled, picturing the scenes in old war movies where divers leaving the boat hammered on the hull with some tool to let those inside know they were okay. Today a submarine's sonar would hear that pounding hundreds of miles away.

"Sir, lockout chamber is dry and atmosphere equalled," announced Lieutenant Polanski from his position at the engineering console.

"Thank you lieutenant." Mike noted that the conversation in the boat had grown more formal from the usual laid back 'banter'. He had seen it happen on every 'special op' he'd been part of as the crew made certain that no order or comment was misunderstood. This was now very serious business.

* * * *

The tepid water pleasantly surprised Jamal Washington as he swam down to the deck of the submerged sub. The tallest member of the squad, he easily released the deck hatch cover and lifted the almost buoyant inflatable boat from the space it had been neatly folded into. When the boat was completely clear he replaced the hatch cover and fastened it back in place securely. Markus reached around and grabbed one of the pull ropes protruding from the zodiac's water-tight covering and finding the release tag hanging from the package's side, gave it a sharp pull. Inside, a CO_2 cartridge partially inflated the boat just enough to break it free from the plastic membrane that had sealed it and the motor from the salt water. Another seal protected the motor which would only be broken once they reached the surface.

Jim Lewis, spread out the folds of rubberized fabric on the deck and with the rest of the men found a hand loop built into the boat's side. Boris turned to them and each gave a 'thumbs up' as he looked into their masks. When he was sure everyone was ready, he pointed up and then pulled the second tab that released a larger CO_2 cartridge that filled the boat in a few seconds. Fully inflated, it rose up the short distance to the surface, bringing the SEALs with it.

Stu looked around, judged the wave height and removed his mask.

"Damn, I love that!" he exclaimed to no one in particular.

"It would be a rush to try from a greater depth but I wouldn't want to risk my lungs on it," quipped Jim, as he removed his mask and climbed into the boat. He helped Stu in and they in turn grabbed the hands of the others waiting in the soft swells to climb aboard.

Lieutenant Boris Martin was the last swimmer to climb in and he clipped the motor to its fibre glass mount on the boat's stern. After removing the three sealing plugs that had protected it from the sea water and seeing that it was fastened securely, he pushed the starter and felt the motor come to life.

"Well, that's a relief," he smiled, lowering the outboard into the water and heading the small boat towards the distant lights on the piers at Toulon. Powering up his GPS, he studied the information he had previously programmed into it and made a small correction to their course. Looking ahead, he found a reference point on the shore he'd be able to use to guide them the rest of the way in.

"You know, if we could sell those motors we'd make a fortune," Stu noted, amazed at how quiet the small outboard was.

"No doubt," laughed Jamal. "But I don't think anyone would pay the price."

"Too bad," Stu replied. "They sure would be great for fishing."

"With what they cost, it seems a shame to just leave them behind like we do," said Jim. "Maybe we could sneak one home someday and just claim it was dumped overboard."

"Don't even think about it Lewis," Boris growled. "Everyone's gear stowed?"

He received four acknowledgements indicating that everyone had properly fastened down their scuba gear to the appropriate fasteners inside the boat for safe keeping. It would not do for them to return to their rendezvous only to be unable to dive down to the sub because someone's scuba gear had fallen overboard during the mission.

It was very dark on the water, with the moon only a tiny sliver in the western sky. The conversation soon dropped off as they neared land, a necessary precaution against being overheard in the stillness of the night. Boris throttled the motor back as they reached the breakwater that protected the harbour from the ravages of the sometimes stormy Mediterranean. The wall of rocks was not needed this night. The weather was exceptionally calm with only a small swell flowing across the water's surface. At this slower speed they left almost no wake and with what little wind there was, blowing out to sea, any sound they made was carried away from the shore.

"See anything Markus?"

"No, nothing yet." Markus had the night vision glasses glued to his eyes as he scanned around them; constantly on the lookout for anyone or anything that might be on the water. He could see a small boat of some kind moving off towards the naval base, but it wasn't heading their way.

"Sure is quiet," remarked Jamal.

"Yeah, too…"

"Don't say it!" Jamal hissed, cutting Stu off, his smile the only part of his face visible in the dark.

"Well it is!" Stu hissed back, his white teeth showing through the camo paint on his face. He had suggested covering their teeth to the commander once, but had been told to just keep his mouth shut and it wouldn't be a problem.

"L-T, boat at ten o'clock."

Boris looked over but could see nothing in the darkness.

"Do you think he sees us?"

"No, it's okay. He's turning away now and heading for the base. He seems to be running in a circle out there but he shouldn't be able to pick us out unless he's using night vision goggles."

"Okay Sanchez. Keep an eye on him. Anything else moving out there?"

"Not a thing L-T. It's really dead tonight. Lucky for us, I guess."

Boris smiled at the thought. Luck was a good thing to have with you on these trips. He guided the boat closer to the shore and they followed the coast keeping a close watch out for any midnight beach goers or moon bathers.

Twenty minutes later the zodiac rounded a small outcropping of rocks and the Toulon dockyard lay spread out before them. Finding their target was easy enough. It was brightly lit and they all looked on in wonder at the condition of the small freighter.

"Damn," remarked Stu quietly. "What a piece of junk!"

"Gee lieutenant, can't we just stick a few holes in the rust with our knives and let it sink right there?" asked Jim.

"Don't let the look of her fool you. Grab your gear and get ready."

The SEALs carefully fastened their equipment to the harnesses they wore. Stu and Jamal carried the satchels containing the detonation devices along with their silenced automatic weapons. Boris guided the boat slowly towards the ship's stern and slipped around to the starboard side against the pier where he shut off the motor. Jamal, grabbing a piece of blackened rope, slipped backwards into the water and swam quietly over to a piling where he carefully made one end of the line secure before returning to the boat. Markus reached down and taking the other end of the rope from Jamal tied it to one of the cleats moulded into the zodiac.

Chapter 10

At Marlant headquarters in Halifax, the phone on Vice Admiral Brent O'Hanlon's desk chirped. As usual, he answered it before it had managed to chirp a second time.

"O'Hanlon."

"Hello Brent, how are things in Halifax?" Caroline Wheeler's voice was trying hard to sound nonchalant on the other end.

"Great minister! How's the weather up there in Ottawa?" Brent smiled at the casual opening remarks with the Minister of Defence. He liked that she wasn't one of those types who jumped right into what was on her mind.

"A bit too warm for my liking." She smiled to herself at the double entendre. "Everything going okay with our project?" she asked from behind her desk on Parliament Hill.

"Just fine Minister. I received word that our passengers have been picked up and are most happy with their accommodations." The cryptic message from *Corner Brook* was still sitting on Brent's desk and Jody had given him a puzzled look when he had handed it to the admiral, hoping for a hint of what was going on. Brent had dismissed him with a wave however and gone back to his paper work. Jody knew better than to hesitate any longer and returned to his desk wondering what the strange message meant and who it referred to.

"That's good admiral. I'll be in my office if you hear anything more. Please let me know or reach me on my cell if I'm away." Caroline was being hounded almost daily by the Prime Minister who was concerned that any day now, the honourable leader of the opposition would stand up in the House and ask what the navy was up to. She couldn't blame the man really. This was far from Canada's first foray into the dark world of espionage, but it was certainly the first one since the cold war ended that carried with it such serious implications.

"I will Minister. Tell the Prime Minister to relax. We won't be embarrassing him this week." Brent knew the Prime Minister well and respected the trepidation he must feel about the mission, especially after the massive increase in spending he had brought forth in the past three years to rearm Canada's military. More than the lives of his men were at stake here. Canada's standing in the international community would take a beating if this mission fell apart and ended up on the front page of the world's newspapers.

"Thanks Brent. I'll tell him you said that. Take care admiral."

Caroline relaxed a little. These kinds of missions did not appeal to the former air force pilot. If they worked, fine. But if anything went wrong, there would be hell to pay at so many levels that…well, it wouldn't be a problem for her, she thought. Hers would be the first resignation expected in the House of Commons.

"Thanks Minister." Brent paused a moment. "Caroline, look, everything will be okay. Our best people are working on this."

"Thanks Brent. I know that. I'm kind of worried for those men as well. I'll be talking with you."

"I know. So am I. Take care." Brent smiled as he replaced the receiver. He knew she was more worried about his men than her career. He respected that. It was no wonder that she was pegged as the person most likely to be the next Prime Minister of Canada.

※ ※ ※ ※

"Boat's secure." Jamal whispered.

"Okay, com checks," Boris ordered quietly inserting his earpiece. His call sign, as always was 'One'.

"Two!" responded Senior Chief Jamal Washington, the youngest and largest SEAL.

"Three!" piped in Chief Jim Lewis, the squad sniper and weapons expert.

"Four!" announced Ensign Stu Cunningham, making it sound like a golf swing warning. He fancied himself the team comedian.

"Five!" Chief Markus Sanchez quipped, while again checking his weapon. He was always the most serious one.

"Everyone's good." Boris adjusted his earpiece a little; satisfied it would stay in place. The custom earpieces each SEAL wore fit tightly into their ear canals, ensuring that no sound escaped from them. He caught everyone's attention and patted his ear piece; the signal that there would be as little verbal communication as possible from here on in.

Looking up he spied the fastening points welded to the hull of the ship that now loomed above them. Most ships had some sort of arrangement of attachment points along the length of their hulls. They were used to attach lines holding crew platforms from where the sailors could perform maintenance or the never ending scraping and painting required to keep a ship afloat. In the case of this ship, no work had been performed on the hull for some time Boris noted, as the first hook he attached a rope to broke away in a cloud of rust. Shit, he muttered to himself. He really didn't want to fire a grappling hook over the rail.

He tried the next hook after manoeuvring the boat a few feet. It held. Pulling himself up, he continued attaching lines to the hooks and testing them carefully until he had reached a point just below the deck. Pausing for a moment, he listened. Nothing. A nauseating odour wafted over him from somewhere on the old craft. He wondered what the ship's last cargo had been and if it had died in transit.

Carefully lowering himself back into the boat, he moved aside as Stu clambered up, carrying a rope ladder over his shoulder. The man climbed like a monkey. Boris smiled to himself as a picture of Stu with big round ears and a tail popped into his mind. In minutes Stu had the ladder firmly attached and like Boris, he hesitated just below the deck level to listen.

"Guess its okay that I forgot my deodorant," he whispered, taking in the ship's aroma. As usual, he was the first to break radio discipline.

Below, Boris gave him the universal finger sign of discontent. Stu remained silent as he returned to the boat for his satchel and weapon.

Boris and Sanchez would ascend the ladder first, weapons ready and cocked. Stu and Jamal would follow after receiving the 'all clear' from the men on deck. Jim would follow last, taking up a covering position somewhere near the ship's stern. Normally the chief petty officer would be carrying his 'baby', a custom built sniper rifle. It was rumoured to receive more tender loving care than his girlfriend. On this mission however, there would be no time to find a suitable 'nest' for him to shoot from and he therefore carried the same silenced 9mm automatic as the rest of the team.

Climbing the ladder again, Boris reached the deck and once again peered over the side. No one was in sight and he checked for portholes along the side of the companionway which would have to be watched for signs of movement inside. There was only one and the light streaming from it formed a round circle on the deck just in front of him.

Good, thought Boris. With the lights on inside, whoever might be in there would have almost no ability to see outside in the darkness. Carefully slipping below the lowest wire on the ship's railing, he crouched against the superstructure and signalled Markus to join him from the position where he had been covering the lieutenant. Holding his weapon firmly, he slipped under the rail and took station a few yards behind Boris.

Boris looked at him and made a quick motion of covering his eyes, signalling he saw no one from his vantage. Looking back to the deck edge, he saw Stu peek over and motioned him up with two fingers upright, indicating Stu could also signal Jamal to follow him.

In a few minutes, all five members of the squad huddled against the superstructure. Boris pointed at Stu and Jamal and motioned for them to head forward to where the deck hatch covering the hold containing the rockets was located. Pointing to the stern, he indicated to Jim that he should stay back and cover their boarding ladder in case they needed to make a quick exit from the ship. Jim gave an exaggerated nod, signifying he understood.

Tapping Markus on the shoulder, Boris pointed ahead to a metal stairway leading up to the bridge. There they'd expect to find someone on watch and taking that person out first was crucial to their mission's success. In most cases the man on watch aboard a ship of this calibre would probably be asleep, but in case he was a keener, they'd have to make sure he didn't look out the bridge windows and see Stu and Jamal heading for the hatches on the deck below.

Slowly and quietly they eased their way up the steps, stopping every few moments to listen. Boris smiled. The door to the bridge was ajar removing one huge detriment to their success. Most doors and hatches on older ships such as this one were so clogged with paint and rust that opening or closing them was usually a strenuous and dangerously noisy operation.

The bridge lights were all on and Boris slowly raised his head to glance inside the window just above them. He saw right away what he was looking for. The man who had the watch was leaning back in an old easy chair reading. His back was to the doorway which was perfect but he seemed to be fidgeting as though he was about to get up.

Boris held up one finger towards Markus indicating only one person visible. Pointing to himself and then to his neck, he communicated he was going in to neutralize the man inside. Slowly he slipped inside, squeezing through the opening carefully to avoid any noise should the rusted door move any further on its hinges. Stopping for just a moment, he then skulked silently over to the back of the chair. The man had settled back in, having found a more comfortable position and was just turning the page of a book. Boris moved quickly but silently, wrapping his arm around the man's neck and holding it until he felt the Korean stop thrashing and lay still. The only sound besides a grunt from the now unconscious sailor was his book hitting the deck. Reaching to move it, Boris noted the Korean script. A fleeting curiosity as to the subject of the book was as quickly dismissed from his mind. Motioning for Markus to join him, he began to tie and bind the slumped body, making sure he stayed low in case someone happened to look up at the brightly lit bridge. One down, he thought to himself. A quick survey of the bridge showed no sign of anyone else being on duty this late and a door to the rear of the space was securely locked from the other side.

Markus quickly glanced at his watch. Six minutes. He knew the odds of trouble developing were directly proportional to the time spent at a 'mission point'. Looking over to Lieutenant Martin he saw that the bridge guard was securely tied and gagged. He'd be no further problem tonight.

"This is One. Bridge watch contained." There was no response. None was expected but the message signalled Stu and Jamal that they were now clear to move onto the open forward deck without fear of a crew member seeing them from the bridge. There were no other vantage points above the forward deck unless someone had taken to sleeping out on the rusted derricks that towered above them.

Motioning for Jamal to follow, Stu quietly made his way to the second set of hatches that rose about two feet from the deck a few hundred feet in front of them. One of them was open but no light appeared to emanate from it. The hatches themselves were about two feet across and had been designed to allow the crew entry into the cargo hold below. The huge cargo hatches that opened to allow large items to be loaded or removed from the holds were both shut tight and secured. Seeing that the securing devices were pinned in place, Jamal felt a wave of relief as that indicated the cargo was loaded. More than once a SEAL team had reached a destination only to find their goal had previously departed or had not yet arrived. He pointed to the securing pins and received a nod and 'thumbs up' from Stu.

Stu was relieved as well. Now it was time to blow those babies waiting for them down below. Reaching the lip of the opened hatch he peered into the darkness. Small naked bulbs hanging from the cargo hold's bulkheads cast shadows on the deck below and he could just make out the crates sitting in the middle of the hold. That would be their target for tonight, he surmised.

Carefully bringing his feet over the edge he felt for the metal ladder that stretched down into the darkness. *I sure hope it goes all the way down*, he thought as a picture of his body smashed to the metal deck below slipped through his mind.

Slowly descending the ladder, he found it was firm and noted it didn't even wobble as he gingerly lowered one foot after the other until he reached out and felt the hard deck beneath his feet. Crouching down he swept the area with his weapon. No one seemed to be around. Not surprising at this time of the night. Reaching into a pocket, he extracted his shielded LED signalling device and flashed it twice up the darkened ladder.

Seeing the tiny blue-green light, Jamal climbed over the hatch and began to lower himself down the ladder. He noted the light bulbs and as Stu had done, realized they would not be able to use their night vision devices down here as an accidental glance in the direction of the naked lights would temporarily blind them. Just as well. The shadows thrown all around the hold would make perfect hiding places if the need arose.

Standing up, Stu moved slowly towards the crate closest to him. There were no markings visible on it. Probably to avoid anyone who was working on the pier guessing what was packed inside, he figured. Jamal touched his shoulder and pointed to the port side of the hold. Stu nodded in acknowledgement and made his way down the starboard side.

Meeting at the forward bulkhead, Stu pointed to a crate and held up four fingers. Jamal nodded and did the same. Perfect. Four boosters dismantled into eight crates. So far, thought Stu, everything was going exactly as planned.

*   *   *   *

Aboard *HMCS Corner Brook*, the same could not be said.

"Shit!" Brad whispered. Mike hearing him, moved over to the sonar position.

"What is it lieutenant?"

"That contact is either making more noise or coming this way sir. He's still too far off for me to identify but the signature is definitely stronger."

Damn, Mike thought. There was no way the other submarine could have detected them stopped dead in the water like this. Maybe the French had installed some sort of underwater security system and *Corner Brook* had unknowingly tripped it.

"Watch him closely Brad. The second you identify him or get a range, let me know."

"Yes sir," Brad replied without taking his eyes off the scope. He called Derek over to his position and pointed out the faint line on the screen, asking him to keep a close watch everywhere else.

"This one is mine."

* * * *

On the *Sariwon's* bridge, Boris was looking over the log book for radio frequencies or any other 'intel' that might be useful. Any extra intelligence gleaned while they were aboard might help someone else later on. Unfortunately the entire book was written in Korean and that was one language he had not mastered.

"One, this is Four, we are setting packages," whispered a voice in Boris' headset. That was Jamal. He knew they had found the crates and were now setting the charges. Excellent. Right on schedule he thought.

Looking over at Markus, he saw the petty officer nod, indicating he had heard the message. Turning back to the chart table where the log book lay, his eye caught something on the panel next to the ship's wheel. Oh hell. A small flashing red light winked at him. Small flashing red lights always meant trouble.

"Guys, I have a warning light on the bridge. We may have activated an intrusion alarm."

No one answered. Hearing his comment, the SEALs immediately sought the closest shelter, looking and listening for any kind of sound.

Stu and Jamal dropped their satchels in a shadow and moved to a dark corner of the hold. Anyone coming near them would be silhouetted against the light bulbs hanging from the overheads.

Jim, alone at the stern, backed into a small space among some boxes that had been piled against the stern railing. From this vantage he could see the top of the rope ladder attached to the railing where their boat was tied. In the dark he doubted anyone would spot it unless they stopped right above and happened to look down. If that happened he'd have to eliminate them.

Down in the cargo hold, Stu pointed at Jamal and then to another space closer to the middle of the hold where the shadows made a dark opening among the crates. Jamal understood and quietly moved across the hold, keeping as low as he could to present as small a target as possible. At that moment Stu saw a hatch on the rear bulkhead swing open slowly.

"Two! Freeze!" he whispered hoarsely into his headset. Jamal stopped moving, quickly looking around for what had alarmed Stu, but there was a crate between him and the hatch that had opened, blocking his view. Seeing that Jamal was not visible from the hatch, Stu called him to retreat back to the shadow he had just left.

On the bridge Boris impatiently waited for word of what was going on down below. Proper procedure called for any squad members in danger to find cover or deal with the threat before reporting to their leader. To tie up their frequency at this moment could be fatal to one of his men.

"One, this is Four, a hatch on the aft bulkhead has opened. There is no light coming from it and no one has come through it," Stu reported, knowing Boris would be wondering what was going on.

"Roger," Boris replied. He'd have to wait while Stu and Jamal investigated the hatch before they could continue setting their charges. He hated waiting. He had always found that the worse things in life happened while you waited.

Stu flipped down his night vision goggles and peered into the hatch. From his vantage point, there was no sign of anything moving in the other space which he calculated was directly below the bridge. Moving carefully, he slipped past where Jamal was concealed and made his way to the last crate, putting him only a few feet from the opening. From this perch he could see that the hatch was part of a water tight bulkhead and had definitely not moved on its own.

He really didn't want to poke his head inside and find someone waiting beyond the range of his night vision goggles, but he had to do something. Extracting one of the extra magazines from his ammo pouch, he slid out a single bullet and tossed it into the open hatch. The 9mm round bounced noisily on the steel deck inside and immediately three sharp clangs rang out. Stu threw himself back into the corner. Shit! A silenced weapon!

"This is Four! We have a silenced shooter down here!" Stu hissed. All five SEALs were thinking the same thing. A silenced weapon meant professional. Their intelligence had reported that only regular crew members were aboard, but obviously that 'intel' was wrong.

Boris found the switch controlling the bridge lights and shut them down. While waiting for his night vision to return, he began to devise who might be doing the shooting. It wasn't the ship's crew obviously, as they wouldn't be using sound suppressed weapons. It might be regular North Korean army, but he doubted that. They would have attacked the hold by now rather than waiting out the SEALs. The Koreans, whoever they were, had all day to play at this. The SEALs, however, were pressed for time. Boris checked his weapon and made sure his own silencer was securely fastened to the end of the barrel.

"Two, this is Four. I'm going to try and get to the other side of the hatch. Cover me."

Jamal moved from the shadow and made his way to the bulkhead where Stu was crouched, his weapon ready.

"Go Four."

Stu moved swiftly. As he crossed over in front of the opening, another clang reverberated through the hold but fortunately the bullet ricocheted harmlessly away.

"Two, this is Four. I'm going to throw a flash ball inside and see if I can spot anything."

"Go ahead Four."

Stu reached into a side pocket and pulled out a small, round device. Turning a small knob on its base, he set the timer and tossed it into the other room. No one fired this time. Flipping up his night vision goggles and shielding his eyes, he counted off the five seconds until a blinding flash poured from the hatch. Uncovering his eyes, he threw himself through the hatch, seeking cover, and then scanned the room for any movement in the dimming light of his flash ball. There! Against the far side someone ducked behind a small pile of boxes. Too slow thought Stu, sliding to his left and firing a short burst into the steel bulkhead behind the spot where the other man lay hidden.

He was immediately rewarded with a scream of agony as his bullets ricocheted off the steel bulkhead and at least one found its mark. Fool, thought Stu, steel walls were not good cover.

"This is Four; one shooter. I hit him but I don't think he's down. No sign of anyone else in this space."

"Four, this is Two. I'm coming in and will move to the right on entry."

"Roger that Two. I'll cover you. Come in NOW!"

Jamal threw himself through the hatch and moved to the right. Flipping his night vision goggles down, he surveyed the large room now returned to darkness. Only a faint aura showed where the wounded man was crouched behind a few boxes. Watching carefully, he moved along the wall to the far corner where he'd have a clear shot at their adversary

"Four, this is Two. I'm moving forward."

"Two, let me try something first," Stu flipped his night vision goggles down and took aim at one of the boxes. Switching his weapon to 'single' he fired one shot and immediately the man jumped up in pain. Tapping the trigger again, he brought him down with a clean head shot.

"Damn good shooting Four!" Jamal was impressed. Only Stu would think to test if the boxes the man hid behind were empty.

"Thought it was worth a try. One, this is Four. He's down. Room is secure."

"Roger Four. Any ID on him?" Boris asked.

"Two is checking now," Stu replied.

Jamal bent over the body, carefully searching for clues to his identity.

"One, this is Two. He's wearing a uniform, but I don't recognize it. No insignia or ID. Taking pictures," he announced turning on the small digital camera all squad members carried now.

"Roger Two," Boris replied. This fellow was definitely not a crew member.

"One, this is Two. The man is hooked up. A really tiny ear set."

"Roger that Two." Okay, Boris thought, he's not alone and he's definitely not regular NK army. They had to find who he was communicating with and fast. He needn't have worried as a bullet smashed through one of the bridge windows sending shards of glass cascading down on the deck around him.

"Shit! Five! Take cover!"

"This is Five. The shot came in the door and blew out the window," Markus answered from behind the chair where he had seen most of the glass blow out onto the deck below.

"Roger that."

"Three, this is One. Can you see the stairs from where you are?" Boris queried.

"One, give me a second." Jim slipped from his hiding place and carefully looked down the deck. Nothing. Crawling further out of his small space amongst the boxes, he peered up the ladder to the bridge. A dark form crouched low against the side of the superstructure, halfway up the stairs.

"One, this is Three. Target is on the stairs. I have a clear shot."

"Take it Three."

Jim would have preferred his C3A1 for the shot, but it was home, packed in its Canadian Army case. He claimed to have 'found' it during a mission in Afghanistan two years ago and had quickly dispelled the rumours about a 'trade' with a friend serving with JTF2, Canada's equivalent to the SEALs.

Bringing up the stubby 9mm automatic, he squeezed off two rounds and watched as the dark form jerked up and then slid limply down the stairs. Jim stood and crept carefully along the superstructure, his weapon aimed directly at the form lying motionless on the deck. He only needed one look at the man's face framed in a pool of blood.

"One, this is Three. He's down." Jim grabbed the man's legs and brought the body around to a shadowed area beneath the steps.

"Three, this is One. Roger that—bad guy down. Return to your spot and keep your eyes open," cautioned Boris.

Dang, and here I thought I'd have a little nap, smirked Jim to himself.

"Two, this is One. Are you guys clear to set the charges?"

"Roger that One. We're going back into the hold."

Jamal motioned Stu through the hatch and covered him as he slipped through. Following, he took a long look around and seeing nothing, returned to his satchel and continued setting the charges.

Across the deck, Stu was already working on the second crate in his row. Carefully removing the small explosive device from its protective case, he fastened it to the side of the crate covered by shadow. At least that way, if one of the charges were discovered before going off, the Koreans would be less likely to find them all before they started to detonate.

On the bridge, Boris had moved to where Markus was crouched behind the chair. Pointing to his eyes and motioning towards the doorway, he indicated that he was going to leave the bridge. He then pointed to Markus and then to the bridge windows, communicating that he was to keep watch on the deck below. Markus signalled his understanding and took a position against the ship's wheel which would offer some cover in case anyone else took at shot at him.

Creeping over to the door, Boris carefully surveyed the stairway down to the deck.

"Three, this is One. I'm leaving the bridge and will be coming down the port side. Watch for me."

"Roger One."

Boris moved cautiously down the stairs. If the two men they'd taken out weren't crew members, then somewhere on the ship, the rest of the crew had to be sleeping, he considered. Or maybe they had been alerted and were now preparing to come after his squad. Reaching the deck, he moved along the superstructure until he reached the open space where the loading hatches spread out before him. Crouching low, he moved across the ship to the port side, and slowly moved down the companionway. It was darker here than on the starboard side, shadowed by the lights from the pier which made visibility far too good on the port side of the ship.

Ahead on his left, an open hatch led inside the ship's superstructure. Peering inside, Boris saw that it was a small open area with a few tables and a television set mounted on the wall. At the rear of the room was a closed door leading to what he guessed was the crew's sleeping quarters. Odd how most ships seemed to be laid out in a similar manner. That was probably good as the crews serving on these freighters tended to transfer often from one ship to another.

Drawing his weapon, he made his way to the door and waited. No noise emanated from inside. He reached down to test the handle and was surprised that it moved effortlessly and quietly. Inside, a dimly lit passageway stretched out ahead, with a closed door on either side.

Grabbing the handle on the door to his right, he slowly pushed down on it and heard a click as the bolt cleared it's housing in the door frame. It was dark inside and Boris felt along the inside wall until he found the light switch. Staring back at the dim light hanging from the ceiling in the hallway, he allowed his eyes to adjust for the brightness that would come and flicked the switch up.

Quickly scanning the room, he used his foot to close the door behind him. Two of the beds in the room were occupied. He waited as the two men, crew members from their dishevelled appearance, stirred slowly and looked up to see who had turned the light on. The younger of the two rubbed his eyes and as they adjusted to the light, he saw a large man, dressed in black, standing in the room. Appearing larger still was the barrel of the weapon the man was pointing at his head.

Boris hissed one of the few Korean words he knew.

"Quiet!"

The young man didn't have to be told twice. Neither did his fellow crewmate who was wide awake now, and not about to risk his life for this decrepit ship or its cruel captain.

Boris pointed to the young man, then to the bedding that lay on the floor and finally to the other crewmember's hands. The young fellow caught on quick, thought Boris as he watched him scurry to the floor to grab the sheets and tie up his crew mate.

After making sure the older man was secured, Boris carefully moved to the remaining sailor and before he could react, clipped him on the neck just above his shoulder. He fell, dazed, and Boris quickly tied him up. Using the electrical cords from a stereo that sat on a rickety stand in the room, he attached their binds to a pipe that ran down the wall. Then gagging them with their pillow cases, Boris pointed the barrel of his weapon against their cheek, each in turn, while whispering 'quiet' in Korean as they stared fearfully up at him.

"This is One. Two civvie crew members down."

"You da man L-T!" Stu's voice rang in his headset.

He was hopeless, thought Boris as he silently left the room and moved across the hall.

Listening for a moment, he carefully opened the opposite door. This time the lights were on and a man lay across the bed reading a magazine. He jumped up startled as Boris entered the room and quickly kicked the door shut behind him. The man just as quickly sat back down as a muffled bullet tore into the pillow by his head, causing a brief flurry of feathers to fall softly around him. Five minutes later, Boris stepped out into the hall, leaving the man inside gagged and bound, but thankful to be alive.

"This is One. Another civvie crew member down." No comment this time.

Leaving the hallway, he returned outside and continued moving towards the stern of the ship. That left the ship's captain according to intelligence, and god only knew how many soldiers, or whatever they were, he thought, moving cautiously down the dark companionway.

*   *   *   *

Aboard *Corner Brook*, Brad could see on his screens that they were about to have company.

"Sir, range to target decreasing. Estimate range now eight thousand yards. No aspect change. He's coming straight for us."

"Any idea yet who it is?" Mike knew better than to ask but asked anyway.

"Computer doesn't know yet, but if I was a betting man, I'd say it's French. Probably a *Rubis*," Brad answered.

"It must be heading for the sub base. Lieutenant Beals, pass the word. Ultra quiet."

"Aye sir," Fred answered, heading for the hatch leading to the torpedo spaces. The message would be passed throughout the submarine verbally, as in 'ultra quiet' mode there was no use of the submarine's address system. Ultra quiet meant no noise of any kind and all unnecessary operations were curtailed throughout the boat.

Told of the order, Cookie poked his head into the junior's mess.

"Guys, ultra quiet has been ordered."

"Damn," muttered one of the men who had been winning a car race on the boat's Playstation3.

"Sorry guys. Probably won't last long. Sit tight and I'll bring out a snack."

The chief knew that good food made everything a little easier to a navy man.

In the control room, Commander Simpson was leaning over the chart and trying to estimate where the other submarine might be located. If it was a French boat, she was probably returning from an exercise off Corsica. He knew the

French navy had some sort of test area around there. Mike's first instinct was to move his boat further from the entrance of Toulon's harbour in order to give the other boat plenty of space. But that would be risky. Although very quiet, his boat would generate some noise starting up. No, he thought. We'll have to take our chances and wait it out.

"Commander, computer just ID'd the other boat. It's a *Rubis* class SSN," Brad announced while keyboarding the name into his digital copy of *Jane's Fighting Ships*.

"Thanks Brad." Mike didn't have to look it up. He remembered all too well the characteristics of the French class of SSNs; one of the smallest and most capable nuclear submarines in the world.

"So monsieur," he whispered looking down at the chart. "Where are you headed?"

*   *   *   *

Stu looked down and confirmed the timer setting on his final charge.

"Two, this is Four. How's it coming?" Stu whispered. The sound of his voice or rather the vibrations were picked up by the combination microphone and speaker in his left ear; the same equipment worn by the presidential detail of the Secret Service.

"Two…is done…now." Jamal answered, grabbing the empty satchel and swinging it over his right shoulder.

Stu motioned for Jamal to cover him while he climbed to the main deck. Bringing his weapon up, Jamal watched as the other SEAL reached the opening above and signalled him to follow. Reaching the forward deck, and keeping low as possible, they scurried back to the front of the ship's superstructure, crouching there for a moment to catch their breath.

"One, this is Four," Stu called. "Charges are set and we are on the main deck forward. Heading aft down the port side."

"Roger Four. I'm just coming out onto the afterdeck. Still no sign of the ship's captain or any more bad guys." That was good, Boris was thinking, although he knew in his heart they had to be aboard the ship somewhere.

"Roger."

"One, this is Five. I'm heading for the stairs and will be going down the starboard side," Markus announced, as he moved carefully across the bridge to the doorway.

"Roger Five. Keep a close watch. Did you get that Three?"

"Got it. I won't shoot him—promise!" Jim retorted. He had a reputation for being a little too trigger-happy.

Jamal and Stu crept slowly down the port companionway, keeping their bodies tight against the ship's superstructure. Boris meanwhile had reached the stern. Turning around, he spied a small stairway leading to a hatch above him. Carefully, he climbed the steps one at a time, stopping on each one to listen. The porthole built into the hatch was dark and it appeared that it might lead to a passageway inside similar to the one he'd just left.

"Four, this is One," Boris spoke quietly. "I'm a deck above you at the stern and checking on a hatch. It might be a passageway leading forward to the bridge."

"Roger that One. I'll come in after you," replied Stu. "Two, cover the hatch from outside."

Boris reached the hatch and grabbing the handle, swung it down carefully and pulled it open. No light was visible. Flipping his night vision goggles down, he peered inside and saw that it was empty. This passageway was narrower than the one below, but had the same door on either side as well as another one at the far end that probably led to an inside space connecting to the bridge.

Making his way carefully down the left side of the passageway, he crouched, weapon ready. Reaching the door on the left, he first tested the knob. It turned easily and giving it a twist, he swung the door open. In the greenish glow of the night goggles, the room appeared empty. It seemed to be an office of some sort. He could see a desk against the far wall, piled with papers. A strong odour of stale cigar smoke filled the air. Must be the captain's office, he thought.

Taking another glance around and satisfying himself that there was nothing of interest in the room, he stepped carefully back out into the passageway, closing the door softly behind him. Checking his watch, he calculated how much time they had before the charges would detonate; forty minutes...no problem.

Outside, reaching the top of the ladder, Stu slipped into the passageway and also lowered his night vision goggles. About halfway down, he made out Lt. Martin just coming through the door on the left.

"One, this is Four," Stu whispered from a few yards behind him. "I've got your six."

The green glowing figure in his night vision goggles gave a 'thumbs up' and Stu saw him reach out and grasp the knob on the door to his right. It didn't appear to move in Boris's hand.

"Four, this is One. Door is secure. I'm heading forward."

"Roger," Stu replied as he watched Boris slowly continue down the passageway.

Chapter 11

On the other side of the door at the end of the passageway, the remaining four members of the Korean Army Special Assault Team huddled together. The commandos had been using the small space as their office since the ship had reached France and had been relaxing together, playing cards, when the security system rigged earlier to the ship's hold had been activated. The leader of the group had heard the warning from his man below but there had been nothing further from him and now he was worried. He had been about to open the connecting door to the bridge when they had all heard the crash of breaking glass outside. There were obviously intruders aboard the ship. He assumed that the man he had stationed on the superstructure behind the bridge, like the man below, was now dead; killed by whoever it was that had come aboard the ship. He had little doubt that the unidentified men were Americans. Carefully examining a layout of the ship, he planned the tactics he and his men would use to kill these western animals.

His leaders had been right to select him for this mission. Now he would eliminate the threat to the precious cargo this horrible little ship was carrying. He was not motivated by a monetary reward as the greedy captain of the ship was, but more dangerously, by a feverish patriotism to his Dear Leader.

His plan complete, he stood and tapped two of his men on the shoulder, pointing at the door leading to the bridge and made a sweeping motion indicating they were to go down to the main deck and check the cargo. The two men rose and unlocked the door to the bridge. Crouching low to avoid being seen, they headed for the stairs on the starboard side leading down to the main deck, ignoring the tied and gagged crewmember slumped in the corner. The North

Korean leader then stood, beckoning to the remaining soldier to follow him as he reached up to unlock the door leading to the passageway aft.

✳   ✳   ✳   ✳

From his position on the stern outside, Jim saw a shadow appear in the bridge doorway.

"Five, this is Three. See him?" He radioed over to Markus, who was just across the deck from him.

"I've got him Five. There's another one coming out behind him." Markus spotted the second soldier stepping through the door onto the stairway.

"Five, you take the first one and I'll take the other guy. On three…one…two…"

A pair of muffled shots rang out and the second man collapsed to the stairs, while the first man faltered but did not fall. The bullet, having missed his head by inches, clanged into the steel superstructure.

"Damn!" Markus fired twice more and this time the man dropped like a stone to the stairs where he lay motionless.

Inside his cabin, the ship's captain was awakened by Markus' shot pealing against the superstructure. Without hesitation he grabbed the shotgun leaning against his bed and cycled a round into the chamber. Quietly unlocking the door that Boris had found locked moments earlier; he threw it open and jumped out into the passageway. In the light streaming from his room, he saw two men dressed in black with their backs to him. One of them started to turn towards him when suddenly the door to the bridge at the far end of the passageway swung open.

"SHIT! HIT THE DECK!" yelled Boris.

At the same instant, Stu seeing the light behind him, had stepped to the left in order to cover Boris and was turning to bring his weapon to bear when a blast from the captain's shotgun sent him flying against the bulkhead. His body stiffened for a moment before crumpling to the deck. One of the Koreans fired his gun on full automatic at the muzzle flash from the shotgun, killing the captain instantly.

Switching his own weapon to 'auto', Boris fired a short burst, bringing both North Koreans down. His ears still ringing from the un-muffled shotgun blast, he got up and kicked at both bodies, making sure they were dead before tossing their weapons back down the passageway.

"One! This is Two! What the hell's going on?!" Jamal had dived to the deck outside as some of the shots fired by the North Korean had ricocheted down the passageway and out the hatch.

"Washington! Stu is hit!" Boris yelled, dropping radio procedure. Reaching down, he dragged Stu roughly down the passageway towards the open hatch. "We're coming out! Cover us chief!"

"L-T, this is Three! All clear outside!" Jim shouted. "Two more bad guys down at the bridge stairway!" He wasn't sure if Boris had caught the chatter between him and Markus in all the action.

Markus was already sprinting for the deck below the hatch where Boris had appeared hauling Stu behind him. With the most medical training of the five men, Markus knew seconds could mean the difference between life and death with a gunshot wound.

Boris literally drug Stu through the hatch and down the ladder by his body armour straps, to the main deck. Laying him down gently, he quickly checked that his breathing was okay. Markus jumped down beside Stu and tore off his vest. Beneath the uniform he could see that some of the shell's pellets had hit him in the small unprotected opening between the front and back panels of the body armour just below his arm pit.

"Stu, can you hear me man?" Markus stuffed the blood stained vest under the injured man's head, propping it up.

"I'm fine. Just…SHIT! Damn! Getting shot hurts! Ya never warned me about that L-T!"

Boris let his breath out. He'd be okay for now, but he had seen that the wound was serious. They had to get him back to the sub, and fast!

※　　※　　※　　※

"He's stopped," Brad barely whispered.

"Are you sure?" asked Mike.

Brad looked up from his sonar screens and nodded.

"Helm, correct for depth only. Let us drift." They would stop compensating for the tidal current trying to pull them away from Toulon and make sure that only their depth did not change.

"Correct for depth only, aye sir. Drift rate is…less than half a knot right now. Still outward." Petty Officer Charley Poulin watched the compass display change slowly as the submarine drifted in the current. At this point in the tide's cycle, they were not really in serious trouble as far as holding their position was concerned.

"What's he doing now Brad?"

"Nothing sir. Just sitting there."

"Okay," Mike said, watching the faint line representing the French submarine. "We'll play their game." He knew however that this game was in the third period, and time was rapidly running out for the Canadians.

* * * *

Markus finished bandaging Stu's wounds and had tried to give him a shot of pain killer, but the young ensign refused.

"Naw, wait 'till I'm really hurting to give me that."

"Fine," Markus answered him, but silently responded, "That time will come sooner than you think my friend."

Boris and Jim took a quick run around the deck, making sure there were no more surprises aboard the ship. Time was running out and they had to be in the boat and away soon and not only because of the explosives they had set. Those would go off with surprisingly little noise and likely wouldn't be heard outside the hold. The rendezvous with *Corner Brook* was another matter. They did not want to be late and more importantly, Stu needed medical attention that couldn't be given on this filthy ship.

"Team, let's get out of here! Three and Five, get down to the boat now!" Boris had regained his composure, although the sight of blood pouring from Stu's wounds kept flashing in his mind. "Two, help me with Four."

Jamal would have little trouble taking Stu down the rope ladder over his shoulders. The man was solid muscle and often surprised the team members with his brute strength. Lowering himself onto the rope ladder, he waited as Boris carefully helped Stu slide under the rail. A few grunts emitted from the ensign as Jamal draped him easily over his shoulders in the classic fireman's carry.

Boris watched as Jamal climbed slowly down the ladder, stopping at the bottom to let Jim and Markus lower Stu to the boat. Markus checked for bleeding and although the bandages were soaked with blood, they were not dripping. That was a good sign.

"One, Two is clear. Come on down!"

Boris needed no further encouragement and slipped quickly down the ladder. Reaching the zodiac he headed for the motor while Jim cut the ropes holding the inflatable boat in place. Slowly, Boris manoeuvred the boat away from the pier and along the rocky shore. A few minutes later, clear of the piers, they looked back at the ship now silent at the dock. Obviously no one on the waterfront had heard anything, or if they had, chose to mind their own business and not alert the gendarmes. All hell would break lose when the harbour authorities finally went aboard the ship in the morning to see why it hadn't left at its appointed departure time.

"Stu, how you doing?" Boris could see how pale Stu's face was in the dim light reflected off the waves from the buildings on shore. The pallor of his skin contrasted sharply with the areas where Markus hadn't wiped off the camouflage paint when he had checked him over.

"I'll be fine L-T. Thanks for not leaving me behind." Stu spoke through clenched teeth. His side felt as though someone was jabbing it repeatedly with a sharp, hot poker.

"Actually, we took a vote and it was a tie," kidded Jamal, trying to distract his friend. "The L-T said if we didn't bring you back there'd be this big investigation though and we'd all be in deep shit because…"

"Yeah, I love you too brother," Stu interrupted, forcing a grin at the big man and then settling back with a grimace. He'd miss these guys. The pain told him his days as an operational SEAL were over.

* * * *

On the bridge of *HMCS Vancouver*, Commander Donnelly looked at the radar plot on the screen hanging from the overhead in front of his chair. He could clearly see the coastline of the nearest island traced out on the high resolution display. A few specks, fishing boats he surmised, moved slowly a few miles from his ship.

"Comms, anything?" he asked pushing the button connecting him to the *Vancouver's* operations room for the third time in as many hours.

"Nothing sir," came the answer from the wall mounted speaker to his left.

The ship was holding station, nestled between Ibiza and the main island of Beleares in the western Mediterranean Sea, waiting for…well that piece of information had not been shared with her CO yet and he was understandably annoyed by that fact.

"So Bishop, you get out this way often?" Commander Donnelly asked the man standing next to his chair.

"Not as often as I'd like to. It's beautiful country around the Med. Everything from the deserts and pyramids to incredible country resorts. Maybe some day, when I retire…" He let the sentence trail off.

Retire from what? Commander Donnelly wondered, but chose not to say anything. He was a professional operator and understood that sometimes you just did what you were ordered to do. It would all make sense later, and if it didn't, odds were he wouldn't be around to worry about it.

∗   ∗   ∗   ∗

"You hangin' in there Stu?" Jim asked above the sound of the waves crashing against the zodiac. They were running much faster than their originally planned speed in hopes of getting Stu to the submarine's medical officer as soon as possible.

"I'm here."

The young man was slumped down in one corner of the boat, his head propped up against his blood stained vest. Markus continually hovered over him, checking his vital signs every ten minutes for any change or signs that he might be going into shock.

Sounded a bit weak, thought Boris. Reaching down, he turned the throttle just a bit higher. They were speeding over the water fast enough now that anyone who happened to look in their direction might see their wake, even in the dark, and wonder who was out on the water this late at night. He checked his GPS and noted they were on course. Another half hour would put them right on top of the sub.

"Sir?"

Boris turned and saw Jim and Jamal looking beyond him over the stern. The skies back towards Toulon's commercial piers were now bright with lights and even at this distance they could hear the sound of sirens and horns. Someone must have gone aboard the ship, or one of the crew had escaped their binds.

"Well, its ten minutes past 'D' time so the packages must have gone off by now anyway," Jamal commented to no one in particular.

"Yeah, we should be fine," Boris replied half heartedly. His mind was focused on Stu right now. He'd never lost a squad member. There hadn't even been any serious injuries previous to Stu's getting hit and he wouldn't be able to relax until they got him to the medical facilities aboard *Corner Brook*.

A short time later, Boris instructed Jamal to start suiting up with his diving gear. He'd go down first, stringing a locator line behind him while looking for the submarine which should be waiting motionless just below the surface. The Canadians wouldn't be expecting them this early but there was always some leeway assumed regarding the schedules, in case something should go wrong.

* * * *

That leeway was meaningless at the moment as *Corner Brook* had drifted almost two miles from her original position.

"Brad, anything?" Like the *Vancouver's* commanding officer, Commander Simpson was unaware how many times he had asked that same question of his sonar operator.

"Nothing sir," Brad answered for the second time in twenty minutes. "He hasn't moved. We're both drifting out at the same rate. I'd say he knows we're close by but he's not sure exactly where. He's no doubt definitely wondering what we're up to though."

Looking at his watch, Mike considered his options. They were all bad. The SEALs would show up at the rendezvous point in about half an hour and wouldn't they be surprised to find the sub missing. He didn't mean to make a joke of it, but sarcastic humour was how he often calmed himself in tight situations.

"Sir, drift is increasing." Charley didn't look up from the helm. He knew it wasn't what the skipper wanted to hear. "We're moving almost a knot now."

"Thanks Petty Officer," Mike replied, without sincerity. Thinking through the developing scenario, it was obvious that something had to be done right now.

Glancing over at his XO, he signalled him into the small space that served as his cabin/office. Once inside, Mike slid the door shut and Fred saw the concern in his commanding officer's eyes while waiting for him to speak.

"Freddy, I'm thinking the only way out of this is to go active, make a high speed run to the west and hope to lose him between here and the Baleares Islands. Then, try to sneak back in and hopefully find the SEALs waiting, or at least run into them paddling on their way to Spain," he added sardonically.

"I agree," Fred answered. "The other boat obviously plans on waiting us out and he has more time and power than we do."

"Okay, let's not waste any more time. Ask me later what I was thinking when I agreed to this mission," Mike said, reaching for the door. Sliding it open he strode over to the sonar console. Brad looked up and could see by his commander's expression that things were about to happen.

"Brad, hit him hard. Full power!"

"Yes sir!" Brad had long been frustrated sitting there listening for someone on the other boat to fart.

PING!!!!

"Helm! Bring us left to two seven zero degrees. Make your depth four hundred feet. All ahead full!" Mike now felt like he was back in charge. This plan had better work.

"Coming left to two seven zero, depth four hundred feet, all ahead full, aye sir!"

"Battery is eighty-three percent sir," came from Lt. Polanski at the engineering console.

"Fine. That will be more than enough." Mike continued the sentence to himself…because we'll either lose them or be sunk before it reaches fifty percent.

HMCS Corner Brook quickly reached her ordered depth of four hundred feet and sped away from the French submarine. The crew aboard the *Amethyst* reacting quickly to her captain's orders, brought the small nuclear boat around in pursuit of the mysterious submarine that had been skulking outside their base and which was now obviously trying to run away. The sonar operator had reported that the sonar signature appeared to be British, but he wasn't sure. This had confused the French captain and he hesitated, just long enough for *Corner Brook* to get a small head start.

"Sir, depth four hundred feet, speed twenty-two knots."

"Thanks Charley! Sonar, where is he?"

"He's still not moving commander. Wait, I have him. Oh yeah, he's kicking it into high gear!" At this close range; Brad could easily hear the reactor pumps furiously moving water through the submarine's propulsion system. He was getting excited now that the chase was on. It would have been more fun though if they were the hunter instead of the prey.

Mike strode over to where Lieutenant Beals was marking up his chart.

"Commander, we're here right now, and he's about three to four thousand yards behind us," Fred spoke without looking up. "He'll catch us fairly quick…I estimate about here, just north-east of Menorca Island in the Baleares chain."

"Okay, that'll buy us some time. I want to go deep just before that point and see if we can throw his sonar off with the Lazcom. Otherwise those SEALs had better hope for a passing cruise ship to pick them up."

"It'll be tricky but we'll pull it off," Fred enthused. One of the XO's primary functions was to encourage his commanding officer. "If we can temporarily blank out his sonar and get far enough away, he should lose us completely."

* * * *

Fifteen minutes later, the black Zodiac containing the SEALs had almost reached the rendezvous spot.

"Five minutes to pick up point!" Boris called out to Jamal who had donned the lightweight scuba gear for his dive down to the sub.

Jamal gave a 'thumbs up' and made one more check of his equipment. He noted the air flask was at seventy percent capacity so he had plenty of time in case a short swim was required to the submarine. With the aid of their GPS they expected to be well within sight of the flashing beacon that would signal them from atop the sub's sail; their only way of sighting the submerged boat in the dark water.

"Stu, you gonna be okay for the swim down?" Boris asked, looking down at the prone figure.

"I'll be fine L-T. I'm a little groggy but the cold water will bring me around," Stu was trying hard to sound confident. "Jim's going to tie a line to me and pull me down if I'm too weak."

"Good plan! Okay guys, get into your gear. We have to move fast when Senior Chief Washington signals us." Boris throttled down the motor and reached for his own suit stored beneath the plastic seat he sat on.

Jamal took one more look at his GPS and confirmed their position.

"Okay L-T. I'm off!" Falling backward off the zodiac's side he disappeared into the dark water. It was colder now than it had been some hours ago when he had first left the submarine. In a couple more hours, the sun would come up and begin to warm the water again.

Diving down about ten feet, Jamal stopped and took a slow look around. Odd, no sign of the yellow strobe from the submarine. Swimming back up to the surface, he pulled out his GPS unit and confirmed the position. It was right on. Again he dived down, this time to twenty feet and took a long look. Nothing. The strobe would have been visible a great distance in these clear waters. Shit! Something was wrong…seriously wrong. Swimming back up to the surface, he spotted the zodiac and swam over to it.

"The sub's not there L-T," he announced, removing his mask.

"What? Are you sure the coordinates are correct?" Boris asked, keeping his voice calm.

"One hundred percent!" answered Jamal. "I double checked and the GPS self test says everything's fine with the unit."

"Damn!"

This was not good. Boris thought back to when they had left the sub, in case he had missed something anyone had said. When they rendezvoused with a submarine, it was the SEALs who were most likely to be delayed. The sub not being there was never a concern because it usually just stayed put…doing nothing but waiting.

"Okay, climb back in and we'll recheck in ten minutes," Boris ordered. *Corner Brook* had probably just moved off the entrance to the harbour a bit. They were half an hour early so the sub would no doubt show up any time now.

"L-T?" Markus spoke quietly. "He's not lookin' good."

Boris looked down and could see that Stu was now unconscious. A lot of blood was soaking through his bandages and the water sloshing around the bottom of the boat was tinged with red adding to his already increased anxiety.

"His pulse is weakening and his blood pressure has dropped," Markus continued. "He's going to need real medical attention soon."

"Okay Chief," Boris responded. "Keep on him. The sub will be back any minute."

Ten minutes passed and Jamal again dove down under the zodiac in search of their ride. Again he surfaced with the same message. Nothing.

"Do you think we should try a noise maker L-T?" Jim asked.

Jim was referring to the small charges sometimes used by a team to signal a waiting submarine to surface in case of an emergency. They sent a loud shock wave through the water and were designed to reach a submarine that had gone deep while waiting for a rendezvous.

"Not yet," replied Boris. "That's going to be our last resort because everyone around will hear it."

Boris was running his mind through their only two options…wait until someone found them or use what power they had left in the motor to make for the shore and take their chances evading the authorities on land. The problem was that Stu would not be able to travel and they couldn't, no, wouldn't leave him behind.

* * * *

"Lost him in the baffles sir," Brad looked disappointed, although he knew this would happen at the speed they were moving.

"Alright then." Mike patted his shoulder. "Helm, we'll give him ten more minutes to catch us and then pull a fast diving turn to starboard on the reciprocal course, hitting him with the sonar and the Lazcom simultaneously."

Both Brad and Charley acknowledged the order and refocused on their respective jobs. Lieutenant Beals looked at his watch and set the countdown timer to ten minutes. Life was going to get very exciting fast when the little beeper went off.

Mike grabbed the microphone for the sub's address system and keyed the button. There was no point being quiet when they were roaring through the water at over twenty knots.

"All hands, this is the commander. In ten minutes we will be conducting extreme manoeuvres to shake off a French SSN on our tail. If all goes well, we'll be returning to the pick up point for the SEAL extraction. Keep alert. Weapons room, clear all unnecessary personnel out of the space and be prepared for reloads." Mike replaced the microphone on its bracket and returned to the plotting table.

"Hot damn!" exclaimed Leading Seaman Gary Steeves, tinkering with the circuitry of one of the Mk-48s on its rack in the torpedo room, "This is what I trained all my life for!"

"You mean the past eight months, don't you?" laughed Chief Darren Cole, punching the young seaman on the shoulder.

"Well, yeah, but that's been like…my whole life," answered Steeves.

"Mess up in the next hour and it might just be your whole life seaman," Darren retorted, seriousness creeping into his voice.

* * * *

Aboard *HMCS Vancouver* Greg/Dennis looked down at his watch. *Corner Brook* would have picked up the SEALs by now and be heading this way. If there was going to be any problems with the French Navy, it would probably be developing about now. He didn't realize that there indeed was a problem, and that it was bearing down on him at high speed.

"Commander, it's time to start moving," Greg/Dennis said to Commander Donnelly. "I'd suggest you sound action stations as well."

"Any particular threat alert or ready all weapons just in case?" Chris simpered. He preferred knowing what to expect.

"I don't know commander. That's the truth. But I can now inform you why we're here."

Chris studied the man, and then led him to the lookout station outside the bridge.

"Okay, I'm all ears."

Greg/Dennis laid out the entire operation to him, and then explained that if the French detected the Canadian submarine, they would vigorously pursue it, possibly even fire upon it. Chris looked at him as though he'd grown an extra head.

"You mean to tell me they would shoot a torpedo at a Canadian warship?" He asked incredulously.

"They wouldn't know who it was," Greg/Dennis replied, "and considering Toulon is their main nuclear sub base, they probably wouldn't care."

"Well sir, you have my respect but I wouldn't do your cloak and dagger shit for all the money in the world. Excuse me now. I have to get ready to fight my ship." Chris shook his head once more in total disbelief and walked back onto the bridge. Sitting in his chair he reached for the ship's public address system.

"All hands, this is the captain. Action stations, all weapons systems. Sonar, call in the extra watch and report anything. I mean anything! Helm! Turn to four five degrees and make turns for ten knots!" Chris turned off the PA system. Bloody hell! This could get interesting! Or maybe they'd just pick up *Corner Brook* in an hour or so and everything would be fine. He smiled remembering Mike Simpson's comment at his house last summer about how he was going to take it easy and enjoy his last couple of operational years in the service. "I wonder how he's enjoying it now", he voiced out loud.

*   *   *   *

"Helm! Hard right; take her down to six hundred feet! Sonar, power up the Lazcom and the minute you think it has the other boat, set it to continuous transmit at that bearing!" Mike leaned into the attack scope mount and held on as *Corner Brook* took on a sharp roll and her bow dropped in a fast dive. The sound of things crashing to the decks came from both the front and rear hatches of the control room.

"Sir!" Brad shouted, unable to control his voice. "I have him! He's coming around slowly. Lazcom is nailing him and I'd say right now he's blind!"

"Launch countermeasures!"

From small tubes in the hull, a pair of cylinders emerged from the submarine and began to spew out noises. From the first cylinder, a cacophony of various sounds emitted in random order. The other decoy transmitted the sound that *Corner Brook* would be making at high speed.

"Helm, all slow. When you reach the reciprocal course, hold it and maintain this depth! All hands! Quiet boat!" Mike moved behind the petty officer 'driving' the boat.

"Aye sir. Back on course in one minute. Maintain depth."

"SIR!" Brad exclaimed and Mike wondered what his sonar officer was doing yelling right after he had ordered quiet…"Lazcom has….*VANCOUVER*!" Brad spun around so fast he lost his balance and ended up standing to avoid falling from his chair.

"Where!?" Mike was surprised but in a decidedly hopeful way and for the first time, he felt that his plan might just work.

* * * *

"Good god! Commander! I have the *Corner Brook* on Lazcom!" the young sonar operator aboard *Vancouver* reacted the same way Brad had but with a little less excitement.

"Excellent! Patch me through!" Chris smiled. His old friend would no doubt gloat about his exploits.

* * * *

"*Vancouver*, this is *Corner Brook*!" Mike tried to sound calm but it wasn't working.

"*Corner Brook*, this is *Vancouver*. Out for a moonlight cruise Simpson?"

"Shit Chris, I wish! I've got a French *Rubis* on my ass! I just pulled a quick one eighty and we're heading east. He's somewhere right behind me! If you guys can latch onto him and harass the hell out of him, I have to get back…" He stopped and then realization that Chris had to be in the know on the mission hit him suddenly…"for the SEALs"

Just behind his chair, Chris heard Greg/Dennis swear.

Chris jumped up and hit one of the buttons on the console in front of him.

"Sonar! Go active NOW! Full power! All freqs! You should find two targets. Lock in the closest one and keep nailing him! Helm! Prepare for high speed manoeuvring!" Without pause he flicked the PA system back on.

"All hands! This is the captain! Prepare to engage submerged contact! Launch the helo!"

Flicking the PA off, he grabbed the com's microphone and spoke to Mike again.

"Okay Simpson. You get going there and pick up those guys." Then a wide smile formed on his lips. "We'll take care of the French boat."

"Thanks Chris! I owe you a big one!"

"And you shall pay!" laughed the commander sitting down again in his padded chair. "I'll be in touch!"

"Roger! *Corner Brook* out." Mike relaxed. He almost felt sorry for those guys on the French boat. Chris loved to harass 'bubbleheads', although he seldom used that polite nickname for submariners.

* * * *

"Bridge! Sonar!" The speaker above Chris's head came to life. "We have both boats! French sub is identified and targeted! Info is being transmitted to the helicopter's data link."

"Bridge, flight control. Cyclone is airborne!"

"Sonar, don't lose him!" Chris ordered. "Helm! Give me twenty knots! Maintain this course."

The frigate dug in its stern and rapidly picked up speed. Above, the dark grey CH-148 Cyclone roared ahead to where it's on board computer, having received information from the ship, said the submarine was located.

The helicopter crew readied the sonobuoys that would be dropped along the French submarine's path and just in case, the weapons officer unlocked the keys for the lightweight torpedoes slung against the side of the sleek new anti-submarine aircraft. All the sonobuoys were set to go active immediately after stabilizing in the water, where they would add their own continuous pinging to that from *Vancouver's* powerful active sonar, thus effectively blinding the submarine and ensuring *Corner Brook's* escape.

"*Vancouver*, this is *Strawberry One*," reported the helicopter pilot. "We are over the target zone. Dropping sensors now."

"Roger that, *Strawberry One*. We still have target on active," replied *Vancouver's* radio operator. Computers aboard the ship and the pair on the Cyclone compared notes over the secure data link. The sonobuoys would soon add their information to the mix and the French submarine would be effectively boxed in.

Aboard the *Amethyst* the sonar operator had completely lost the unidentified submarine they had been chasing in the massive sonar barrage from the Canadian warship which had unexpectedly appeared on the scene. Within minutes, the

French sonar team was deafened by more 'pings' as the *Cyclone*'s sonobuoys, dropped all around the boat, switched to active, relentlessly searching them out. The captain contemplated surfacing but instead headed deeper and ordered a turn to the south.

"Bridge, sonar. Target has changed course. Now heading south. Range thirteen thousand yards."

"Good work! Keep on him!" Chris grinned. "Helm, come right to one eight zero degrees. Pick it up to twenty-five knots."

The French had completely given up on *Corner Brook* and were now desperately trying to lose this warship and her possessed captain who seemed intent on running them down.

Chapter 12

▼

"Helm, make your speed ten knots," ordered Commander Simpson. "Bring us up to four hundred feet. Okay guys, let's try this again." Mike grabbed the address microphone. "All hands, ultra quiet."

Forward in the torpedo spaces, Gary looked at Darren with dejection.

"Guess we're not going to see any action today chief."

"Hey," Darren answered. "Let's hope not."

"Sure was scary there. At least we don't have to worry about that French boat any more."

"Don't get too complacent seaman. Remember we're heading back to their sub base and they must be on full alert by now," said Darren, his face registering concern.

"I guess you're right," replied Gary and for the first time Darren saw fear in the young man's face. Good! He thought. It was time for him to realize that in this game, people get hurt.

✳ ✳ ✳ ✳

"STU!" shouted Markus for the third time.

"Wha…"

"Wake up you lazy bum!" Markus tried to sound annoyed but inside he was worried. Stu had passed out a second time and that was not a good sign. He looked over at Boris and they exchanged a look that told the lieutenant they needed to get him help very soon.

"Jamal…"

"On the way L-T." Again he let himself fall backwards off the zodiac and again he searched fruitlessly through the cold, dark water for the flashing amber light that would signal the arrival of the long overdue submarine.

"It'll be light soon," said Jim, to no one in particular. Indeed, the eastern sky was more defined against the horizon as the first shards of daylight began to appear.

"We won't be here much longer," Markus responded. "Once daylight comes, we'll have to head for the beach or be sitting ducks with all the traffic going by."

In the past half hour a few ships had gone past, not seeing them in the fading darkness. But that would soon change and the protection given them by the radar absorbent materials in the zodiac would be gone.

"Geeze," muttered Stu barely coherent. "What I wouldn't give for a Coke."

* * * *

"Commander, five minutes to the extraction point," announced Lieutenant Fred Beals.

"Thanks Fred. I hope they're still up there waiting." Mike knew if they weren't it was because they were probably uninvited guests of the French Government and any moment now he'd receive a VLF signal requesting that he raise his antennae to receive a message telling him to clear the area immediately.

"They'll be there. It will be daylight soon so we'll have to be quick."

"We will be that Fred," Mike answered. He already had that part planned out.

"Helm, all stop. Bring us up to periscope depth...slowly"

"All stop, coming up to periscope depth, aye sir." Charley repeated.

"Battery at sixty-seven percent," announced Lieutenant Polanski.

"Our little excursion used less power than I expected," Fred commented, impressed with the performance of the new batteries.

"Good thing we have them," Mike replied while grabbing the address microphone. "Duty divers to the control room!" he announced as quick and as quietly as he could.

Forward in the weapons space Darren looked up. That was his duty this watch and he waved over to Chief Marcel d'Entremont that he was leaving.

"Sure," Marcel laughed. "YOU get to go for a swim!"

"I hope not chief!" Darren preferred diving on scenic reefs, not the cold ocean outside his boat. Maybe Heather would like diving...he quickly banished the thought as he grabbed his scuba gear and started changing.

In the control room everyone waited expectantly for what would happen next. No one spoke until Commander Simpson broke the silence.

"Here's my plan," he started. "I'm going to surface the boat right alongside the SEALs. It will be daylight real soon and we won't have time for them to dive down and come in through the lock out chamber." He stopped speaking as Darren and a seaman entered the control room already dressed in their scuba gear. "Hey chief, you have the duty? Good. I need you and Seaman Truman to get out the main hatch the instant we come up. I don't know what shape the SEALs are in but they've been sitting out there a lot longer than planned so be ready to render assistance if they need it."

"No problem commander." Darren patted Truman on the shoulder and headed aft to the ladder leading up to the main hatch.

Mike watched them go, then turning back to Lieutenant Beals, ordered the attack scope raised, although they were not yet at periscope depth.

*   *   *   *

"Hey look guys. A shooting star. Make a wish." Stu mumbled, barely understandable, as the sun started to rise.

"No Stu. Must be a satellite. See how slow it's moving?" Markus responded, increasingly worried about his squad mate. He'd started acting more incoherent and was beginning to show the first signs of shock.

"Shit guys!" exclaimed Jim. "A periscope!"

Markus thought for a moment that maybe Jim was losing it as well, but turned around and spotted the dark grey form slowly rising from the water less than a hundred feet away.

"Jim! Signal him!" Boris ordered. "And pray that it's *Corner Brook*!"

Jim flashed his light at the periscope and was immediately rewarded with a quick flash of the signal light built into the metallic tube.

A few moments later, a rush of bubbles appeared on the water and the periscope climbed higher into the dawn sky.

"He's surfacing!" Jamal yelled. "Hang on guys!"

HMCS Corner Brook rose slowly from the water. As her hull cleared the surface, the SEALs saw the hatch behind the sail swing open and a pair of divers come out on deck. One of them crouched down, took aim with a line gun and fired, sending a rope flying over the zodiac. Jim reached out and made the line secure to one of the eye hooks on the inflatable boat.

"Alright! Start dumping guys!" Boris ordered as the men on the submarine's deck began pulling the zodiac towards the steep hull.

As they had been trained to do, the SEALs made cuts into their scuba suits before throwing them overboard. Specially designed valves on the air tanks were turned and any remaining air hissed out in a few seconds before they too were tossed into the ocean. Last was the motor, unclipped from its stern mount and allowed to drop into the depths. Designed to corrode quickly, it would be useless in a matter of hours to anyone who might come across it lying on the bottom.

"Hey guys! We thought you forgot about us up here!" called Boris to the figures on the sub's after deck.

"Not a chance fellows! They have dumping regulations in the Med and I can't imagine the fine for polluting it with the likes of...!" Darren stopped suddenly when he realized one of the SEALs was laid out across the bottom of the boat.

"Cole!" Markus was never so glad to see someone. "Stu's been hit. We need to get him down fast!"

"Grab the line Truman and heave!" Darren called out. In moments they had the zodiac secured to a deck cleat and had dropped a rope ladder down the steep sloping side of the submarine to the men below.

Boris and Markus carefully lifted Stu to the ladder and prepared to climb with him.

"I can make it L-T" Stu sighed. "It's not much of a climb."

"Okay, but I'm right behind you," Boris answered, not at all sure Stu could make it.

Stu grabbed the ladder and pulled himself upright. Slowly he lifted a leg up and had almost reached the next rung when a large swell lifted the zodiac against the side of the sub, causing him to lose his balance and fall into the water.

"God dammit!" exclaimed Darren as he dove in. Quickly he grabbed one of Stu's arms and brought his head clear of the water.

"Take it easy man. We'll have you aboard in a second," Darren spoke soothingly while spitting out the water he'd ingested.

"Sorry guy...slipped..."

"No problem. Truman! Drop a line to me! We're going to have to pull him aboard!"

"Here you go!" shouted Truman, throwing a line to where Darren was treading water while supporting the wounded SEAL. Cole grabbed the line and made a quick loop under Stu's arms, noticing the red soaked bandage for the first time.

"Hang in there pal. We've got you now," he spoke softly to the wounded man.

On deck, more sailors had joined Truman and were now slowly pulling the line attached to Stu bringing him to the submarine's hull.

"Okay, slowly now!" commanded Darren to the men on deck as they carefully lifted Stu from the water. He then swam over to the rope ladder and held the bottom of it as the last of the SEALs climbed aboard and formed a small circle on deck while waiting for their team mate. Looking up from the water, he called out to Boris. "You guys have everything you need from here?"

"We do!" Boris called back, catching a glint of light reflected from the diving knife in Darren's hand. He heard the swish of air as the zodiac deflated and quickly disappeared below the surface. After making sure it had sunk, Darren climbed up the ladder.

"Good work chief!" Darren looked up to see Commander Simpson on the bridge giving him a 'thumbs up'. He waved and then leaned down to see how Stu was doing.

"How bad?" he asked.

"Not good," Markus responded quietly.

"Okay, let's get him below." Carefully they lowered the wounded man down the ladder to the area behind the control room that had been quickly set up with a cot and medical instruments by the submarine's medical officer. There, with his remaining uniform cut away, Lieutenant Neil Oland examined the SEAL's wounds.

"I tried to bandage him as best I could," Markus said quietly.

"You did a good job lieutenant," Neil replied without looking up from his work.

Markus relaxed, assured now that he hadn't done anything to aggravate Stu's injuries.

On the bridge, the first rays of sun were glinting off the still raised periscope as Mike confirmed that the decks were clear and climbed down the sail to the control room. After securing the hatch he dropped to the deck.

"Helm, dive the boat! Make your depth four hundred feet and make turns for ten knots. Heading two three zero degrees. Lieutenant Beals, you have the con." Mike ordered, heading aft to where the SEALs were waiting for word on their mate.

"Lower attack 'scope!" ordered Fred. "Sonar, keep a close watch."

The SEALs made room as Mike entered the space aft of the control room and looked down at the injured man.

"How's he doing doc?"

"Okay commander. I've disinfected the wound and given him some blood. His pressure is coming up nicely but he'll need a hospital to have the pellets removed."

"Okay, we're dropping these guys off at Gibraltar. They'll take good care of him there." Then turning to Boris, "Lieutenant, get your men below. Cookie's got some special chow for you down there. I'll be along in a minute."

"Well, I just want to…"

Mike cut him off. "Stu will be fine. Now get some food, that's an order." Boris, realizing there was no point in arguing, directed his men below.

Mike returned to the control room and looked over the charts Lieutenant Beals was working on.

"You have us plotted to Gib, Fred?"

"All set commander. Sonar has nothing in the area that we have to worry about and ECM didn't pick up much when we were on top," he informed Mike. "Seems odd the French don't have a full scale alert on," he added. "Looks like we might just pull this off. How's the ensign doing?"

"Not great but he'll pull through. I'm afraid his operations days are over though," Mike commented sadly. "But he'll no doubt end up in a training command somewhere. Be a shame not to pass down that experience."

"That's true."

"Well Fred, you have the con. I'm going down to explain what happened to the SEALs."

"Aye sir," he replied turning to the helm and checking their status.

* * * *

Aboard *HMCS Vancouver*, Commander Donnelly was leaning over the bridge lookout studying the French submarine surfaced off the frigate's port quarter. After a long chase with the expenditure of almost all the sonobuoys they had on board, the French captain had finally relented and surfaced.

"Tiny little thing for a nuke," he observed.

"Sure is, but very capable," responded Greg/Dennis, also looking the submarine over carefully with a pair of binoculars.

"Sir?" a sailor appeared at Chris's elbow.

"Yes Chief."

"The launch has returned from delivering the food that you ordered sent over and the French captain sends his compliments along with this package."

The chief petty officer handed over what appeared to be a tube covered in bubble wrap. Taking his pocket-knife, Chris carefully cut away the protective covering. The French captain had obviously received word from his base that all was well and he could stand down from his hunt for the submarine. As if he had a choice, with the hunter-killer team of *Vancouver* and her Cyclone chasing him down. Someone in Paris must have had a change of heart; he smiled to himself, and then whistled as he saw the label on a bottle of very expensive French wine.

"Damn, send him my regards and lie that he gave us a tough chase," Chris laughed out loud. "Well Bishop, if you'll join me in my cabin…"

"Absolutely!" Greg/Dennis followed the *Vancouver's* CO through the bridge hatch. He hoped the SEALs were okay. There hadn't been any further word from *Corner Brook* because they were now well out of Lazcom range, but he had a good feeling about it. And his feelings were usually pretty accurate.

* * * *

"Attention on deck!" Boris shouted as Mike strode into the junior rank's mess.

"I told you before lieutenant, we don't do that here," Mike reached out and shook his hand. "Welcome back."

"It's really good to be back sir. You had us worried there for a bit"

"We had a little problem with a French SSN but we took care of it," Mike smiled wryly.

"Sir?" Boris queried, not sure what he meant by 'took care of it'.

Mike sat down and explained what had happened and how, with the help of *Vancouver*, they had managed to evade the other boat.

"Sounds like your little Lazcom box is quite the toy sir," Jamal commented when Mike had finished speaking.

"It is that, senior chief. We wouldn't have been able to pull this op off without it. I suspect you'll see it soon on your own ships. We tend to share that kind of technology."

Mike looked at his watch. "We should reach Gibraltar tomorrow morning and we'll be setting you guys loose there. The official story is that this is a 'show the flag' visit and we'll be using the same plan getting you off the boat as we did getting you on. As soon as we can, we'll be radioing ahead for medical facilities for Stu. He'll have to masquerade as a Canadian petty officer with an acute case of appendicitis, requiring immediate hospitalization. Doc has assured me he'll be fine," Mike added, seeing the concern in their faces.

"Thank you sir. It was pretty crazy out there," Boris remarked. "I guess the North Koreans will be plenty pissed...err...sorry sir...upset, about what happened."

"No doubt," Mike said quietly. The North Korean ambassador was probably on his way now to register a formal complaint to the French government. They might even demand the money back that they had paid for the boosters. The French meanwhile, would have their secret service digging around to find who had carried out this little espionage mission.

"Get some rest guys," Mike said to the tired looking men. "You all look like shit!" He grinned and left them to their meals. Cookie was hovering over the young men like a mother hen, making sure they were well fed before sending them off to get some sleep.

Climbing the ladder to the upper deck, Mike suddenly felt very tired. He really was getting too old for this kind of thing but he had to admit; it was a stellar way to end a long and successful operational career. A nice desk and padded chair at Marlant would be a welcome change.

* * * *

HMCS Corner Brook's transit to the Royal Navy's naval base at Gibraltar went smoothly and without incident. Surfacing just outside the harbour, Commander Simpson stood on the bridge and directed the crew as they tied up his command at pier fourteen.

"Bridge to engineering, all manoeuvring complete. Shut her down."

An acknowledgement came from his headset and he ordered the shore guard set and liberty granted for all off duty personnel. The crew had cleaned up as they expected some high ranking visitors and the boat would be open to tours by the general public to allow the same ruse to distract from the SEAL's departure.

Mike had gone down to the mess earlier and said his good byes to the team. He'd stopped and chatted with Stu who looked considerably better and was now wearing his 'borrowed' Canadian navy uniform.

"Thank you for everything sir," Boris had shaken Mike's hand firmly.

"It was our pleasure lieutenant! Anytime! Just don't call for another sixteen months, eh? I'll be sailing a desk by then."

The SEALs had laughed and begun changing into the civvies they'd worn coming aboard in Yarmouth. Seems like so long ago, thought Boris as he dumped his uniform into a plastic bag. The SEAL's equipment and tactical clothing would all be discreetly shipped back to Little Creek some time after *Corner Brook* returned home to Halifax.

Now climbing down the ladder to the control room, Mike headed to where Lieutenant Fred Beals was locking up the last of his charts and tools.

"So Freddy, you ready for supper with the admiral?"

"Absolutely sir! It's not everyday I get a chance to hobnob with Royal Navy brass. I want to see if they're as uptight as they act in the movies," he laughed.

"Not any of the ones I've met," Mike chuckled.

"I don't care either way, as long as they give me a decent meal," Fred smiled and grabbed his hat. They had both changed into their dress whites and now climbed carefully out the main hatch, to avoid any grease on the hinges.

Mike walked over to Darren who was standing on the after deck watching the first group of visitors coming aboard to tour the boat.

"Take good care of my boat chief!" he smiled.

Darren returned the smile and gave a crisp salute, "You can count on it sir."

Walking down the gangway, Mike and Fred headed to a waiting staff car. The commander was sure that more than just supper was on the menu this evening. The British brass would want answers to the rumblings they'd heard. A Royal Navy frigate had picked up all the active sonar pings, and had recognized their former boat's signature.

One of the four admirals present was also more than a little curious about a mysterious submarine, apparently flying the Royal Navy ensign, which cleared the strait a few days ago. All however were envious of the Canadian's adventure.

On *Corner Brook's* after deck, a detail carefully brought Stu up the ladder and rested the stretcher he was secured to on the deck. Darren walked over and chatted with the SEAL while a Royal Navy ambulance backed slowly to the gangway.

"You take care 'chief', " Darren laughed, calling him by his 'Canadian' rank, "and take some driving lessons when you get home!"

"I might just do that," Stu smiled. "And if you manage to hook up with that girl in Virginia, you make sure to look me up!"

"I will," Darren smiled. "Just be sure to get some rest and let all those holes heal up. You want to be water tight before you go playing in the ocean again."

"Yeah…" Stu paused. "I don't think I'll be playing anytime soon, Cole."

"Don't write yourself off yet man." Darren stood aside as the ambulance attendants lifted the stretcher onto a wheeled gurney.

Something hard pressed into Darren's palm as they shook hands for the last time. When he opened it, a small gold US Navy SEAL Trident pin glinted in the sunlight.

* * * *

A couple of hours later, the last of the tour groups were being ushered off the submarine. Walking back to the open hatch, his deck officer duty completed, Darren descended the ladders down to the senior ranks mess and grabbing a Coke, sat back on the couch, stretching his legs. Cookie, having seen the solemn look in his eyes as he passed by, came in with a plate of cookies that were more chocolate chip than cookie and placed them on the table in front of Darren.

"Damn Cookie," Darren asked, taking a bite from the still warm cookie. "Where did you find chocolate chips this late in the cruise?"

"HA!" laughed the big man. "Like I'm going to share that info with the likes of you! So, the SEALs all get off okay?"

"Yeah. Jim just left with the last group."

"That's good. Bet they can't wait to get home."

"I'm looking forward to going home too," Darren said, half to himself. His apartment would be just as he'd left it, neat and tidy and…empty.

"Well you munch out and give me a holler if you want some supper." Cookie rose and headed back to the galley.

"I will and thanks chief."

Darren reached over and grabbing the well worn remote, turned on the television. He flipped between the only two channels available and saw that one of them appeared to be a British all news station. A picture of a weather beaten old ship he'd seen once before back in Little Creek, Virginia filled the screen. Reaching for the remote control he turned the volume up.

"…official French news source also reported that the French Military Police who boarded the ship found the crew tied up and the ship's captain dead. We were able to confirm that the captain had been shot but no other information is available as the French Navy, now leading the investigation, have closed off all access anywhere near the ship and…"

Darren stood with his eyes transfixed on the screen. "Cookie! Come see this!!"

"…rumours abound that whatever cargo it had been carrying was destroyed in a commando raid during the night. The ship, the *MV Sariwon*, registered in North Korea had been due to leave this morning. The North Korean Ambassador, contacted earlier today, refused to be interviewed or provide us with a comment. We will bring you further information as it becomes available. In other world news, the European Union has…"

Darren muted the set. "Good work guys", he whispered under his breath.

* * * *

Two hours later, a dark grey US Air Force C-17 touched down at the air strip just outside the Gibraltar Royal Navy base and taxied over to one of the hangers. Inside, four men in civilian clothes watched as the aircraft stopped and the side door opened.

"Now get on board so we can get the hell out of here!" Boris hollered at the SEALs who had been horsing around inside the hanger.

The pilot notified Air Traffic Control that their flight plan was set and their destination with a cargo of spare parts was Norfolk, Virginia. A few minutes later, having received clearance, the jet took off.

* * * *

The next morning, her decks cleared, *HMCS Corner Brook's* crew cast lines and steamed out of the harbour. Commander Simpson and Lieutenant Beals had been questioned relentlessly by the British admirals, anxious to learn about their mission. Finally recognizing the futility of their attempts, they had toasted the Canadian officers late into the previous night for the success of their mission, whatever it had been. For Mike and Fred this was frustrating as they were limited by the morning departure to drinking colas. The world media, who had taken to the story like a pack of wolves, had just as quickly dropped it when there was no further information forthcoming.

The protests by the North Korean government had continued in Paris but they fell on deaf ears. The official French government response was that the rockets were aboard a North Korean vessel and therefore their security and protection was solely the responsibility of the North Korean captain. Since all of his crew were either dead or awaiting the results of their applications for political asylum however, the case was closed as far as the French government was concerned.

The French navy had also reported the successful conclusion of a recent joint Canadian/French naval exercise in the Mediterranean Sea, furthering relations between the two countries.

On *Corner Brook's* bridge, Mike leaned back, enjoying the fresh air. Beside him, Fred scanned the horizon one more time as he sent the watch below and prepared to leave the bridge.

"See you below commander."

"Thanks Fred. I'll be right down." Alone, he let the sun warm his face one more time, then flipped his headset to transmit. "Bridge clear! Prepare to dive the boat!"

*   *   *   *

Due east of *Corner Brook*, *HMCS Vancouver* was about to enter the Suez Canal on her way home to British Columbia. On the afterdeck, Chris stood chatting with Greg/Dennis as the ship's boat was lowered into the water.

"Guess you'll be heading home too?" Chris asked.

"I'm never sure commander. Thank you for your hospitality and have a safe journey back."

With that they shook hands and Greg/Dennis climbed down to the waiting boat. He gave a final wave and thumbs up to Chris as the boat pulled away towards shore.

*   *   *   *

On a sunny morning two weeks later, *HMCS Corner Brook* cruised on the surface a few miles south of Halifax. Commander Simpson was on the bridge and he beamed as he always did at the first sight of Nova Scotia. Soon he would be home again with Ann and the kids.

"Sir?" A head appeared in the open upper hatch.

"Yes, what is it?" Mike answered.

"Message from Marlant sir."

"Thank you seaman." Mike unfolded the note and read the message. Smiling he folded the piece of paper and stuffed it into a pocket. "Not a word of this to anyone seaman!"

"Yes sir," replied the young rating as he turned to climb down from the bridge.

"Con, bridge. Decrease speed to ten knots. Steady on course," he commanded as another harbour marker slid past the submarine. Below, the radio operator, in touch with Halifax Harbour Traffic, received clearance for the submarine to enter the harbour.

A short time later, *HMCS Corner Brook* slid along the west side of McNab's Island, entering the inner harbour. Mike called the port detail out and in no time the crew had 'manned the rails'. Seeing that they were in their proper positions, he called below again and in minutes Petty Officer Trask's pirate flag snapped freely from a line rigged to the ESM mast.

Looking ahead along the docks, nothing he saw appeared different from any other arrival home. Nor had he expected it to. Where they had been and what they had done would remain undisclosed, probably forever. Only a select few who shared their secret would ever allude to it by offering to buy a drink for any of *Corner Brook's* crew.

Mike reached down and switched his headset from 'com' to 'announce'. "Chief Petty Officer Darren Cole to the bridge immediately!" He chuckled to himself, remembering the message in his pocket.

A few minutes later, Darren poked his head through the hatch and requested permission to come up.

"Granted chief," Mike answered, standing aside to make room in the small confines of the bridge.

"Chief Cole reporting as ordered sir," Darren didn't know what else to say. He'd never been called to the bridge during docking before.

"Cole, your request for thirty days leave is approved. Thought you'd like to know before we dock."

"I'm sorry sir. I didn't request leave."

"No? Are you sure? Wonder how that happened?" Mike did his best to look puzzled. "Well you're up here now. You might as well stay and watch us dock. Here are my glasses if you want to take a look around."

Thank you sir. I appreciate it," said Darren taking the binoculars and examining the Halifax waterfront. There were a few ships moving around the harbour and he examined them, trying to guess their nationality or what they held in the containers piled high on their decks. He looked over as they slowly sailed past the camouflaged stern of *HMCS Sackville*, rendering honours to the small, but feisty World War II Corvette that was a proud reminder of the Canadian Navy's wartime successes.

As the submarine moved closer to the dock, he examined the crowd of people waiting for them. It was somewhat larger than usual, probably because they'd been out for so long. A lot of brass as well and one of them looked familiar to Darren…too familiar. Standing next to Admiral Brent O'Hanlon was Admiral George Carroll, the Chief of Naval Operations for the US Navy. Oh shit! He thought.

"Hey, isn't that your buddy the CNO?" Mike asked, trying with some difficulty to sound surprised.

"Yes, it is. Maybe I'll go hide in the battery compartment until he's gone commander," Darren joked sheepishly.

"Oh, I don't think you'll want to do that," Mike smiled. "Anyone else down there we know?"

Puzzled now, Darren brought the glasses up and looked again. Both admirals were looking up at the approaching submarine's sail now and he knew they could see him looking down at them. In unison they moved apart, huge grins on their faces, revealing Heather who was now waving up at him enthusiastically. Amongst the cheers and calling out between the families on the dock and the men aboard the submarine, Commander Simpson still heard the dull thunk as his binoculars dropped to the deck below and bounced into the harbour.

"Oh shit! I'm sorry sir! I…"

"That's okay chief," Mike sighed. "Now, about that leave…" He gave Darren a wink and without waiting for an answer dropped down the hatch.

A few hours later, the boat securely tied up and her crew off to join friends and family, Mike relaxed in the senior rank's mess, entering the last few details of the mission into his personal log. After seeing Admiral Carroll, Darren and Heather off, Brent O'Hanlon had come aboard and was taking a quick tour through the boat, after which he planned to buy Mike a well deserved drink.

Brent had just entered the torpedo spaces and looking around noted the Mk-48 torpedoes were all safely stored in their racks. Then something on the side of the nearest one suddenly caught his eye…

A deck below, his shout reverberated clearly.

"SIMPSON!"

The End

CPSIA information can be obtained at www.ICGtesting.com
Printed in the USA
LVOW131109070313

323167LV00001B/22/P